THE LIGHTHOUSE ROAD

THE
LIGHTHOUSE
ROAD

PETER GEYE

UNBRIDLED BOOKS

This is a work of fiction. The names, characters, places and incidents are either
the product of the author's imagination or are used fictitiously, and any
resemblance to actual persons living or dead, business establishments,
events, or locales is entirely coincidental.

Unbridled Books
Denver, Colorado

Copyright © 2012 by Peter Geye

Library of Congress Cataloging-in-Publication Data

Geye, Peter.
The lighthouse road / by Peter Geye.
p.   cm.
ISBN 978-1-60953-084-6
1. Domestic fiction.   I. Title.
PS3607.E925L54 2012
813'.6—dc23
2012009270

3   5   7   9   10   8   6   4   2

BOOK DESIGN BY SH · CV

Second Printing

Again, For Dana

And

In Loving Memory Of
My Mother, Susan Geye
(1943–2011)

I will greatly multiply thy sorrow and thy conception;

In sorrow, though shalt bring forth children.

GENESIS 3:16

THE LIGHTHOUSE ROAD

I.

[*November* 1896]

*S*ome ancient cold had taken root in Thea Eide's belly, a feeling she'd not yet had but one she knew meant the time was nigh to deliver her baby. She wanted to walk, felt she must walk. So she rose and stepped into the mess hall and lit a candle. She steadied herself with one hand on the long table, cradled her belly with the other, and began pacing up and down the hall, measuring her contractions by those laps around the board. The contractions started in the small of her back and reached around to her belly, where they paused and clenched. She paused, too, when the contractions burrowed in, and in the throes of each the absolute chill of the large room was brought down on her. In Norwegian, her mother and only tongue, she said, "My God, what now?"

She decided to start a fire. From the tinderbox she took the last scrolls of birch bark and set them under the wood already piled in the stove. She struck a match and lit the birch bark. The fire flared directly and before her next contraction the room was already warming. The mice sought the heat beneath the stove without the least fear, gawking at her with eyes the size of pencil tips.

She heard the wind raging outside but was unaware of the snow until she unlatched the door and pushed it open. The dark night was gleaming with snowfall. So much snow that she realized the impossibility of crossing the camp to the jakes. She said, "Mercy," then hiked up her nightdress and leaned against the mess-hall wall.

When she stepped back into the mess she saw Abigail Sterle readying water for tea. "I'll wake the brothers," Abigail said. The sound of the old woman's voice was a revelation. For more than a year Thea had worked beside Abigail without having heard it plainly. Abigail said no more, only braved the blizzard herself, leaving Thea to wonder why the brothers needed to be woken.

Since Thea discovered her pregnancy, she had avoided its consequences entirely. She had not made plans of any sort, had not prepared herself for the child's arrival, had not considered how she might keep cooking for the jacks and raise an infant, much less how or where she might deliver the babe. Pacing the mess hall again, the candlelight casting eerie shadows over the pine-board walls, the fire rasping in the stove, she realized how imprudent she'd been. She thought, *I'm foolish*. Even as she reprimanded herself, another contraction—the strongest yet—clutched her womb.

What little she knew of these goings-on came from two memories. The first was of her mother in labor when Thea herself was but five years old. This was back in Norway, in their hovel on the treeless banks of Muolkot, across the harbor from Hammerfest. Candlelight flickered there, too, and her mother braced herself in bed, alone, while she labored. Her mother never made a sound beyond her harried breathing, and when the child was born still, she merely wrapped it in a blanket and set the corpse on the puncheon floor.

The second memory was more recent. As Thea voyaged across the Atlantic just more than a year before, her cabinmate had gone prematurely into a terrible labor. Thea fetched the ship's surgeon herself, and during the tailing hours of a rough storm, she watched that child come into the world stillborn, too, so small the mother could hold it in the palm of her hand while she wept. In the early throes of her own labor, Thea understood the silence of her mother and the ululations of that woman aboard ship equally.

Abigail Sterle returned, bringing with her a gust of cold air and snow. She paused to feel Thea's forehead, to make them each a cup of tea. "Drink this," she instructed, then slunk into their chambers. When she returned to the mess hall a moment later she came carrying Thea's eiderdown, her cape, her woolen hat. "Dress," she said. "We'll cover you with the goose feathers for the ride to town. I forgot your boots."

Thea was about to take another step in her birthing march, but stopped. There was a sluice between her legs, an almost audible *pop*, and her socks were soaked with something warm and thicker than water. And then there was mud on the dirt floor. Abigail came with the boots, knelt before Thea, and said, "You've broken water." She pulled Thea's wool socks from her feet, put on her boots, and laced them up.

Outside, the camp foreman's horse stood harnessed to his sleigh in the first inkling of light. The snow had buried everything. Thea was set in the sleigh, Abigail sat next to her, and the taller of the Meltmen boys took the reins and stood between the women's four feet. His brother went into the mess to start the baking. As the horse pulled the sleigh past the jacks' quarters, Thea saw the old bull cook walking toward the mess. No doubt on his way to help with breakfast in her absence. He was the last thing Thea saw before they turned up the ice road and into the trees.

She didn't open her eyes again until they reached Gunflint a half hour later. Closer to the lake, the blizzard had a different shape and unruliness. Snow had drifted into sharp ridges all along the breakwater. In town—or what passed as town—the roads were covered in snow, so even the horse had trouble passing. There was no sound from the mill. The lights in the Traveler's Hotel lobby were unlit. Even the dogs that usually ran the streets were nowhere to be seen. At Grimm's apothecary, though, the large front window was aglow. The only sign of life in town. Frost crept down from the corners to cloud the glass.

Thea was by then in agony, but still she bore it. The Meltmen boy picked her up and trudged through the knee-deep snow to Grimm's door, where he hammered on the glass. Before a minute passed he hammered again, and Hosea Grimm's daughter, Rebekah, came hurrying across the storeroom floor. She opened the door and said, "Oh, dear," and turned and hollered, "Hosea! Hosea! It's Thea. Hurry."

Inside the store the smell of roasting capon hanging in the air sickened Thea. She said, "Stink." To which Rebekah replied, "That's Thanksgiving dinner already in the oven."

The Meltmen boy set Thea on her feet, tipped his hat, and left as though he'd just delivered a parcel.

Hosea Grimm, dressed only in his union suit and a matching toque, came down the stairs two at a time. "None of us was sure we'd get you here in time, Miss Eide. How far along are you?"

Thea, answering, fell into Grimm's ready arms.

She labored to the reassuring sound of Hosea Grimm's deep voice. He bent beside her, dressed now minus the collar he usually wore, his shirtsleeves rolled to the elbow, an apron cinched around his waist. Next to him, resting on a music stand, Hunter's *Anatomy of the Gravid Uterus* stood opened. He read from it while Rebekah listened intently and arranged a tray of medical implements. Thea's pain was rising now—she thought she could see it coming, swell after swell—like storm breakers on the shores of Hammerfest. She moaned as the contraction passed and then settled back into the cushion of pillows Rebekah had placed behind her.

By what strange calculus could she measure the distance between the shores of her childhood in Hammerfest and her laboring on this table in Gunflint? For all of Rebekah's tenderness, Thea wanted her mother now. More than anything she wanted her mother. She called her name.

Another contraction gripped her, and she was brought back to the bed, to Rebekah's steady hand on her own. Grimm was speaking now of his years at the Sorbonne, of his studies with the great Jean-Philippe Armand, of the accoucheur's duty. He had studied two years with Armand, had even cowritten several articles with the man. Or so he said.

He was in fine form, Grimm was. He lectured on the curative powers of ground stag antlers and dried rabbit wombs and a dozen other equally strange remedies for everything from infertility to gonorrhea. He suggested that when the child finally came they ought to read its skull—caul forecasting, he called it. Finally he spoke of his great affinity for Soranus, a second-century Grecian who had been Grimm's first introduction to the science of gynecology. He held forth while he worked, as though his monologue would both edify and distract. Thea, of course, could hardly understand a word he said.

*G*rimm had two pots of boiled water beside him now, and he was soaking the instruments that Rebekah had earlier arranged. He said, "Well, Miss Eide, what say we welcome this child before dark? Let's earn our sup."

He spread her legs gently, sliding the sleeping gown over her knees. "We must have a look, child." Then he reached into her and pressed and she thought surely this was the first touch of death. She put her hands around her neck and pressed and felt her pulse like hammer blows on the palms of her hands.

"Very good, child. Excellent. You must be halfway there. No doubt you'll be done by suppertime," Grimm said.

She looked at him uncomprehendingly, looked at Rebekah, who had not moved from her side for many minutes. Outside the window she could see the snow still falling.

The morning passed with difficulty. Several times Grimm consulted his library, and his discourse on the history of childbirth gave over to more imminent concerns. He twice sent Rebekah to his stores, once for morphine and later for a vile of scopolamine. Thea closed her eyes at noon and did not open them again until two hours later, when Grimm injected her with another syringe of cold drugs. The moaning that had issued from Thea for hours ceased, and she felt nothing, only that she no longer existed.

It was in this state that the child was born. The umbilical cord was tangled around him, and when Grimm held him up by the feet, even the blood coating him looked blue. The child had a huge shock of hair on his misshapen head and his eyes were but slits. Grimm reached for a long-bladed scalpel. He gripped the umbilical cord and sliced through it as though he were cutting tenderloin from the shoulder, catching the child in the crook of his arm. He unwound the cord, first from the infant's neck and then from his legs. Almost instantly a flush of paleness washed over the boy and he was alive.

Grimm laid the child on a blanket and Rebekah bathed him, she suctioned the mucus from his throat and nose, and when she did he let out his first wheeze. While Rebekah tended to the boy, Grimm stood aside, rubbing his own furrowed brow. He watched the child open his eyes, he counted the lad's fingers and toes, he noted his hair. He documented his findings in a notebook and set the notebook nearby and when the child was cleaned and swaddled, he took him from Rebekah and handed him to Thea, who looked wan but relieved. She held the boy. Smiled. Then wept silently. He recorded this in his notebook, too.

"You'll need a name for this one," Grimm said in stuttering Norwegian. He'd been practicing her language that season.

Thea looked at Grimm. "A name?" she repeated. She looked at her child, pulled him from his place nestled in the warmth of her neck, and rubbed his cheek. It was so soft it could have been satin. "Odd Einar," she said. "I will call him Odd Einar. For my father."

Now the child began a long, wheezing lamentation. He clutched the air with his balled fists and kicked under his swaddle. Thea tried putting him back in the crook of her neck but the child still wailed. She looked at Grimm. She looked at Rebekah, who ushered Grimm from the room and returned to her bedside. The child still cried.

"Thea, the child is hungry. Here," and she pulled the loose sleeping gown over Thea's shoulder, exposing her breast. "The child wants to eat." Rebekah took the child from Thea's arm and told her to sit up. Then Rebekah positioned the child in Thea's lap and said, "Offer him your breast. Milk, Thea. He wants milk."

When Thea looked up uncomprehendingly, Rebekah cupped the baby's head in one hand and Thea's breast in the other and brought them together.

And before Thea could fail, the child opened his mouth and leaned toward his mother's breast. The child sucked with astonishing vigor. He sucked and he sucked and Thea felt the life going into him, drop by precious drop. In that instant she realized she was famished herself.

The smell of the roasting birds was delicious now, and she felt she could eat a whole hen.

But she watched her boy suckle instead. He ate and ate. And Thea wept. And wept. And was elated.

And would soon die.

II.

[July 1920]

Odd stood out on the point, watching the distant lightning in the east, watching the moonrise in the vacuum of the leaving storm. He could feel the booming surf under his feet, vibrating up through the basalt. He could feel the weather lowering, too, behind his glass eye.

Another swell pounded the beach. He looked behind him, at the water in the cove, at his fish house and skiff. He checked his wristwatch against the moonlight. Just past eleven.

He stayed on the point long enough to imagine star trails. Long enough to imagine everything that could go wrong out there. He didn't have a choice, though. If he balked, Marcus Aas and his brother would get the next job. Odd needed the next job.

He checked his watch again. The lightning was now just flickering over the horizon, like a premature and sputtering sunrise. He knelt, put both hands flat on the rock, felt what it told him: He'd get wet, no doubting that. But there was moon enough. And he was game.

Back in the cove he emptied his skiff, brought the fish boxes up to the fish house. He grabbed line from a hook on the wall and his spray hood. He made a cheese sandwich and wrapped it in wax paper and put it in his pocket. He took the teakettle from the stovetop. It was sweltering inside the fish house and he wiped sweat from his face and cussed. But he smartly donned his oilskin pants and jacket.

At the waterline he untied his skiff and walked it down the boat slide and into the cove. He lowered the Evinrude and turned for the open water. He rounded the point as far offshore as possible dodging the swells as much as he could. But still he was wet right away. He motored past the breakers and in the open water the seas spread out and his ride smoothed.

He passed a set of his gill-net buoys and kept the nose of his skiff pointed east, using Six-Pine Ridge as his marker ashore. The moon was above him now, its light pooled over the lake, over the hills. Twice he checked his watch and when it was finally one o'clock he lit his lantern and hoisted it up one of the oars. He lashed the oar to the gunwale. He settled into the shipping lane bearing northeast, taking the swells on his port bow. He took the cheese sandwich from his pocket and ate it. The pulsing behind his glass eye kept a steady pace with the rolling seas.

He cruised for another hour before he saw the far-off light of his rendezvous. It was nearly two o'clock by then and he knew he'd be lucky to beat the dawn getting back to shore.

The oncoming boat made steady progress. She'd done the lion's share of traveling that night, forty or fifty miles up from Port Arthur. He could see that the boat—as big as a towboat, and cut like one, too—was suited for seas like these. Much better suited than his skiff. He thought for the millionth time of the boat in his mind. Could see it damn near plain as day. Could see himself in a cockpit, the spray over the bow spattering glass instead of his wincing face.

They called sooner than he'd expected, their voices carried on the stiff breeze. "Ahoy! That Grimm's runner? What're ya, in a canoe there?"

He heard drunken laughter as the Canadians slowed beside him. When the lines came over and after he triced up the boats, he saw there were three men.

"Old Grimm sent a runt, Donny. Look at this one."

"You shits are late," he said. "It's no night for sitting in a skiff."

One of the men had come to his gunwale and stood looking down at him. "But it's a fine night for moonshine! Just look at her up there." The man gestured at the luminous sky. "Don't piss on me about being late, runty. We're here, we got the hooch."

"Six barrels?"

"That's what Grimm ordered, that's what we got. How 'bout the dough? Hosea send it along?"

Odd reached into his pocket and withdrew the wad of bills. He handed it up to the man at the gunwale.

"It's all here?"

"It's all there."

"Donny! Over the side. Let's load these barrels."

The one named Donny came over the gunwale and into Odd's skiff. He offered his hand and they shook and when he looked up they were ready with the first barrel.

"Good Christ, friend, six of these barrels might damn well sink you."

"Don't worry," Odd said. They each took an end and lowered the barrel, the boats rising and falling like a pair of drunken dancers.

They took five more barrels aboard his skiff and Donny scuttled ass back up onto his boat. "I've seen sunken boats with more freeboard than that," he said.

"Say your prayers, runty," one of them said. "By God, you'll need more than luck to get back to Gunflint."

Odd was already covering the whiskey barrels with the spray hood, lashing it as the wind played hell with the canvas. "Don't worry about my luck."

"To hell with him," one of them said.

"Tell Hosea good night," another shouted.

"Tell him we'll be up to see his daughter!"

"You shut the hell up," Odd said at the mention of her. He gave them a fierce look before he unfastened the lines that held their boats together. He hurried to the rear thwart and started the Evinrude before he lost the shelter of their lee.

And then he was taking the swells astern and wet all over again. They were right about the freeboard. There wasn't more than two feet of it. Though the whiskey was good ballast, it was too much. "As true in the belly as in the boat," he said aloud.

He'd have a hell of a time the next three hours, that much was sure. He pulled the lantern down, stowed the oar, and extinguished the light.

W as it really possible for the pressure to fall and rise and fall again all in the same summer night? The wind coming around now from the northwest, the moon fading behind a lacework of clouds, and the pulsing behind his glass eye all told him yes. He'd been a half hour heading upshore, running before the seas, and though the swells were shrinking they were running closer together, too. None of this good news. A couple of times he'd come off a crest and into a trough and the Evinrude's propeller had come out of the water and raced and whined. He eased up on the throttle each time but when he slowed the boat would yaw, and he was good and goddamn tired of getting pooped.

He thought if he shifted the barrels he might run a little easier, so he untied the spray hood and unlashed the barrel closest to him and rolled it back to his feet. The skiff heeled as the other barrels came free, all five of them following the first.

"You're as goddamned dumb as Hosea says you are," he said aloud, the sound of his voice barely audible above the wind.

He throttled down to an idle and on hands and knees rolled one of the barrels up toward the bow. He set it upright and lashed it quickly and, like a housecat, crawled amidships and lashed another pair of barrels to the thwart. All the while water was washing into the skiff and before he could get back to the Evinrude and his cruise home, he spent fifteen minutes with his bail bucket, the cold, cold water numbing his hand even as lightning flashed to the north.

"Christ almighty," he said, shaking his head. "Good Christ almighty, I'm about done wrestling this goddamn lake."

But the lightning—even with all it implied—was a turn of fortune: Without it, he'd have had a hell of a time keeping the shoreline in view, for the clouds were back with the change of weather and he was in a new kind of darkness, one relieved only by the flickering sky. By the time he had the barrels lashed and the skiff bailed and was back on his rear thwart with a wad of snoose stuck in his mouth, he realized that accounting for the squally seas had slowed him by half, and the lightning showed the hills above Gunflint still twenty miles before him. He ought to have been safe in the cove by now, safe in his bunk for a few hours' sleep. Instead he had two more hours of lake water swamping his boat, soaking his trousers and boots.

He spent those hours fighting sleep and swearing there had to be a better way. Hosea had it all figured out. Send a sap like him out to fetch the goods, give him a hundred dollars for his trouble, then turn around and distribute the rye for ten times the runner's share. That was five hundred dollars a week easy in Hosea's purse. And that on top of his other schemes.

"I just need my boat," Odd said to himself. Now he was using the sound of his voice to keep him company. "A bigger boat and I can fish more and deeper and make the run up to Port Arthur myself. Pocket the five hundred and to hell with Hosea Grimm." He even figured he could work with Marcus Aas and his brother, figured they'd be damn near friendly if they weren't tussling for the same scant share of Grimm's whiskey dollars.

The lightning quivered again and he could see the hills above town. He could see, from the top of the next wave, the lights of town. Twice as many now in the hour before light as there'd been in the hour of his leaving. No doubt the other herring chokers were up now, standing on the shore, taking stock of the lake. Most of them would leave their nets for another day. He would if he were standing ashore, reading the water.

But he'd been out in worse than this, he told himself. Last March, his first haul, northerly seas so sudden he'd been thrown half from his boat. He'd lost a boot in the bargain. Theo Wren's boat had come back without him that day. He'd orphaned two little boys and widowed his wife, Theo had. "Yes, sir," Odd said aloud, "that storm was worse. I'll be home in half an hour."

And he was. His watch read four forty-five behind the blurry crystal. As blurry as he himself was. He managed to navigate the skiff into the cove. But even as he coasted across the gentler sheltered waters he could still feel the swells lifting and settling him. He steered the nose of his skiff onto the boat slide and tied her quickly to the winch line and on unsteady legs hauled her out of the water.

He removed the Evinrude from the boat and set it on the grass ashore and then one at a time he rolled the whiskey barrels up and over the transom, let them roll into the cove and then floated them in knee-deep water to the very crux of the cove and the large boulders that sat there. He wrestled the barrels ashore and then rolled them behind the rocks. He'd deliver them that night. Now he sat atop one of the barrels and caught his breath. For a moment he looked at the dark silhouette of his fish house, sitting under the tall pines, his place in the world. He'd built it himself. Paid for it and built it with his dollars and his sweat. And him come from nothing.

Before he went inside he put the Evinrude back on the transom. He brought the gas can up to the fish house and set it at the foot of the steps. He walked to the boat slide and checked the knot and line holding the skiff. And last thing, he took the teakettle from under the slide, walked the hundred paces to the whiskey barrels, and cut the oakum from the top of one of them. He pried the lid from the barrel, the aroma oaky and fine. He dipped his finger into the hooch and brought it to his lips and licked his finger. That taste alone made the whole night worthwhile, he felt sure of that.

"But we'll take this for good measure," he said aloud, and he dipped the teakettle into the barrel, filling it to the brim.

He hammered the lid back onto the barrel and carried the whiskey to the fish house.

*H*e wasn't expecting to see her inside but was glad when he did. Sitting under the open window, in the guttering candlelight, her hair down the way he liked. There she was. He stood in the dark corner of the fish house looking at her, she looking back. Neither spoke. It occurred to him, as he untied his bootlaces and kicked them off, that the candlelight was doing the same work inside that the lightning had been doing out: throwing just enough light to lead him where he needed to be.

Before he went to her he stopped at the end of the workbench he used as his kitchen counter and found two clean coffee cups. He poured a finger of hooch into a cup, swallowed it quickly, then poured another finger in each.

He stopped short of her, stopped short of the light from the candle, stood there with the coffee cups. His very favorite thing was to watch her rise, to watch her long arms and legs and hair simply *move*. She moved—in the middle of the night, in candlelight—with the almost imperceptible slowness and suppleness of the seiches.

When she flipped her hair and looked down, he said, "What's this, Rebekah?"

She glanced up at him, pouted. "Only a fool who didn't care about anything would have gone out on that lake tonight."

"A fool, you say?"

"A proper fool. Yes."

He stepped to her, set the coffee cups on the floor, and lifted her from the chair on which she sat. "I'd never convince you or anyone I wasn't a fool, but I didn't have a choice. I don't make that run and Marcus Aas does, then he wins favor. Aas wins favor and I lose the skiff. I lose the fish house—" his voice trailed off. He thought better of saying, *I lose the fish house and we've got nowhere to go.*

She looked up at him for the first time since he'd stepped in from outside. The look that came over her face was as a mother's. She reached up and feathered his damp hair away from his eyes.

They looked at each other for a long moment before Odd set her down. He bent and picked the whiskey off the floor, handed her one and they stepped to his bunk. They drank their whiskey together, two sips apiece and in harmony. He slid off his soaked pants and hung them over the back of the chair. Did the same with his shirt. He lifted first his left foot to remove his sock, then his right. He lay down. Though he was a short man—only five foot five—he was also long-armed and broad-shouldered, he had a chest like a woodstove, was as hairy as a bear. Swallowing her up was as easy as putting his arms around her, which he did as she lay down beside him, using his bare arm as her pillow.

He took a deep breath, closed his eyes. It occurred to him that he conducted all the best and easiest hours of his life here in the fish house: his heavy slumber, what few idle afternoons he had whittling and carving, the poker games, the long winter mornings spent mending his gill nets. And now his hours with Rebekah, here under his arms, her impossibly soft skin and the attar of rose in her hair. Their life together went back to the hour of his birth, and he supposed their time together now was something like religion.

"How long can you stay?" he said.

"He was soused at four o'clock when the card game ended. He'll sleep until at least nine. I've time."

Outside he could still hear the wind rocking the trees and the pounding surf out on the point. If there'd been no wind or breakers on the lake, he'd have heard the Burnt Wood River running hard with fresh summer rains.

"A bigger boat would make life a hell of a lot easier." He reached to the upturned fish box beside his bunk and took his carving from it, held it up to the candlelight, rode it along the shadows on the wall. The carving was of a boat, the boat he dreamed about. He'd spent all of Christmas week whittling it from a birch bole, whittled the finest details: the motor box, the canopy, the gunwale, and even a toe rail. He'd fashioned a couple of fish boxes and set them in the cockpit. "Something with a little bow to her, a strong, high sheer. A cockpit instead of that goddamned spray hood. A Buda inboard. A thousand pounds of keel and skeg." A gust of wind blew through the open window and the candle shadow raced up the wall. He moved the carved boat with it. "And a bell. I damn well want a bell. You'll know I'm home by its ringing." He felt her nestle into him, she loved this hopeful part of him, thought it innocent and childlike. "So big I'll need a berth in the harbor, next to the tugs and charter boats."

A strong breeze came through the window and blew out the candle. He set his carving down and looked out at the night.

"A boat like that and I could make the runs down to Port Arthur myself. I could do business directly all up and down the shore. Could take a boat like that clear across the lake. Clear across to the Soo. We could go anywhere. *Anywhere*, Rebekah."

"I'm too old to go anywhere."

"That's nonsense."

"Nearly twice your age."

"So what? You're the prettiest gal in Gunflint."

Now she smiled and looked at him again. She kissed him lightly on the lips. "Tell me more about the boat. Where would you take me?"

"Where'd you want to go?"

She took a deep breath, was thinking earnestly about where she could get. "What's the place farthest away in the world?"

"I guess Norway's a fair piece."

"Where your mother was from."

"Sure, where she was from."

"Let's go to Norway, Odd. In your boat. What's it like, do you think?"

"I've heard tell it ain't unlike it is here."

"Oh, Lord! Let's choose someplace else, then."

"I told you we could go anywhere."

"Anywhere," she repeated.

They lay in silence, each picturing *anywhere* as though they might someday get there. She fell asleep. He could tell by how she warmed. So he tilted his head back and looked out the window.

Here was the daybreak, the first promise of light, coming as deliberate as Rebekah crossing a candlelit room. And there were the pines, swaying in the old wind as though this aubade were played in the slowest of time.

III.

[*July* 1893]

*T*wo days and two nights of oblivion ended on a Friday morning when Hosea woke from a dead man's sleep. A dozen champagne bottles littered the floor in a swath of dull sunlight. He pressed his eyes and imagined he could feel the dream retreating to its place in that part of his mind he could only access in a state such as he'd roused those days in the Chicago bagnio.

He found his pants under the bed and checked his pocket watch. He checked his billfold, too, which still held a stack of fifty-dollar banknotes. He kicked the threadbare bed linens from his legs and swung his still-stockinged feet onto the floor. The rush of blood to his head was swift. He was so parched he could not swallow. He needed a drink of water, so he rose and stood still until he found his balance.

But for his socks he was naked. His drawers hung over a lampshade, his linen shirt was tangled with the duvet on the floor at the foot of the bed. As he dressed, memories of the last forty-eight hours came back to him piecemeal, each more lecherous than the one before. When he was dressed he took stock of the room. Not bad as such rooms went. A carpet on the floor. A bed with a proper headboard. An electric lamp. An enormous mirror on the wall opposite the headboard. A brass ashtray. A table and chair in the corner with an empty decanter and four used snifters, three stained with lip rouge.

At this hour of the morning the hallway was quiet, the water closet vacant. He stepped into it and closed the door behind him. He washed his face without looking in the mirror above the basin. He slicked back his hair and then put his mouth to the faucet and drank copiously. He drank until he thought he'd vomit and then rested a moment and then drank as much again. Already he was feeling better, the fire in his gut just smoldering now.

When he reached the bottom of the staircase he was surprised to see five women lounging on the divans. There was a barman behind the counter. The window looking onto Wrightwood Avenue was covered with crushed-velvet drapes, the only daylight coming in from the rose window above the entryway door. There was a young girl tending the coatroom, and Hosea stopped for his jacket and suitcase. She came from behind the half door and offered to assist with his jacket, but Hosea declined. He fished a bill from his wallet and put it neatly into her palm.

"You're Ava?" he said.

She looked over Hosea's shoulder at the barman, then looked at Hosea. She nodded.

"Well," Hosea said, then thought better of it and said nothing more.

She returned to her spot behind the half door and nodded again and Hosea crossed the lounge to the bar.

He asked for a soda water and after he paid he packed his pipe and the barman lit it. The barman also placed a copy of the morning *Tribune* before Hosea, who looked at the headlines but was too distracted by the thought of Ava behind him to read beyond the banner.

"Say," Hosea said, "might I talk to Mister Hruby?"

The barman grunted and disappeared into a doorway at the end of the bar. A minute later he returned, Hosea's old friend Vaclav Hruby trailing behind him in a cloud of cigar smoke.

"You've made it out alive, friend," Vaclav said.

"Alive and clearer of mind," Hosea said.

Vaclav watched the barman resume his spot at the end of the counter, watched him pick up a newspaper and light a cigar himself.

When the barman was out of earshot, Vaclav said, "That's the lass." He nodded in the direction of the coatroom.

"Yes, I know," Hosea said.

"She's a good girl. She won't cause trouble."

"I'd like to speak with her. Alone," Hosea said.

Vaclav stubbed out his cigar. "I told her the score. But if you want to talk to her, go ahead. Why don't you wait upstairs in one of the rooms? Leave the door open. I'll send her up."

"Maybe it would be better to talk to her outside. Tell her to meet me at the artesian well in Lincoln Park. Give me a few minutes to get ahead of her."

"You're the boss, Grimm."

So Hosea walked out of the bagnio, pausing outside to look back at the inconspicuous brownstone. He knew of a dozen other such places in cities on the water, places as far away as Acapulco and Bombay. He walked up Wrightwood Avenue, crossed the trolley tracks at North Clark, and reached the park five minutes later. It was a hot morning, humid, with low clouds hiding a hazy sun over the lake.

Hosea pumped the well until a steady flow of the sweet water poured from the spigot. He bent at the waist and let it pour into his mouth. When he was finished he removed the handkerchief from his coat pocket and wiped his lips and brow. He took a seat on a bench near the well, adjusted his hat, and turned his attention up the gravel path.

It was fifteen minutes before she arrived, wearing a different dress than she'd had on in the coatroom. She walked quickly, a parasol over her shoulder. She wore white gloves. She was lovely.

"Good morning, Mister Grimm," she said, offering a slight curtsy.

"Good morning. Thanks for joining me."

"I'd do *anything* to get out of that nest of harlots," she said.

"'Nest of harlots,' you say?"

She closed her parasol and stood before him. "Call them whatever you want."

"Please, sit down."

She sat on the bench beside him, crossed her legs and adjusted her skirts.

"Vaclav has informed you of my reason for being here, is that right?"

"He's a pig."

Hosea sat back and looked at her. A smile played across his face. "I'll save you the trouble of a lifetime of discovery and tell you that all men are pigs."

"You think I don't know that?"

"How old are you, Ava?"

"I'm thirteen."

"Thirteen."

"I'll be fourteen at Christmastime."

"Tell me, how did you end up in the employment of Vaclav Hruby?"

"I'm his slave is more like it."

"Is your tongue always so sharp?"

"I'm sorry. I don't mean to be wise."

"So you're unhappy working for Vaclav?"

"It could be worse."

"Yes, I suppose it could always be worse." Hosea tried to read the meaning of her quips. "I wonder, has Vaclav spoken of me?"

She uncrossed her legs and put her elbows on her knees. In that pose she looked every bit the child she was. "He said you want to adopt me. Move me up to Minnesota." She looked over her shoulder at him. "Is that far away?"

"Minnesota? No, not far at all. Where I live—I should say where I'll *soon* live—is on a lake much like this one—" he gestured at the wide waters of Lake Michigan "—a lake called Superior. Though the town is much smaller than Chicago. The whole of it would fit in Lincoln Park." He looked south. "Might fit twice."

"I don't mind a small town. I was born up in a small town in Wisconsin."

"What happened that you ended up an orphan?"

"Can't say. I never knew my parents. I was born into that godawful orphanage. I ran away as soon as I thought to."

"And came to Chicago? Why?"

"I stole two dollars from the orphanage. Chicago is as far away as I could get."

"I see."

"Don't think I'm a thief. It's the only time I ever stole anything. I had to. The headmaster at the orphanage was awful. I've worked for Vaclav for two years and never stole a red cent. And I could have. It would be easy."

"That's good. That's good. I wouldn't want to adopt a thief."

"Why do you want to adopt anyone?"

Hosea looked at her, knew from the look in her eyes that it would be easiest to tell her the whole truth now, that any omission or lie would come back to haunt him tenfold. "I hope you'll let me ask you a question, and I hope you'll be honest. I put great stock in honesty."

"Okay," she said.

"I want to know what life has been like for you at Vaclav's."

She looked at him, confused.

"You've been a hostess, yes? And worked in the coatroom I see. Anything else?"

"Oh! No, nothing else. Well—"

"You must be completely honest, remember."

She didn't so much as flinch when she said, "I said Vaclav was a pig."

"Do you mean to say he has made you available to his clients?"

"He made me available to himself, is what I mean."

"Dear God," Hosea whispered. "You poor child."

"It was nothing the headmaster at the orphanage hadn't done."

Hosea put his hand on hers and looked her firmly in the eyes. "I want you to know that I will never, ever treat you that way. I will protect you as though you were my own flesh and blood."

"Why?" she said.

"Why?" he repeated.

"You don't even know me."

"Do you have any idea what fate awaits you at Vaclav's? Do you know what your life would be like a year from now?" He stood up and buttoned his coat. "I can offer you a life free of that fate. I would like to." He knelt before her. "Tell me, Ava: Why haven't you run away from Vaclav?"

"It's a warm bed and hot food."

"There's more to life than that."

She looked at him as though she were the adult. "Not when you don't have it. Let me ask you a question, Mister Grimm: How do I know you're honest as you say you are? You said yourself all men are pigs. You just spent two days tangled up with some of Vaclav's best girls."

"A fair question. Fair indeed." He stood again. "I am a man of resources, Ava. I've traveled to all the corners of the world. I'm educated." Now he sat next to her. "I'm not religious, even if I once was, but I do have a meditative streak. Places such as Vaclav's serve as my

Asclepieions. Places where I can restore myself." He paused, considered whether to continue in such a vein but thought better of it. "All of which is to say that though I have my—how shall I say this?—uncouth tendencies, I am also a man more capable than most to subvert those tendencies. I am, at heart, a simple man." He nodded his head in self-approval. "I have enemies, though. It's probably not a good idea for me to be in Chicago in the first place. But I needed to see Vaclav. I needed to see about you." He straightened up. "I have represented myself to the people of Gunflint as a family man. They expect me to return with my daughter."

"Do you have a real daughter?"

"No, no. I wish I did. I was married once. Many years ago. In Paris, France. My wife passed. We never had children."

"Who are these enemies? Why won't they follow you to Minnesota?"

The thought of telling her the whole story occurred to him. It would be easy enough to do. Easy enough to tell her about the stud game turned deadly, about running through the levee with fifty thousand dollars in his briefcase, two Polack hoods chasing him, the knife still bloody. The fact was, the particulars of his fleeing became more remote the closer he got to leaving, seemed to matter less and less. Whatever ambition had once been in him was now satisfied by the mere notion of what he was building in Gunflint. So instead of answering her question he said, "My enemies are my own business. But they won't follow me to Minnesota. They won't know I'm there." He said this matter-of-factly. "Now, Ava, let's get back to you—"

"Tell me what your business is there," she said interrupting him.

"Why, I own an apothecary. Or I should say I'm building an apothecary. I'm also a trained dentist and surgeon. In France I was trained as an accoucheur."

"What's that?"

"A deliverer of babies. Like a midwife. I will be the town's general physician."

"And what's an apothecary?" She had trouble pronouncing the word.

"A place where cures are sold. Medicines and suchlike."

She nodded and began fidgeting with her parasol, opening it half-way and snapping it shut. For a long minute she said nothing, only toed the pebbled pathway and played with her parasol. When finally she did speak, it was very softly. "I don't care to go to school. I'm not a very good cook."

"Going to school won't be required. I hope you'll learn to cook. I also hope you'll help me at the apothecary. Otherwise you'll be free to do as you please."

Now she looked at him as she said, "And you'll leave me be? Won't do what Hruby and the headmaster done?"

"On my life."

He thought her face brightened. "All right," she said. "When will we leave?"

Hosea clapped his hands as he stood. "Excellent! Excellent, Ava! We'll collect your things at Vaclav's and leave at once. I believe there's a train at noon. Let's hurry along."

So together they walked back to the bagnio. It took her only moments to gather her belongings, all of which fit into a small suitcase.

Hosea paid Vaclav five hundred dollars. The two shook hands and agreed that the rest of their business could be conducted via the post. Together they were going to operate a brothel near Gunflint, the place the Shivering Timber would become. They would hire a stable boss and pay him twenty-five percent and split the remaining seventy-five percent. This was a condition of their bargain concerning Ava.

At ten o'clock in the morning Hosea and Ava boarded the trolley on

North Clark and rode it downtown. At noon they were sitting in a first-class berth on a train pulling out of Union Station, bound for St. Paul.

It was in that berth as the train trundled across the state of Wisconsin that Hosea laid forth his plan. They would spend the night in St. Paul, using the following day to outfit Ava. She would need a new wardrobe, one more in keeping with a girl of her standing. He informed her of the type of airs she ought to affect, counseled her on manners, spoke for what seemed hours on the merits of fine posture. Though he talked too much and of things she thought boring, she found Hosea to be an affable companion. He was witty sometimes, and at least he was never coarse.

They arrived in St. Paul after midnight, took lodgings at a hotel near the station, and in the morning went shopping for Ava's wardrobe. When they boarded another train that afternoon, this one bound for Duluth, they carried an extra trunk loaded with dresses and furs and a hundred fine undergarments.

"When we reach Duluth, we'll have to take a ferry up to Gunflint. We might have to wait a day or two. But Duluth is a nice city. If we must wait, perhaps we'll pass the time by finding a few more dresses for you."

"I don't think I need any more dresses," she said, but he could tell from her blush that she would happily take them. Though she'd been demure in accepting his gifts at first, he saw that she was quick to prize the soft things in life.

"One of my hobbies, Ava, is portrait photography. Have you ever had your portrait taken? I presume not."

"I never have, no."

"I'm having a studio added at the apothecary. It's a large building. Will be the largest in Gunflint. Our living quarters will be a flat on the third floor. The second will have my offices and the studio."

"What's a studio?"

"A place to take pictures. I hope you'll be a good subject."

"I can't imagine it'll be too hard to have my picture taken."

No doubt she had her charms. "I suppose not!" he said.

Six hours after they left St. Paul the conductor came through to announce their arrival in Duluth.

"We're nearly there," Hosea said. "Are you excited?"

"It's been a real fun time so far," she said, her childishness blooming.

"There are a few more things, Ava. Important things."

"Okay."

"I want people to believe you're older than thirteen."

"All right."

He smiled, looked her up and down in the seat across from him. "You've certainly got the figure of a young woman."

She didn't even blush.

"And though you've a beautiful name, I think I'd like to call you Rebekah instead. It was the name my poor lost wife had always intended for a daughter. From this moment forward, you'll be Rebekah Marie Grimm."

"Rebekah," she repeated. "Rebekah. *Rebekah.*" The name put a smile on her face. "A new dress," she said, smoothing the pleats of her gingham gown. "And a new name. Here in Minnesota. I'm all new." She looked up at him. "Rebekah it is. Father." She flashed a knowing grin. "Rebekah Marie Grimm."

IV.

[*July* 1920]

*W*hen he woke at noon the pillow still held the imprint of her head, still clung to the scent of her hair. The air in the fish house could have been bottled, it was so heavy. Still lying on his bunk, Odd rolled a cigarette and set it between his lips. He paused before lighting it, knowing the smoke would erase the lingering scent of her, wanting it to linger longer. So instead he reached over and brought the boat carving back. He sighted the boat's bottom with his good eye, tried to convince himself that the keel and skeg could be fashioned the way he thought. It was there to be seen, even with only one eye.

The first notion of a boat had come to him the summer before, as he'd whittled a piece of driftwood into a gently curved keel. He did it without the least intention, but when he was finished he held it before him, sighting it with his good eye as if he'd just aligned every crooked thought he'd ever had. A couple weeks later, while he was cutting and splitting firewood, he left a five-foot length of birch on the sawhorse while he ate lunch. When he came back he saw the birch log as the next version of the keel scale and spent a week at it with his crosscut saw and adze, then his gouges and chisels, and finally a sanding block. It was then he knew with all the certainty he possessed that he would be his own keelmaker.

He rose now, finally lit his cigarette, and went to the window. He knew it was time to get to work.

The cupboard was empty but for a can of coffee and two jars of soused herring, the heel of the loaf of brown bread. There was an apple on the windowsill. He thought of making coffee but remembered he'd filled the teakettle with whiskey the night before. *This goddamned life of mine*, he thought, taking the apple from the windowsill and wiping it on his drawers.

He ate the apple as he walked to the shore, a towel over his shoulder, a bar of soap in his hand. The apple was tart and hard and grown in a place unsuited for apples. But he ate it anyway, his face puckering with each bite. When he got to the shore he threw the apple core into the lake.

The water in the cove had warmed some with the week of hot weather, but the night before the rollicking seas had brought in more of the cold water, and when he stepped into the lake beneath the boat slide the chill felt electric. Outside the cove he could see the big waters had slowed, had almost synchronized with the dying wind. The rollers came weakly and slow now, like a herring's last few gill flaps in the bottom of his skiff.

He washed quickly and toweled off and went back into the fish house to shave, which he did with his straight blade after honing it on the strap he had tacked into the counter. There was a small mirror hanging beside the window and he watched himself as he shaved. The lines in his brow led to it like streams to a shaded pond. Only twenty-three years old and already he had a face like a map. He could have passed for a man twice his age, even with his youthful grin and fine full hair.

Before taking his hidden trail to town, he checked on the whiskey. It sat as the night before among the rocks in the cove. He'd stashed it there in the past and was fine leaving it until nightfall. If not for that census taker, he could load it onto the bed of the pickup right now. Lord knows Mayfair didn't give a damn about a few barrels of whiskey; he imbibed himself. But the rumors of feds masquerading as civil servants were rampant in the Minnesota wilds, and this fellow up from St. Paul was as fishy as a jar of roe.

How long, Hosea asked one night over cards, did it take to count two thousand folks? Much as he questioned Grimm, Odd had to admit the old man had a point. There weren't more than two thousand people in all the great county, and the census taker had been in Gunflint since March.

I need something to keep the skeeters off my neck," Odd said, standing at the counter in Grimm's Apothecary.

"It grows by the bushel on every lake shore, you can't pick some?"

"I'm no goddamned flower picker."

Grimm turned and pulled one of the glass canisters from the shelves that lined the wall behind his counter. There were a hundred such canisters, full of everything from catnip to balls of spiderwebs to lemon drops and horehounds.

"You went rowing last night?"

"A little breeze is all she had."

Hosea put a small bouquet of catnip into a paper sack and handed it to Odd. "Christ, Odd, you'd wrastle a black bear, wouldn't you?" Hosea winked.

"To hell with you."

"But you landed the juice?"

"I'll bring it around come dark. Couple of barrels here, couple more over to the Traveler's, the rest up to the Timber. I'll roll yours down to the cellar."

Grimm's awful smile came across his whiskered face. "Drop mine first, I'll join you up to the Timber."

"Sure."

Rebekah appeared from the hidden staircase behind the shelves of canisters. Despite the fact that Odd had been raised in this place, a person appearing from the narrow staircase always shocked him, especially when, as with Rebekah now, her skirts sprang fully like an umbrella as she made the last step into the apothecary.

She walked over to him and kissed him on the cheek and said, "Hello, little brother."

Odd blushed, he couldn't help it.

She looked into the wax-paper sack. "What are the flowers for?"

"I'm going up to the farm today. Skeeters are hell with all this hot."

Hosea counted twenty five-dollar bills onto the counter. "For your trouble," he said. "I'll see you at nightfall."

"Hosea's making deliveries with me tonight," Odd explained.

"Boys on the town."

"Something like that," Odd said.

"Can I come?" she asked, a wink for Odd.

Hosea stood up straight. "The Timber's no place for a woman of your standing," he said.

"A woman of my standing. Yes, well. I know all about the Shivering Timber," Rebekah said sharply. "A woman of my standing," she added, this time under her breath.

*T*he way up to Rune Evensen's farm was a palimpsest of old logging roads and game trails, the abandoned rail bed, the ice road they were talking about turning into a certified highway, one that went all the way up to Canada. Middle summer now, the forest's undergrowth was tall and unruly and giving Odd hell. The grabby brush even annoyed the horse he'd rented from the livery keeper. A big beautiful Percheron sired by one of the old Burnt Wood Camp haulers.

Odd urged her along, tugging on the bridle reins and saying sweet things. The horse was already in harness and excited about the afternoon ahead, even hot as it was. The skeeters and blackflies were awful, as Odd knew they'd be, and when he reached Rune's old fence he stopped and buttoned his shirt at the wrists and collar and took the catnip from his rucksack and rubbed the dried flowers all over his neck and hands and face. They continued along the fence line until they reached the gate, where Odd stamped the ferns and brush and pulled it open. The horse neighed and shook her head and stepped into the paddock. Odd slung the bridle over the horse's neck and hit her on the rump. "I'll fetch you a bucket of water. Then we'll get to work, you hear?"

The horse answered by pushing Odd with her long face and neighing again.

In the barn Odd found the wood bucket he used to water the horse and walked the fifty yards to the well pump in the middle of the paddock. It took fifteen minutes to get water, and Odd was as primed as the pump by the time he did, but the water was frigid and delicious and he soaked his head and slaked his thirst before filling the bucket for the horse. He set the bucket next to the fence, and the mare dropped her neck and drank and when she finished she took a long and heavy piss. He tied the horse to the fence and gave her a nosebag of oats and finally turned to survey the farm, the barn, the house now fifteen years abandoned, his at the age of eight. An awfully young age to be a private landowner.

When Rune Evensen died intestate—drowned in and washed down the Burnt Wood River—Hosea hired the best attorney in Duluth, who'd convinced Mayfair that Odd, as next of kin, deserved the property and chattel and that Hosea, as Odd's guardian, should hold the trust. It was one of the many piebald gestures Grimm had made on Odd's behalf after his mother died. No doubt the property established Odd. He'd mortgaged his fish house and length of shoreline against it fifteen years after Rune's death, upon Grimm's suggestion. But how much money had Grimm skimmed off Odd's holdings? And had Hosea known Odd would be beholden to the odd jobs he was employed in on Grimm's behalf? The whiskey running, the mail fraud, the chopping of half-a-dozen cords of firewood each summer, the carpentry work on the apothecary. Odd often felt he'd never be out from under Grimm. "Which is why I'm out here hunting wood now," he said to himself.

He walked into the old farmhouse. It was hard to imagine that anyone had ever lived here. Two small rooms. Two windows. Six-foot ceilings. Odd didn't know much of the history, only that Rune was his mother's uncle. He knew of the misfortune that had come to pass here, knew of the ghosts said to haunt the place. He knew it was a goddamned eerie place, no doubt about it. Knew that a farm in these climes was doomed at the outset. But he loved the place, and not only because it belonged to him alone. No, his attachment to the farm stemmed from a single sudden day eight years ago.

It was late November and he and Rebekah had been hunting

34

rabbits up at the old Burnt Wood Camp. Rebekah was as sharp a shot as he, maybe even sharper. Rabbit stew, that was the idea. His favorite dish. Rebekah was like a mother to him. She'd done more to raise him than just about anyone. She and the Riverfish family. She'd bagged three snowshoe hares, he a pair, the pelts turning from brown to white. They were easy to pick in the already dormant tall grasses around the abandoned camp. Odd had gutted them and strung them and they were halfway home when the wind came up their backs, a fierce and out-of-nowhere blow that was trailed five minutes later by the unlikeliest blizzard. In the half hour it took them to get from where the wind hit them to Evensen's farm, there was already three inches of snow on the ground, and coming down harder. They hurried into the abandoned farmhouse, Rebekah laughing, thinking it a frolic; Odd dazed, knowing just how dire the situation could have been.

They lit a fire in the woodstove, trusting the tin chimney for no good reason. They stoked the fire and in spite of the broken windows and the wind coming up through the floor, the place warmed.

And there was Rebekah, her hyaline eyes, her beautiful hair coming free of her hat when she took it off, still girl-like in every way despite being almost twice his age. Odd had always been the whole town's child, the gamin who could find supper at any doorstep on Wisconsin Avenue, but on that late afternoon he felt a hundred years old. Their shotguns leant one on either side of the door, the snow outside coming down heavy enough to snuff out the last twilight. Inside there was the light from the open stove door but none other. It shone dully on the puncheon floor.

He unbuttoned his coat, doing as she did. He shook the snow off it and slung it over his shoulder. The rabbits he'd laid on a bench. There wasn't much else in the cabin: a rocking chair, a small kitchen table and one stool, a woodbox, a chest of drawers without the drawers.

They'd taken their silent inventories, stood facing each other in front of the fire. She took a very deep breath. Her eyes narrowed, she looked sleepy. The floor was freckled with mouse droppings and he swept them away with the hem of his mackinaw coat. He laid his coat across the floor in front of the fire. He gestured at the floor, at his coat, a place to sit. She looked at him again with those eyes of hers, a look of uncertainty, perhaps curiosity, in any case full of questions. He started to say something, he couldn't remember what, but she stepped to him.

And then she kissed him, a kiss as unexpected and sudden as the snow. And as full. She stopped and her breath caught when she stepped back so she stepped forward and kissed him again. In a flurry they undressed and sooner than either of them knew what they were doing they made love. It was the first time for him and the first time in many years for her.

He was staring at the place on the floor now, heard the horse's happy neigh outside. He counted back to make sure he had the years right. Eight years ago, right, and only once. Until two months ago, when it got regular.

He counted back the time to that day in May. He'd walked into the apothecary after breakfast, expecting to find Hosea. He found Rebekah instead, standing behind the apothecary counter, her fingers deep in a rabbit pelt. There were a dozen pelts spread across the counter. She didn't even look up as he walked toward her.

"Hey there," he'd said three steps from the counter.

She'd looked up slowly, smiled, shook her head to clear her daze. "Odd? What are you doing here? I thought you were out for your nets."

"I'm about to head out now. What's with the pelts?"

"Inventory," she said, then looked back at the fur. "Why don't you come over for dinner tonight? Hosea's down in Port Arthur. We can act like kids again."

His breath caught. Since that day here at the farm years before, there'd been a constant uneasiness between them. They couldn't look at each other when they were alone, could hardly say hello.

But that day in May, she lifted her eyes from the rabbit pelts and said, "What do you say?"

"All right. Yeah. That sounds swell."

"Come over as soon as you're finished out there."

"I will," he said.

And he had. She'd baked popovers and set them on the table with a bowl of herring roe and gherkins. Sliced cheese. It all looked delicious, but they never got to eating.

She poured them each a whiskey and water. They sat on the davenport with the windows open, the lake breeze coming across the pink sky at dusk.

After their first cocktail she mixed a second and sat back down. "Do you ever think of that day up at Rune Evensen's farm?"

"We shouldn't talk about that," he said.

"Do you?"

"Of course I do, Bekah."

"I've been thinking about it. I can't stop thinking about it."

He looked out the window. "What have you been thinking?"

"That we've wasted enough time," she said quickly.

"Wasted time?"

And that was when she came across the davenport and kissed him. She kissed him and unbuttoned her blouse while he unbuttoned his shirt. It was as simple as that.

If he stopped to think about it he started feeling dizzy. So he cleared his head of her and stepped back outside. He took the stone path to the barn and heaved the skidding tongs and chain and an ax back to the horse.

"Yup," he said to the horse. "Yup, yup. Let's find a bit o' wood." He shouldered the ax and untied the reins and together they made for the stand of birch under the shadow of white pine up behind the barn.

*T*hough he spent most of his time on the water, Odd loved the woods too. He knew the wilderness—the paths and meadows, the bear dens and beaver lodges, the blueberry bushes and eagle aeries—as he knew his own fears and desires. From the time he was but seven or eight years old he'd been free to roam. So he did, often alone but just as often with Daniel Riverfish. They were days of freedom, hunting or simply beating the summer heat in the shade of the tall pines, but even in the freedom Odd knew something was missing. He'd always known it. It took him years to understand the void, but when he did it was as if the mysteries of the wood were amplified. He saw in the wilderness a reflection of his motherlessness. It was *easiness* that was missing; the orphan's onus, never seeming whole. It was as if he ran and hiked through the woods without his feet ever hitting the duff, as though his own ankles never felt the brush of the ferns.

But now it was different. Now, with the horse trailing him up the game path and into the woods, the weight of his task as heavy on his mind as the ax over his shoulder, he felt wholly less alien, as though his purpose gave him life and his prospects with Rebekah gave him a future. The thought quickened his step.

When he reached the top of the hill and looked down over the slope of birches, onto the overgrown barnyard and up at the slice of river the vantage held, he felt a new absence. The sun was high and hot, the birds shrill and all around. The hilltop here was narrow and as he stood there, he felt the sensation of someone watching. He shrugged, hoping to shake the feeling. The horse stepped toward him and when he turned to look at her, he realized that the sensation of being watched was only the sun warming his back. A stand of white pine that had once loomed from the western slope of the hill was gone. Just gone.

He stepped to the other side of the hill and looked down at the blown-over white pines. There were a dozen of them, trees that had grown from the hilltop, subject to the prevailing winds and their own heft, and so begun a slow bowing. Together they'd formed a gentle arc fifty years in the making. And now they were all down, the air above the heap redolent of the pitch oozing from the thousand broken boughs. He stared down on the tangle of trunks and limbs for a long time, as though somewhere in that crude geometry lay proof that his errand was not a fool's. And proof took form, there, the tree that lay atop the pile, its boughs most intact and cloaking the others. He studied the curve of trunk, cocked his head, childlike, curious, first mystified and then bothered that he hadn't thought of this on his own.

Convinced he'd found his keel, he plotted his day's work. In his mind he trimmed the boughs and cut it to length and set the skidding tongs and rapped the horse on the ass. He turned to look at the trail heading back down the hill, judged the bend against the length of white pine in his mind, hauled it down the ghost of the ice road and meandered through the trails to his fish house, caught only a couple of times. He wondered how long it would take to bleed the pitch.

And then he saw himself with the whipsaw and planes, the keel materializing in the molds he'd fashion, he saw a whole winter of building the boat up from the keel, saw the beautiful sheer, the transom with her name hand-carved and lacquered and riding across the lake, with only the memories of them watching from the breakwater in Gunflint, waving themselves good-bye.

"You willing to wait a few hours while I cut, old girl? Get up in the shade," he told the horse.

Then he put the ax over his shoulder and descended the hill to the heap of blown-over trees.

*I*t was past suppertime by the time he'd finished, the task unfolded just as he'd imagined. The white pine ran the length of the fish house now, outside against the western wall so that it might take the afternoon sun. The horse had been returned to the livery; a bowl of venison stew had for dinner at the saloon in the Traveler's Hotel; and now Odd sat on the stoop outside the fish house with a teakettle of whiskey and lake water to rout his thirst.

He sat there all of twilight, watching the gloaming fall, realizing in the deepest part of himself—the least part of himself—that he was watching something holy, this turn of day to night. He finished his drink and packed and puffed his pipe. When he finished smoking he tapped the ash out and got to it.

He covered the barrels in the bed of the pickup with a canvas tarp and covered the tarp with stacks of empty fish boxes. The trail up from the fish house was rutted and overhung with tamaracks, but he managed to get onto the gravel road and into town.

The truck was Hosea's, but Hosea didn't often drive. Aside from the six or eight streets in town and the gravel trail that led three miles up the hill to the Shivering Timber, the roads in and out of Gunflint were mere sleigh roads, fit for dog teams or horse-drawn wagons but not rubber-wheeled flatbeds. Grimm's latest initiative, brought before county commissioners and the state legislature, was to transform the North Shore Trail into a highway built from Two Harbors clear to the Canadian border, insisting that people would come in droves given the chance. He had the big lodges in Misquah and Portage to bolster his argument on the grand scale, and the myriad hunting camps scattered all over the forest on the smaller scale. The ferries that ran all summer from Duluth, the pleasure craft that docked in Gunflint harbor from June through September, the anglers who were willing to hike from Gunflint up to any of a hundred lakes in the bush, all of this had convinced Hosea that given the highway, the area would become a tourist draw.

Odd had already delivered a pair of whiskey barrels at the Traveler's Hotel and now parked the pickup behind the apothecary. He opened the cellar doors. Walked down the stone steps and found the lantern hanging in its spot and lit it and checked there was room in the false floor for the whiskey. Then he went back to the truck and from beneath the tarp removed two more barrels and walked them one at a time down the stone steps and into their hiding spot. He extinguished the lantern and replaced it on the hook. Before he fetched Hosea, Odd packed another pipe and smoked it while he rearranged the tarp and fish boxes.

Grimm stepped out the back door. "There's our boy!" he said.

"Hooch is in the floor."

"Very good."

"Already dropped it at the Traveler's, too."

"Then we're up to the Timber."

"I guess you're all dressed up," Odd said. Hosea wore a seersucker suit with periwinkle-blue pinstripes. He wore white patent-leather brogues and a sharp white hat. His tie was mint green and pinched under his gaunt chin in a collar the color of the pinstripes. "You think those girls'll like you better if you dress like a clown?"

"A clown, you say?"

"Some damn thing."

"Odd, lad, the reason you spend all your time whittling and running whiskey is because you don't take care in your appearance. You've been wearing the same shirt all week. And it's been hot. Maybe if you bathed and put on a hat and a pair of proper trousers, you could get one of the little ladies in town to whittle for you." He winked.

"The little ladies," Odd said, his secret blowing through him like a cool breeze. "Guess I'll worry about that, and about wearing a proper pair of trousers."

"You're my charge is all. I promised your mother I'd raise you right."

Odd stepped to the truck and opened the door. "I'm a grown man. I'll dress how I please."

"Suit yourself," Hosea said, joining him in the truck. He withdrew a pocket flask and unscrewed the cap and sucked a long drink. He offered it to Odd, who took a draft himself.

"Now," Hosea said, "let's get to the strumpets."

*T*he Shivering Timber was an unabashed brothel and whiskey parlor that had evaded the reach of the pious Gunflinters and constables by catering to their weird and secret proclivities. It housed a dozen or so prostitutes and was guarded by two woodsmen brothers from Wisconsin on Grimm's payroll. They were mild-mannered behemoths who abstained from the whiskey and the whores and buried their considerable fortune in coffee cans and burlap all over their ten-acre parcel.

Odd had never visited for any purpose other than this evening's errand, but Hosea had a forty percent stake in the place. He also kept the girls in calomel and morphine, gave them abortions, and pulled their rotten teeth. And he supplied the whiskey. So he had a king's reign.

There were three girls sitting under the gaslights on the porch as Odd and Hosea carried a barrel around back. They smoked and drank from glass lowballs and when Hosea stopped to greet them on the way back for another barrel they rose and kissed him on his freshly shaven cheek from over the railing.

By the time the last barrel was in place Hosea was in the room behind the bar, standing at the glass of the one-way mirror, looking back past the bar to the dimly lit lounge and taking inventory of the whores reclining on divans or standing at the bar with their long cigarette holders and watered-whiskey cocktails. There were only a handful of other men in the lounge, men unknown to Hosea, likely sportsmen up from the Twin Ports or even come through the Soo. A long way from home in any case, from their wives and children, and playing at being their younger, wilder selves.

"You want a plate of roast venison?" one of the brothers asked Grimm.

"Thanks, no, but I'll have a whiskey, up." And then to Odd, "Nothing strikes your fancy, lad?"

"I ain't dressed for it, doubt they'd even take a gander."

"Don't patronize me, Odd. I'm offering is all. My treat."

"I think not." Rebekah on his mind, her stories, their secret stories, took on a little extra heft in the Shivering Timber.

Larue returned with a whiskey in one hand and his ledger in the other. He and Grimm stood at the glass and went over accounts.

"We'll need extra the next couple of months. Busy summer. Six barrels next week?"

Hosea looked over his shoulder at Odd, who nodded. "Six barrels it is."

"What do you fellas know about this census taker?"

Hosea said, "He stinks. Rotten. But he's having a fine time up here in the wilderness. I doubt he wants his good summer to end. I'll see that it doesn't."

"I knew that son of a bitch was a nark," Larue said.

"He'll be easy enough to manage. You see his shoes? They're falling apart. He wears the same trousers day after day. He's got a wife in St. Paul, she'll grow fond of what those few extra dollars each week will bring. I see new crockery in her kitchen cupboards, new dresses for church on Sunday. Maybe even a beaver-pelt coat."

"I was you, I'd tell him to keep the hell away from us. Strange things happen to the uninitiated up here at the Timber. There're lots of places to fall and break a leg, lots of hungry critters in the woods happy to make a snack of boys fallen down."

Hosea smiled. "So violent, man!"

"I don't want to see him. That's all I'm saying. I'll make things bad for him if I do."

"Once I've pocketed him, I'll pass your message along."

Odd liked this talk. He knew that Hosea would indeed pocket the fed and that a summer of running whiskey lay ahead. Enough money to outfit his boat and maybe make a run for it next spring. He and Rebekah gone forever.

"Odd, you want a whiskey? A gal?" Larue asked.

"No, thanks. I'll be on my way."

Hosea, speaking to Larue, said, "Don't worry, he isn't queer. Just principled."

"There were more principled men in this world, the Timber would be on the Lighthouse Road, we'd be selling whiskey on the board-walk," Larue said.

Odd smiled. "There'd be no fun in that, though," he said.

Larue patted Odd's shoulder. "Point well taken, friend."

Odd took a few minutes to study the lounge, the women in their negligees or cheap dresses, their vacant eyes and slumped shoulders. Odd could not see the pleasure in any of it.

V.

[*January* 1896]

*T*hea learned first to tend the scullery fire, to warm water for the dish scrubbing, to make tea for the other cookees. She was up at four every morning, rekindling flames as she mouthed her silent prayers.

Between the stovewood and the kitchen sink carved from white pine, she had splinters enough that her hands looked like porcupines. But she was tireless and dispassionate and worked without complaint. Within two weeks of her arrival at the camp she was paring potatoes and rutabagas and opening tins of milk. Before Thanksgiving she could soak the beans and boil cabbage. Now, in the new year, she was in charge of baking: biscuits and rye bread and larrigan pies. She could slice the loaves and ready the pea soup before the other cookees could set the tables and replenish the woodpile.

Because he could not speak Norwegian the camp cook taught her by demonstrating, speaking only in rudimentary terms fit for a child or simpleton. In this way she came to know the language of the kitchen as a series of words in isolation, nouns and verbs independent of each other. *Herring, oleo, roux, apple, mutton, cellar, sowbelly, stove.* And *clean, stew, stir, cut, serve.* Though he was terse and strict, she knew that she pleased him, and not for the reasons she pleased the hundred other men in camp. In the cook's estimation, her diligence and sub-ordination would have been enough. What came after that was gravy. As for Thea, she understood his authority instinctually, and though she had no great opinion of the man, he was at least not mysterious.

Those others in the kitchen were entirely more beguiling. There was Abigail Sterle, whose croupy hosannas sung into the enormous vats of sowbelly stew were the only evidence of any voice at all. She bunked and worked beside Thea while keeping her stare in a perma-nent study of the shanty floor. They made the only pair of women in camp. For this reason alone Thea withstood the elder's coldness, and after washing the morning dishes the two would sit on either side of the cook stove sipping tea sweetened with pilfered sugar.

During these quiet, stolen moments, the brothers Meltmen—the other cookees in camp—would sometimes join the women. They were fine-haired and lean and their skin was so pale as to appear poached. Another shade paler and they might have been albinos. Like Abigail Sterle, they were pious and humorless. But unlike the crone, they were sixteen years old and possessed the vigor of boys their age. It would have been easy for Thea to shrink under their unabashed ogling and sniggering. But she didn't. Her life was difficult enough without the Meltmen boys' attention.

Only when the codger bull cook passed through did Thea feel any sense of curiosity. If that was what she felt. She would never know his name, that old man so timeworn by his life in the wilderness. The whole liquid part of his eye—sclera, iris, pupil—was white as pearl and set deep in his wizened face. He might have been blind but for how he stepped around camp with complete sovereignty, less a cook than a bull. His position among the men puzzled Thea. One moment she'd see him hauling water up from the river, the yoke over his shoulders an ungodly cross for a man his age, and the next he'd be in private consultation with the camp foreman. He would feed the horses, brand the lumber, tend the wanigan while the clerk took his evening constitutional, even distribute the mail on occasion. But whatever his errand or task, every man in the camp regarded him with the utmost respect.

Her only reprieve from the kitchen crew came from the hundred ravenous jacks. For fifteen minutes three times a day they descended on the mess, arriving in single file and leaving the same way. They all looked the same at a glance, so she learned to identify them by their grotesqueries: the missing fingers or hands, the peg legs, the hunchbacks, the harelips, the sunken chests, the pruritus and scabies. It seemed as if each of the men possessed some defect or wound. They did not speak but greeted her with grunts or pleasant nods, depending on their age or mettle. Some were churls, some gentlemen, but most had about them a halo of resignation so heavy as to mask character of any sort. Their ambivalence followed them into the mess and weighed heavy on the mood. Silence was the rule of the mess hall. So despite the clattering of tinware and shuffling of boots, despite the sighs and audible yawns, their presence at chowtime only made the dumbness of her days more oppressive.

The quiet might have been tolerable were it not for the close quarters. When word had come to the camp foreman that he would have two women in his charge—he'd been alerted only days before the crew of sawyers and teamsters had reported at the end of October—he'd had to fashion their accommodations quickly. Trond Erlandson had worked the northwoods for years and could remember the camboose shanties of the seventies. Therefore, he saw no reason the men should need separate bunkhouses and mess halls. He likewise could not come to peace with the idea of two women toiling under his watch. Unless they were selling hospital tickets or accompanied by their proprietor husbands, women were to be unseen. That was his belief. As such, he put little effort into their billet, ordering the bull cook and two others to extend the root cellar behind the kitchen.

In a single rainy afternoon they dug a den not seven feet deep. They fortified the dirt walls with pine planks and built a roof of the same. They tarred the seams of the roof and hung a curtain between the cellar and their hovel. Against opposite walls they built bunks with no more thought than they gave the woodbox, which they stashed beside the potbelly stove. Above each bunk candle sconces were hung without the least consideration for where the paraffin might drip. A pewter pitcher and basin were set atop the stove, a barrel opposite the woodbox on the floor, and a pail without a handle intended to suffice as chamber pot was tucked behind the curtain. As dusk settled the rain gave way to drizzle and each of the three men carried a bale of hay from the stable to the new burrow. Having spread half of the hay on the floor, they padded the bunks with what remained. Finally, they stood back and considered their work. One of the jacks said, "I'd not unbutton my britches to make water here, but it'll do."

The first days in camp the quarters actually appealed to Thea, contrary as they were to the ship's berths where she'd spent so much of her recent time. At least here the squalor did not pitch and roll, was not rank with the smell of vomit, had not, in those first few days anyway, been infested with rodents and lice. Though it was true she could not stretch her arms fully above her head, though her bunk was barely wider than her thin hips, though it was true that when the autumn winds came howling through at night they sawed through her eiderdown as if it were no more than mosquito netting, she still possessed a sense of relief for having found a place to rest.

It was a mere ten sleepy steps from her bunk to the stove in the kitchen. She could retrace half of those steps to fetch stores from the cellar. And unless she was setting tables or making a trip to the privy she did not much move beyond that scant domain. By the time of the first snowfalls, she had begun to feel caged.

Each day after Thanksgiving the hours of daylight shriveled until it seemed there was hardly any purpose to the sun rising at all. And with each short day a definite restlessness settled into her. The jacks returned for lunch and for dinner with frosted coats, their faces hoary as ash, wraithlike. As their coats melted in the mess hall's heat, they appeared to be vaporizing. Where once she had needed all her powers of concentration to perform her tasks, she now found herself with time to daydream. While plating their slices of pie she would puzzle over their evanescence as though it were a religious rite. Day after day they entered and took their seats and began their disappearance. It saddened her and scared her some, but mostly it simply mystified her.

She spent all her spare thoughts on the men, and what she discovered—for the first time in her life—was simple desire, as if their warming, their steaming, their appetite, the way they smelled, all of it fed this new thing in her. Each night, after the camp had settled, after she had finished her own duties and lay in bed exhausted, she would recall the subtlest moments: the way a man would rub the cold out of his hands, for example, or the way he would blow on his stew, any of a hundred such mundane habits. In her revisiting them, the moments became profound, delicious, and she would often find herself caressing the bottom of her belly or tracing her fingers up and down her neck, feeling for her quickening pulse.

*W*ith the New Year came the cold. Colder even than the bitterest days in Hammerfest. The first week of January Thea hardly slept for the whining from the horse barn. The accordion music from the bunkhouse that had been a Saturday night staple since her arrival ceased. And if such a thing were possible, the men found new measures of silence as they filed into the mess for their meals. In a vacant gesture the foreman began making rounds during breakfast, glad-handing the men as they sulked over their porridge and coffee, reminding them of their fortitude and stoutheartedness. Of course they left each morning into the frigid darkness, but the purpose in their step was visibly reduced.

The second week of January was colder still. Twice the temperature dropped to forty degrees below zero overnight, and on those mornings following, the murmurs in the mess hall began. Any speech at all was rebellion, but even the hardened bull cook seemed reluctant to enforce the rule of silence. From his stool at the head of the table, he looked thoughtful, judicial, even, as he contemplated the new boundaries of his order. The taciturn resignation in the men had given way to anger. They griped about the cold, about frostbite, about the snapped saw blades and shattering ax handles. The teamsters lamented the horses' agony and their own. In all of this the bull cook and foreman indulged the men.

Thea was not so alarmed by the cold, partly because most of her day was spent near the comfort of the ovens and stoves and scullery fires but also because of her arctic childhood. So despite the turn to peevishness in the jacks, and despite the fact that she understood almost none of what they said, she actually welcomed the sound of their voices.

It was during the third week of January that something completely unexpected happened to Thea. After supper on Sunday, after most of the men had filed out of the mess and trudged back to their bunkhouse, one of the jacks stopped by the kitchen to address Thea. He was an old man, his lips cracked to the point of bleeding. He said his name was Rolf and that he had been asked by the bull cook to speak with her. He spoke in Norwegian, and the sound of her mother tongue after months of its absence almost made her cry. The old man must have sensed as much because he paused and smiled and patted the back of her hand. He then told her what he had to say was important. He reiterated that he was speaking on behalf of the bull cook, who was speaking on behalf of the foreman. Thea composed herself and sat down.

Rolf said that there had been reports from the jacks and teamsters of wolf sign. He said there were many wolves in the woods, and that in all his years of working in the forests, he'd never seen one himself. Given the horrendous cold, the wolves were perhaps getting desperate, and that was why they were encroaching on the camp. Were, in any case, coming nearer and nearer. He told her about the tracks on the river, about the scant moose and caribou, and that she was not to use the latrine without being accompanied by the old lady. The bull cook thought it best for the women to move as a pair until further notice. And then the old man nodded and left.

VI.

[*March* 1910]

*I*n mid-March, along the river's frozen waters, two thirteen-year-old boys shattered the glaze on a knee-deep and moon-shaped snow. They wore snowshoes they'd made of bent ash and moose gut. Their hats were beaver fur, trapped and skinned and finally sewn while they sat around the fire in the wigwam.

Odd and Danny Riverfish. They wore bowie knives on their belts and carried shotguns over their shoulders and they dragged a toboggan behind them. They were on their way to Danny's traplines on Thistle Creek and in the beaver ponds above. Their play at being men was grave and full of purpose and hardly premature anymore.

"Maybe there'll be some otter or marten, too," Danny said.

"Otter's good to eat. Pelts will fetch a fair price at the trading post. Maybe at Hosea's," Odd said, trying the woodsman's banter he was just learning that winter.

"Loony Hosea."

Odd smiled. "Yeah."

Danny smiled back.

"How's marten roasted up?" Odd said.

"We don't eat marten."

Odd nodded, committing to memory this new knowledge.

They went into the woods east of the lower falls. The water had cut through the snowpack and fell thunderously, icy mist rising into the clear, hard morning.

"You think Miss Huff will miss us today?" Odd asked.

"Miss Huff could make a forest fire boring. Besides, I don't plan on ever going to that schoolhouse again. I've had enough of her goddamn Bible. Goddamn arithmetic. Arithmetic never got a beaver tail to fry up, did it?"

"Or a pelt to sell," Odd said, then fell silent for a moment before he added, "She tells Hosea I'm truant and I'll get the belt."

"Someday you'll be doing the belting."

"I'll never be able to whomp Hosea."

"Sure, you will. Someday we'll whomp him up together, steal his money."

The mere thought of this made Odd despair. His feelings about Hosea were as complicated as his own true history. The only thing in his life that held any semblance of order was his friendship with Danny. They'd been fast friends since they could crawl. Miss Huff had been their teacher since kindergarten.

"I don't mind her lessons," Odd said. "Those Old Testament stories are about as scary as hell."

"None of it makes the least damn sense. Fire and brimstone and a bunch of things to be scared of. Bunch of impossible rules. And she's ugly as a pile of bear shit."

"That's plain meanness. She can't help how she looks. And her Bible stories ain't that different than those stories your grandpap tells around the fire."

Daniel looked over his shoulder and smiled at his friend. It was his best feature, that smile. It conveyed a minute's speech in a second's time. "Grandpappy never whipped you if you doubted him, though, now, did he?"

Odd tried his turn at a smile.

"Did he?" Daniel persisted.

"No, he did not."

"And besides, you think Miss Huff could tell you a damn thing about these woods? You think there's secret directions in that black book of hers on where to set your traps? Where to tap the maple trees come spring? Where to go ricing?"

"The woods ain't everything, Danny."

Daniel stopped, held his hands palms up. "What else do you see?"

It was true: The wilderness was ubiquitous, in all its guises. From where they stood he could see the cedar swamp east of the lower falls, knew it went from bog to basalt in a few mere steps, the rock rising sharply into bald outcroppings too steep to climb. This late in winter the lichen would have been eaten away by the surefooted caribou, their tracks were all over the place.

The outcropping went on for a mile, and they walked its base in silence until they heard the river falling at the Devil's Maw.

"We'll take a break at the river, eat those biscuits and bacon," Danny said. They each had a pair of sandwiches in the pockets of their wool coats.

"I'm about hungry enough. That gruel Bekah cooks up in the morning is the worst."

"You know, you can come live with us anytime you want."

"I don't think Hosea would like that very much."

"Hosea. Pap says he's two men at once."

"I believe he might be."

They walked through the edge of the woods to the river's shore. Odd said, "It ain't that I wouldn't want to."

"Want to what?"

"Live in the wigwam village."

"It's better than town," Danny said.

"Sure is."

They stood on the shore and unwrapped their sandwiches and drank cold coffee Odd had carried in the deer-hide wineskin.

"You got the land and farm now," Danny said.

"It ain't so bad at Hosea's. Except he makes me go to school."

"Plus you got Bekah."

"Yep."

"Well."

They finished the coffee.

Odd said, "I'm going to apprentice with Arne Johnson in springtime."

"A herring choker? That Hosea's idea, too?"

"Hell, no, it ain't. It's what I want to do."

Daniel Riverfish wore his rascally grin.

"The hell's so funny?" Odd demanded.

"It's just that you're a bit of a chickenshit, is all. I don't see you out on the lake by yourself. Least not when the wind comes on down."

"A chickenshit?"

Still that grin.

"I'm no chickenshit, Danny."

"You mess your britches and run for Bekah when an owl hoots. What's it gonna be like out on Gitche Gumee?"

Odd turned inward, began to think about this, was readying some sharp response. But Daniel spoke again first. "We got a ways to go, let's walk."

So Odd stowed the wineskin in his coat and put his mittens back on and adjusted his hat.

"You make the trail now," Odd said crossly. "I'll drag the sled."

*A*nd so they climbed the northern rim of the outcropping in silence, Odd sulking, Daniel cutting trail.

It was true Odd was a fearful boy. He was scared of almost everything, but especially of the fact that he'd never had a mother. At night, up in the third-floor apartment at Grimm's, in the closet-sized room, under the down ticking with the moonlight blaring through the window, in his socks and his union suit, he passed his sleepless hours mulling the life he didn't have. He didn't know it, but he was possessed by an old man's fears. He missed his mother—the mother he'd never known—the way an old widower might miss his wife of fifty years, he'd worked his mother up to those heights. Her ghostly presence colored so many of his thoughts.

And because of the hole she left in his life he was timid, and that timidity might have come across as fear.

Odd looked around the woods, at Daniel's back before him, at the enormous sky pitch blue and getting bluer. He had always taken these woods for granted. But in that quarter mile before Thistle Creek he realized that if there was anything to fear it was this wilderness, not his missing mother. He'd heard it said there were thousands of miles of the same woods to the north, and temperatures colder, and colder longer, the farther you went. He knew about the wolves and bears and moose that roamed these trees. He suddenly felt vulnerable.

"I guess I'm afraid of some things," he said from out of the blue.

Daniel Riverfish stopped, turned to face him. "Some things? You flinch at your shadow, bud." He turned to move ahead but stopped. "All I'm saying is that's hellish work, out on the lake. Much harder than trapping or standing behind a counter selling aspirin. I ain't saying you couldn't do it, but—"

"I never thought I was afraid of these woods, but I am. I think."

"Hell, yes, you are. And you should be. These woods are the world and the world ain't an easy place. That's what Grandpap always says. And he ain't ever wrong. About nothing."

"I know it now," Odd said.

"Good."

*T*histle Creek came down the gully off Peregrine Hill and emptied at the oxbow just north of the Devil's Maw. Daniel's first trap was a hundred paces up the creek and marked by a cedar tree grown out over the frozen water. They stopped at the tree and unlashed their shovels from the toboggan and dug through the snow. The trap was empty, as Daniel presumed it would be. He thought they'd be empty clear up to the pond, two miles upstream. But he was dutiful and they spent three hours digging and resetting traps.

By the time they reached the beaver pond Odd's neck and shoulders were burning and taut and he took the firmness for a sign.

"Watch me be brave," Odd said aloud.

"What do you mean?"

"Just watch."

Daniel smiled. "I will."

*W*hereas the otter traps were baited with fish, the beaver traps were baited with poplar poles two feet under water. The beavers would find the poplar and as they sat back to eat it fall on the trap and drown. Daniel had a dozen traps in the pond and they worked the first ten of them into the late afternoon. It wasn't until the eleventh trap that they found a beaver, a middling male. Odd pulled him out of the pond and tossed him onto the snow, released the trap, and reset it underwater.

Daniel huzzahed from across the pond, where he'd found a second beaver in the last trap. He likewise released the trap and reset it and joined Odd near their toboggan.

"Ma will love this tail," Daniel said. He could already taste it, fried up in bear fat, so hot it would scald the roof of his mouth.

"I'm coming for dinner," Odd said.

Daniel smiled.

They unsheathed their bowie knives and each of them gutted a beaver, tossing the offal aside for the ravens and wolves. If they were making a living they'd have been poor and disheartened, but because they were only boys in the service of becoming men they were thrilled, and they lashed the gutted beavers to the toboggan and turned down the same trail they'd cut on the way to the pond.

When they reached the Burnt Wood River and the Devil's Maw Odd finally spoke. "You think you can just decide to change?"

"Yes. Someways."

"I believe I can do it. I believe I will. No more chickenshit."

"Grandpap would tell you be careful."

"Be careful—"

*O*dd saw it first, heard or saw it, he couldn't say. Just under the Devil's Maw, about a hundred paces off the eastern shoreline of the river, from somewhere along the craggy cliff face came a plaintive cry just above Daniel's whistling and the river purling beneath the ice. The cliff was lit with the setting sun, blazing really, but for the dark recesses of the shallow caves that dotted the river's edge. Daniel was well behind him, pulling the sled. The cry grew with each step until Odd found himself slowing, then finally stopping twenty paces short of a curious declivity in the rock. He looked back, saw Daniel still trailing.

He felt himself welling up, recognized the feeling as faintheartedness, and bit down. He walked to the opening in the stone and felt his heart running as there rose from the rocks a musky odor he'd never smelled before. He took a half step back and tried to place the scent but could not. The bawling had stopped. Now only a kind of whimper came from the rocks.

Years later, whenever he tried to reconcile the defining moments of his childhood with the man he had become, he thought of that moment on the precipice as a divine one, when he became, for better or worse, the person he would always be. He would recall with utter clarity Daniel's voice telling him no, would recall his dizziness and the imaginary hand he felt pushing him as he knelt and removed his snowshoes, as he took his shotgun from over his shoulder and laid it against the cliff wall, as he shifted his bowie knife hanging from his belt to the small of his back. It would be strange to think about in later years, the way he knelt on the rocks without thinking, the way he crawled to the sound from the cave, the way he could never have done it again, how he had acted on the most animal level, curious in a way he'd never be again, not even the first time he made love with Rebekah. Strange to think there were moments when you could live completely outside your mind, stranger still to think how seldom those moments came to pass.

He crawled closer to the sound, to the cave, and then slithered into it. He noticed first the warmth and then caught the smell, rank now, whereas from above it had only been faint and musky. Taken together, the warmth and stink made his already swirling mind swirl more.

It took a moment for his eyes to adjust to the darkness and what it held. In that time he felt and heard the chthonian rhythms: the coursing waters, the earth's beating heart, his own pulse heavy in his head, the bears' slow, slow breath. They were two, a sleeping sow and her yearling, awake with the warm day. It must have been the yearling's cry he'd heard, for the cub's small white eyes were on him, wide and in a frenzy, its murmur grown to a full yell. A desperate yell.

And there was no way to explain what Odd did next. He reached his hand across the distance between them and touched the sleeping sow's shoulder. She was the source of all the warmth in the world, and that warmth was his now, too. For a moment he left his hand there, leaning closer and closer toward the bears as though drawn by some magnetic force. The yearling's screaming had become everything with the warmth. Everything until the sow woke as though from a warning dream. She rolled over and in a single motion came up at his face with her right forepaw. She swiped the side of his head with such force that he was thrown back into the light of day, a bleeding hole where his left eye had been.

Daniel was upon him, his shotgun raised to his shoulder while Odd scrambled up, screaming, his unmittened hand plugging the hole in his face. The bears were both screaming now, the earth rumbling. Daniel hurried Odd onto the sled, shouting, "Let's go, let's go, let's go!" as he pulled the lead ropes of the toboggan with one hand even as he kept his shotgun ready. He told Odd to hold on. To hold on tight. And he ran with the sled behind him, ran away from the sound in the earth, his best friend half blind.

VII.

[August 1920]

*H*e had spent a month watching the white pine not dry fast enough, the pitch bleeding like icicles dripping from an eaves trough.

At the end of the month he rented the horse again and dragged the log up to the mill, where for two dollars he had it kiln dried. He had felt, as he stood in the lumberyard smoking half-a-dozen hand-rolled cigarettes, like a cozener; like having the lumber dried was a desecration of his vision. But he'd also spent enough nights with Rebekah to know that time was more important than principle.

Since that day at the mill he'd lived as a hermit. He tended his nets and ran the barrels but otherwise spent his time in the fish house: by day working on the keel and, on those lucky and unforeseeable nights, in the company of Rebekah. The rhythm of that season was unlike anything he'd ever known. It was almost as if the long, steady work with his saws and adze continued in the dark with Rebekah, and since he took as much pleasure in one as the other, there were nights his felicity seemed endless. Boundless. And so he mistrusted it even as he gorged himself.

Now he had the keel on a strongback, leveled with shims on the floor of the fish house. He'd built the temporary ribbands and he could see, as he stood back with a fifth cup of coffee on those hot August nights, the bones of it, could see with his eye what he'd seen in his mind for years. He had a flitch of cedar sitting under a tarpaulin where the keel had sat before, he'd built a steam box of planks sawn from the white pine and fashioned a steamer from an old five-gallon kerosene bucket and hose line ordered from the automobile-parts catalog Hosea received each spring and fall. He'd also ordered two dozen C-clamps and a hundred dollars' worth of tools—rabbet planes, chisels, wooden mallets, nippers, a spokeshave, a sharpening stone, an assortment of ball-peen hammers and bucking irons and wrenches and screwdrivers—from Arneson's Hardware. On the fish counter a dozen well-fingered boat-motor catalogs sat beneath the plans, which were hand-drawn by Odd on huge sheets of onionskin paper. There were pencils and rulers scattered on the counter, and a new lamp shining down on it all.

He'd spent fifteen hours a day working on the boat since he'd gotten the keel dried, days he'd not eaten more than an apple, a bacon-and-onion sandwich, days that turned into night without a moment's notice or pause. At the end of those days he found himself exhausted but unable to sleep for the anticipation Rebekah might appear. And because her visits were unscheduled and the waiting interminable it was during these hours of night that he'd stop the physical work and resort to culling the catalogs, to his drawings and plans. He'd redraw the lines, up the sheer, recalculate the amount of lumber he was going to need, the barrels of oakum; double-check the weight of the motor he was considering against the strength of the motor box he had planned. All of these things raised in him an apprehension that was redoubled by the uncertainty of seeing her.

The waiting gave him a feeling deep inside. It was not heartache or longing but rather a definite pain, a throbbing in his bones. Some mornings he'd wake from his few fitful hours of sleep hardly able to walk. He'd brew a pot of coffee and stand at the counter scratching his beard, considering the boat. Considering his achy bones. He knew these first strips of wood were the most important, and the thought of his own life at the mercy of his workmanship filled him with doubt. On one such morning, after three nights without Rebekah, he decided to visit Hosea to see what he could learn about bones.

As a boy he'd been forbidden to enter certain rooms at the apothecary. Hosea's bedroom on the third floor was off limits, as were his offices on the second floor. There were doors with padlocks on them in the basement, rooms he knew now as the storage cellars for the hooch. Even Rebekah—so wont to disobey Hosea, so quick to conspire with Odd—was firm on the banishment.

But even as he'd been forbidden entrance, Odd had been a young boy left often to his own devices and full of a child's inquisitiveness. He'd made his romps through the apothecary governed by his curiosity, reveling in his cunning more than the discoveries made. The room Odd thought of now was Grimm's medical office. He wanted to see the skeleton that stood in the corner.

When he entered the apothecary on that August morning it was a place bustling with customers. By then Hosea was peddling garments and dry goods along with his cures, and the townsfolk were out in force. The Lund boy was behind the cash register in an apron to match Hosea's, Rebekah nowhere to be seen.

When finally there was a lull, Hosea met Odd at the counter. "Hello, young man," he said. "Business is brisk. It is indeed."

"I see that," Odd said.

"I'm a fool for not introducing this line of clothes sooner."

"They're in a frenzy for them, sure enough."

Hosea took a moment to delight in his savvy, then turned his attention back to Odd. "To what do I owe the pleasure?"

"I'm wanting to learn about bone disease."

"Bone disease?"

"Yup."

"As in diseases of the human skeleton? That sort of bone disease."

"That sort."

"Why? Are you not well?"

"I'm fine. Curious is all."

"Well," Hosea began, lapsing into a fatherly role that had never once suited him, "there are many diseases that afflict bone and marrow alike. Jean George Chrétien Frédéric Martin Lobstein was a professor and pathologist at École d'obstétrique du Rhin inférieur. He discovered the root causes of osteoporosis. Brittle bones, essentially. There are cancers of the bone marrow. Rickets, of course. And—"

"What about that skeleton up in your office?" Odd interrupted. "That bunch of bones have any disease?"

"Why, no, of course not."

"Can I go up and have a look at it?"

"Why so curious about bones in an attic?"

"I just want to see the skeleton."

Hosea looked around the shop, told the Lund boy he'd be back in a moment, and led Odd up the hidden staircase behind the wall of shelves above the counter.

Upstairs, he took a key from above the door frame and unlocked the door. "We don't often venture into these quarters anymore," Hosea said. The room was windowless, hot and close, dark but for what light followed them in from the hallway.

It was hard to see at first, but everything in the room was covered with white bed linens. As Hosea went from object to object removing the linens, a whole world of antique curiosities came into dim view. There was Hosea's old phrenology machine, his dentist's chair, his surgical table and glass-cased surgical tools, several volumes of medical books all bound in calfskin and stamped with gold lettering, a model of the planets aligned, held in place with bronze rods. Under the last sheet stood the skeleton. It was on a cart with wheels and Hosea rolled it toward the light from the hallway.

Odd glanced at the leg and arm bones, at the feet and hands, but settled quickly on the ribs and spine. As he studied the skeleton, Hosea launched into a lecture on what he called osteology. Hosea's bloviating was something Odd had long since learned to ignore, so as Hosea prattled, Odd studied the delicate curve of the ribs, the intricacies of the spinal column, the interconnectedness of the entire system.

He interrupted Hosea midsentence, "It's a complicated thing, ain't it?"

"The skeletal system?"

"What the hell else would I be talking about?"

Without suffering Odd's question for a moment, Hosea continued as though this had been the thread of their conversation all along. "When an infant is born there are many times more bones than the skeleton of the adult. They fuse. The system simplifies. Though of course it remains a wonder."

Finally Hosea stopped talking. The two of them stood in the afternoon light in the hallway and studied the skeleton.

Odd thought of the boat, the latticework of bent wood it would require, the hundred hours he'd spent shaping the keel, its perfection. He thought of the worst Lake Superior could offer and found satisfaction in his confidence in the white pine that just the winter before had stood in the forest. He decided he would be less cerebral about the boat. Less susceptible to his longing for Rebekah.

"What's brought this curiosity on?" Hosea asked.

Odd looked at him, thought better of telling him, but did anyway. "I'm building a new boat. A bigger boat. I just wanted to see the skeleton." He paused. "I've got the ribbands all set up. The keel is made. It's one piece, carved it out of a white pine log."

Hosea appeared interested. "How long is the keel?"

"Eighteen foot."

Now Hosea appeared interested and impressed. "A single-piece keel eighteen feet long? The wood is sound tip to tail?"

"It came from a chunk forty foot long. It's sound. It's a goddamn work of art, what it is."

"Why a new boat?" Hosea said.

"I'm tired of being wet."

Hosea smiled, remembering the night of the storm last month, Odd's willingness to risk his life in the skiff. "A little more cargo room?" Hosea pressed.

Now Odd smiled. "Yeah, a little."

"But why the skeleton?"

"I've been achy. I don't think I'll be anymore."

Hosea wheeled the skeleton back across the office. He covered it with a sheet. "I'll tend to the rest of this later."

Odd stepped down the hall and Hosea closed the door. After he turned the lock, he put the skeleton key in his pocket and led Odd downstairs.

VIII.

[*January* 1896]

*T*he moon hung gibbous and low, casting the snow in the gorge in bronze light. The only sounds were the wind and the flowing water beneath the snow. In an hour the sun would break over the lake.

Trond Erlandson and Hosea both wore fur coats and moose-hide mitts and hats pulled over their ears. They wore woolen socks beneath their sheep-lined boots and they covered their boots with felt. They stood on snowshoes and carried loaded Winchesters. The foreman withdrew from the inside of his coat a pair of field glasses that he trained first upriver and then down. The only thing they seemed to magnify was the cold. This was the eleventh night below zero and still two weeks until February.

Whispering, Hosea said, "We saw the otter scat smeared around below the lower falls. The wolf sign's up and down this river like they couldn't care less about you."

Trond looked into the downriver darkness, measuring their whereabouts against a woodsman's markers: deadfall, beaver lodge, muskeg, eagle aerie. "We're only six miles from camp," he said. He shook his head and spit the wad of snoose from his mouth, spit twice more and said, "Goddamn. Where was the bull moose they found?"

"Up on Bear Paw Lake. Just ten miles as the raven flies. And those ravens have been around."

The bull moose had been found by a crew of sawyers working the northern parcel two days earlier. Frozen solid, its graying dewlap blowing in the stiff wind, leaning against an enormous white pine, it was but the most recent evidence of winter's provenance. They'd found other creatures similarly dead. Each carcass a portent of hungry wolves.

The foreman followed the moonlight up the gorge once more. New snow had fallen the day before and in that light the drifts appeared lit from inside.

"I've been in these particular woods for three years and not seen them yet," the foreman said. "I've heard them, I've messed my boots in their scat, I've seen what they can do to a caribou weighing four hundred pounds. But I've not set my eyes on them." He spoke as much to himself as to Grimm. "But if they're this close to camp—" His voice trailed off and he shook his head. "We're not talking about hugags or agropelters here." He closed his eyes hard against the wind and when he opened them the moon was gone, swallowed by clouds.

He turned to Hosea. "You want the wolves why?"

"The bitches are in estrus, their glands are spilling with curatives."

"I wouldn't believe it if I'd never seen some of those potions you peddle."

They hiked another quarter mile along the palisade's edge, hoping for a better view of the river. They stood against trees not four feet from the precipice, the wind rising to their faces. They were silent now, waiting for the clouds to pass or the morning light to rise. The foreman already knew he would send for the dogs down in Two Harbors. He knew, also, that any wolf sign closer to camp would sharpen the auguries forming in the minds of the men.

There was no longer any reason to be standing on that cliff with Hosea Grimm but that he wanted to see the pack. So they waited. He knew the hour to be near five, the time of day he usually rose from his bunk and stepped outside to piss.

"There!" Hosea Grimm whispered, clutching the foreman's shoulder. "There, below the falls."

The foreman craned to see but found only dark.

"There again. Christ. Christ, yes." Hosea Grimm lifted the Winchester to his shoulder and aimed downriver.

Still the foreman searched, pleading silently with the morning for light. But none came.

And then the flash of the gun, the concussion traveling up and down the gorge, trapped.

*B*y the time they reached the lower falls the morning light was up. The clouds that had engulfed the moon stuck, so the day broke grainy and dim. But no matter, all the light in the world would not have illumined the wolves. Nor any tracks nor any sign at all.

"Fools persist," the foreman said. "I lost a night's sleep for what?"

"A vigorous hike is good for body and mind," Hosea countered. "Cold air clears the lungs."

"I get plenty of cold air, to say nothing of hiking around these woods." The foreman checked his pocket watch. "This damn watch. It's froze up on me."

Hosea Grimm checked his own. "It's nearly seven thirty. I'd best turn for town. Who knows what the peaked will require today. Yesterday it was Mats Barggaard with a nosebleed."

"What did you prescribe?"

"Spiderwebs. A ball of spiderwebs."

The foreman smiled. "I wouldn't believe it if I hadn't heard about the ox shit you slathered all over that boy's back after he fell into his family's stove."

"It worked—both the dung and the spiderwebs."

"Tell me, with what would you remedy a frozen timepiece?"

"For that you'll want Joshua Smith. He'll be passing through before long."

The foreman took a deep breath. "Sorry you didn't get your wolf."

"I'll get one yet."

"I believe you will."

Hosea offered his hand. "I'll see you in town."

"Soon enough."

As the two men parted ways on the river, an unkindness of ravens decamped from the high boughs of a white pine and flew up the gorge. Their cries were horrible and their moving shadow cast yet another shade on the snow.

Hosea Grimm turned back to the foreman and shouted across the river, "What did I say about the ravens?"

*T*he ice road cut through the tallest stand of white pine along the river. Before the upper falls, the road veered south and plunged into Gunflint. The next morning Trond Erlandson sat his horse on the crest of the road looking onto the morning over the lake. A mile offshore the vaporous open water cemented his doubt. It clouded the sunrise. He looked down the shore for Isle Royale, but it was gone in the sea smoke.

He had once been a peaceable man—not given to the agitation that was so much a part of his daily routine now—and the vista, though it complicated things, reminded him of that quiet part in him. When he had first arrived in these wilds, now thirty years ago, he'd looked on the country—in all its enormity and ungoverned beauty—as if it were his own private opportunity. Though he had worked tirelessly and with unchecked vigor, all he had to show for his labor was his authority. And his responsibility. He took neither lightly. He spit a stream of tobacco juice into the snow and spurred the horse forward.

In all that cold the leather saddle creaked with the first stride. The horse sidestepped into the soft snow on the edge of the road and began his cautious descent. Some few paces down, the wind paused and when it did the horse paused, too, and the foreman craned his head toward the river. He heard the water coursing under the ice and over the falls and into the Devil's Maw. He cursed it and spit in its direction. Were it not for the falls and that hole in the river he could have rafted the harvest down to the mill instead of hauling it on the treacherous road. The horse stepped again without prodding and in half an hour Trond heard the whine of the mill and saw the mountains of stacked pine in the mill yard.

Instead of hitching his horse outside Grimm's, he stabled him at the livery to be blanketed and fed. Before leaving the horse he took his Winchester from the saddle scabbard and unloaded it and put it over his shoulder. He asked the livery keeper to water the horse, too, and he patted the Appaloosa's mottled hindquarters and walked to Grimm's.

By any definition Grimm's store was more than an apothecary—if it was an apothecary at all—though that was what the signboard above the door advertised: GRIMM'S APOTHECARY. The first time Trond Erlandson entered the store had been in the late spring of 1894, a few months after it opened. His piles had become insufferable and he submitted to his embarrassment and sought counsel. Grimm prescribed oakum, to Trond's dismay, but it worked. He'd been a reliable customer since.

The store was as much a testament to Grimm's eccentricity as it was a place of commerce. When Trond entered that midwinter morning, the whole of his beard was coated with ice stained amber from the snoose dribble. For as often as he frequented Grimm's apothecary, and as fond as he was of its proprietor, Trond did not feel, now more than a year after his first visit, any closer to knowing Hosea Grimm.

The door closed behind Trond Erlandson, sucking much of the heat with him. He stomped his feet and took off his mittens and hat and nodded at Rebekah, who darned socks in a chair beside the box stove. There was a basket of socks on the floor beneath her. Hosea himself stood behind the counter, his felt derby squarely on his head, his apron starched and hanging to his ankles. The store was, as always, impeccably clean. At this hour there were no other customers.

"Trond, my good man. Every time I see you you've ice on your face."

"Thirteen mornings in a row below zero," Trond said, stepping forward and cupping his beard in his hands. He stood above the spittoon and waited for a moment while the ice melted, dripping into the slurry. "I see you survived yesterday's hike out of the woods."

Hosea stood before the beakers and vials and canisters lining the shelf behind him. "I guess I'm hardier than all those frozen moose."

"That's why I'm here," Trond said. "Will you show me that advertisement again?"

Grimm checked a pair of drawers behind the counter before he found the week-old Two Harbors *Ledger* in question. At the bottom of the back page an outfit in Castle River advertised the dogs. Grimm asked Rebekah to bring Trond a cup of tea and left him to the classified.

The headline read, WORLD'S BIGGEST DOGS! Two droopy-faced hounds were drawn muzzle to muzzle, looking not unlike the foreman's

St. Bernard. Trond read the rest of the ad: RUSSIAN OVCHARKA WATCH-DOGS, BEASTS OF THE BRAVEST ORDER, FEAR NOTHING AND NO ONE. BRED FOR OUR KILLING WINTERS. GUARD YOUR LIVESTOCK OR FAMILY. $30. LITTER OF SIX YEARLINGS READY FOR YOU! It then listed the name of the breeder and an address at which to contact him.

"What can you tell me about this Olli?" Trond said.

"He's a Laplander," Grimm began. "Used to run a trapline way the hell up the Bunchberry River, but he lost a foot winter of '93. Now he raises these dogs. And a little hell if truth be told."

"On one leg he gets around?"

"He limps and curses, but he does get around. Got a stump made of hickory. He runs a ferry up to Duluth in the summer months, keeps butter on his bread."

"And what have you heard about the dogs?"

"Joseph Riverfish tells a story how one of them giant mutts treed a bear this fall. Way up a white pine. Then waited the bear out. When it finally came down, the dog and it squared off. The dog won. Olli's got the pelt to prove it. I guess it's true they're two hundred pounds. Feet the size of skillets. Probably wouldn't want to curl up with one, but might keep the wolves at bay."

Trond read the advertisement again, then asked, "When does Joseph make the next mail run?"

"Not until Friday. But he can't bring those dogs back. He'll be fully loaded. He always is."

Trond ran his hand through his beard again. "I can't spare the men or the time," he said.

"For the right price his son would make that run."

"He's what, fourteen years old?"

"He might be, but he's been helping his father with the mail route. He can look after himself."

"What do you suppose the right price is?"

"Christ, Trond, they live in a wigwam. Eleanor is pregnant. It's been a long, hard winter. I imagine any price is right. Just be fair."

"Could he run up the lake?"

"I've not heard reports from along the way, though you can be damn certain I'd not do it. You can see the water's still open just a mile off-shore." He peered out the big window in front of his store. "But the trail is fast, from what I hear. The cold, you know. He could have those dogs back here in three or four days."

"The dogs, you think they could run the trail?"

"I imagine those dogs dictate their own terms. If they can't handle the trail, they'll let the lad know it."

Trond walked to the window. He didn't have a choice, he reckoned. The jacks would tolerate about anything, but not wolves in their back-yard. He turned to Grimm. "Where can I find the boy?"

IX.

[*March* 1910]

*I*n the middle of the night, exhausted, over a finger of Canadian whiskey, Hosea paged through Howe's thirty-year-old *Manual of Eye Surgery* for the fourth time. Odd lay sedated on the same table on which he'd been born, the bleeding from his eye stanched, the hole in his face where his eyeball had been like a potato gone to mush.

Rebekah slept in a chair at Odd's side. The cuffs of her blouse sleeves were stained with blood. Hosea set the manual down on the bedside table and stepped into the next room, returning with an afghan that he placed over her. He thought he could see her settle into a deeper sleep under the warmth of it. To what dreams he could not imagine. These two children, he did love them. Which was what made Odd's pain so difficult to bear. He was still just a boy. A boy whose only chance had been Hosea.

Hosea looked down on Odd, the ether having blanched the color from his cheeks. *I have offered him a chance, haven't I?* This question had been dogging him since Danny had delivered Odd twelve hours earlier.

Danny had left Odd unconscious on the toboggan outside the apothecary while he bounded up the steps and into the store. Breathlessly he shouted, "Hosea! Hosea! It's Odd! He needs help! Quick!"

Hosea had been taking his evening inventory, up on the ladder counting the contents of the canisters on the shelves behind the counter. He jumped down and hurried around the counter to meet Daniel.

"What is it, lad?"

Danny still had his snowshoes on and he sat on the floor to take them off as he panted, "Odd, he's outside. He's hurt bad."

Hosea ran outside, down the steps, and found the boy lying there. One of the town dogs had sniffed Odd out and was poking his cold nose into the wound on his face. Hosea kicked the dog away.

"Daniel!" he shouted over his shoulder. "Daniel! Get out here."

But Danny was already hurrying back to the toboggan.

"What in Christ's name happened?"

Danny's breath was coming back to him. "It was a bear."

"A bear?"

"Odd went into a den. It's my fault."

Hosea stood quickly and removed his apron and balled it and put it firmly over Odd's eye. He turned to Daniel. "Listen to me carefully. Go inside. Tell Rebekah to put water on to boil. Lots of it. She's upstairs. Tell her to put fresh linens on the table in the surgery. Go."

Daniel was back inside the apothecary before Hosea lifted Odd off the toboggan. By the time he'd carried him up to the second floor, Rebekah and Daniel were already preparing the table. Hosea laid Odd down. Though the boy was still unconscious, Hosea was relieved to find his pulse steady, his temperature, to the touch, normal.

"Rebekah, listen."

Rebekah could not take her eyes off Odd.

"Rebekah! Listen to me."

She finally looked up.

"Do you have water boiling?"

She nodded.

"Go upstairs. As soon as it's ready, as soon as it's hot, bring it down. Put more on to boil. Do this as quickly as possible. Do you understand?"

Rebekah answered by walking backward from the room, her eyes not leaving Odd until she'd stepped out.

"Now, Daniel, I need you to tell me slowly and precisely what happened."

So, while Hosea sedated Odd, while he stanched the blood and cleaned the eye, while he clipped away Odd's shaggy hair and shaved his eyebrow, Daniel told him the story of Odd climbing into the bears' den. Danny spoke slowly, as he'd been instructed, and tried to remember every detail. Hosea listened intently while he worked.

"I tried to stop him but I was too late," Danny concluded. "He was half in the den when I realized what he was doing. It's my fault." Danny started to weep.

Hosea stood up and checked Odd's pulse again and then looked at Daniel. "I don't understand how it's your fault," he said.

"I told him he was a chickenshit," Danny said. "Odd said he was going to be brave." Danny wiped the tears from his cheeks, wiped the snot from his nose. "I didn't know he was going to climb into a bear den."

Hosea put his hand on Danny shoulder. "Daniel, any fool who climbs into a bear den deserves what awaits him. This is not your fault."

These words only sent the boy into another fit of tears.

Hosea tousled the boy's hair and said, "Go help Rebekah with the water, Daniel. We'll fix your pal up good as new."

But Hosea had no confidence this was true. Since his arrival in Gunflint he'd set countless broken bones. Cleaned the bullet wounds of many men clipped accidentally in the shoulder or back during pheasant or turkey hunts. Delivered all the babies born here over the past ten years and stood over more than a few slow deaths. Never mind his effort at curing Thea, the poor lad's poor mother. But Odd's injury was different. It was out of his purview, for one. This skull injury, he wondered if he was actually seeing the outer recesses of Odd's brain when he looked into the wound. And then, it was Odd.

Hosea walked to Odd's bedside and carefully removed the bandage covering the boy's eye. Blood pulsed slowly from the wound with each beat of Odd's heart. Hosea put two fingers on his neck and opened his pocket watch. After a minute he wrote the boy's heart rate on a chart on the bedside table. From his pocket he removed the ophthalmoscope and trained it on the empty eye socket. He had identified the essential components. The extraocular muscles had been severed. The ophthalmic artery was intact. The bundle of optic and sclerotic nerves was horribly frayed. Hosea could not imagine the pain. It made his skin crawl to think of it. He wet a clean cloth in the bowl of warm water and washed the wound for the tenth time. Odd stirred but did not wake, the drugs staying consciousness.

He replaced the ophthalmoscope and walked to the window. The sun was near to rising over the lake. He had to catch his breath looking on the horizon, thinking about the boy and how from now on he'd only ever see half of what he ought.

*A*fter lunch, after Hosea had been up the Lighthouse Road to the telegraph machine in the lighthouse keeper's office, after he'd exchanged telegraphs with a physician friend in Chicago, after two more hours spent with Howe's *Manual* and another hour studying Gray's *Anatomy*, after he'd administered another dose of ether, after all this, Hosea performed the surgery. With a speculum holding Odd's eyelids wide open, Hosea trimmed the frayed nerves and cut back the extra-ocular muscles. The bear's claw had entered at the corner of the boy's eye and broken the bridge of his nose in the process. Hosea removed several tiny fragments of bone that he'd not seen until then. For an hour he labored over the boy's injury and when he was satisfied he stitched the gash extending down from the outer corner of Odd's eye, bandaged it, and wrapped his head with gauze. Finally he gave him a last dose of morphine and left the boy to sleep.

Danny had been sitting outside the surgery since early morning, and when Hosea stepped out of the room Danny stood with a questioning look on his face.

Hosea took a deep breath, he cracked his knuckles. "Hello, Daniel."

"How is he, Mister Grimm?"

"I think he'll be fine. He's lost his eye. It will take him some long time to recover. He'll need visitors. I hope you'll come see him."

"I will. Every day."

"I believe you will."

"Can I go in and sit next to him?"

"Don't touch or otherwise disturb him. Do you understand?"

Danny nodded.

"And if he wakes, or if anything seems strange, come up and fetch me."

"I will."

Hosea turned to leave as Danny stepped into the room, but Hosea paused and turned. "Daniel."

Danny paused in turn. "Yes?"

"Where were you boys when this happened?"

"Up on the Burnt Wood. We spent the day on my trapline."

"Why did you call Odd a chickenshit?"

Danny blushed.

"I already told you it's not your fault, son."

"He told me about learning to fish with Arne and I couldn't help it. I just don't see him out on the big water all by himself."

Hosea considered this for a moment. "So he went bear hunting."

"Mister Grimm, I wish I wouldn't have said it."

"I'm sure. Go on in there, sit next to your friend."

Danny did.

*T*wice each day Hosea cleaned the wound and changed the bandages. He administered smaller and smaller doses of morphine until finally none was needed. Danny came every day and sat on the bedside chair. Rebekah brought Odd his meals and watched over him when Danny wasn't there.

After a week Odd was well enough to convalesce up in the flat, so Hosea moved a chair to the front window and piled books around the boy and in this way Odd ushered in spring. Danny still came often and the two boys spent the first days of April playing chess or card games rather than romping through the woods.

On one such day, as the boys sat in the flat putting new backing and line on their fly reels, Hosea joined them.

"I've something to show you, Odd."

Three weeks had passed since the surgery and except for the regular, dull throbbing in his eyeless socket Odd was feeling fine. The boys set their fly reels down and looked at Hosea standing above them. He held a metal box.

"What is it?" Odd asked.

Hosea set the box on the coffee table, knelt on one knee, and opened the box. He withdrew one of a dozen silken handkerchiefs. He peeled the silk back as though it were a banana skin and withdrew from its center a glass eyeball. He offered it to Odd, who took it and held it close to his good eye.

"What is it?" Odd asked again.

"It's a glass eye, son. I have several here. Wanted to see whether any of them might fit."

Odd was transfixed by the eyeball. He held it up to the sunlight in the window and rotated it as though he had in his hand a precious jewel. The sunlight caught the glass and flashed brilliant penumbras on the floor.

"I don't understand," Odd said.

"You put it in place of the eyeball you lost to the bear."

"Will I see from it?"

"No, it's cosmetic. It will look just like a regular eye, but it serves no purposes for sight."

"So he won't have to walk around with a patch over his eye for the rest of his life?" Daniel ventured.

"Precisely," Hosea said. He removed another of the silk handkerchiefs and extracted a second glass eye. "If none of these work, we'll have to order one."

Odd reached into the box himself now, pulled another out, and unwrapped it. He couldn't imagine it in his eye socket. For that matter, he couldn't imagine that he'd lost one of his eyes. The thought quickened his heart and the pulsing behind the bandages intensified.

"We'll have to wait another month or so, until the eye has healed some. But I wanted to show you. What do you think?"

"I don't know what to think."

"It's a good thing, Odd."

Odd said, "What if it shatters? What if someone hits me in the eye? What if I slip out on the boat, hit my eye on the deck?"

"I believe they're quite durable, though I suppose there's always a chance of the eye shattering. Or cracking. In which case we'll replace it."

Odd was now holding the second glass eye up to the light. The quizzical expression on his face suggested he'd heard none of what Hosea said.

"In any case, wearing a glass eye will be better than walking around looking as though your face were half melted away. Hell, it might even help you find a wife someday."

"Hosea?" Odd asked a moment later, as Hosea was wrapping the eyes back in their silk handkerchiefs.

"What is it, lad?"

"Will I still be able to apprentice with Arne Johnson this spring?"

"I reckon you will, yes."

"Because it's time I got started earning my share."

"There will be plenty of time for earning your share," Hosea said. He put the eyeballs back in the box and clasped it shut. "You boys finish with your fly line. I'll talk to Arne Johnson soon."

*A*rne Johnson saw no reason Odd shouldn't start learning the ropes, so five weeks after he'd climbed into a bear den Odd straddled the forward thwart of Arne's skiff as they headed out to haul the first set of the season.

Arne was a widower, childless, and the least garrulous man in a town full of reticent men. That Odd was in Arne's skiff at all was a testament to the boy's standing among the villagers. From the first days of his life, Odd had been the whole town's ward. All his sweaters were hand-knit by the fishermen's wives; his haircuts given under a bowl by the innkeeper's wife; the men took him hunting and handed down their own sons' outgrown boots and shotguns; Christmas morning always found twenty gifts intended for Odd on the apothecary doorstep. The godly wives took him to church on Sunday mornings, and the schoolteacher stayed after class to help with his lessons.

That brisk April morning in Arne's skiff was just another version of those Christmas gifts and haircuts and Odd was as grateful for this as he'd been for all the kindnesses bestowed on him over the years. As Arne pulled for the open water beyond Gunflint harbor, he said, "You watch what I do. If your hands get cold, keep it to yourself. If you get hungry, eat the sandwich in your pocket. Watch the shore closely, that will tell you where we are. If you fall overboard, God rest your soul."

Odd listened intently, coupling Arne's terse lecture with what Danny's father had told him about the big water. Arne's thirty-second speech was the first of only a few short speeches that season, but what Odd learned that summer would last his lifetime. They rowed an hour offshore to Arne's buoys, where Arne secured his oars and set immediately to hauling the net. Odd knew to sit still at first, to watch, as Arne had put it. Odd likewise knew that as Arne choked the herring through the net it was his job to box them. The fish were cold and slippery and the wind coming up his back might have dissuaded other boys, but Odd relished it from the first moment. The fear Danny had diagnosed that fateful day on the Burnt Wood River never entered his thoughts.

Five hours they hauled, tending fifteen thousand feet of nets at two different sets. They worked in harmony in a way Arne found unbelievable. The boy with the patched eye was as natural under the rolls of the boat as the water itself. When they got to shore that afternoon, after they'd hefted the boxes into Arne's harborside fish house, as Arne gutted and salted the fish and Odd packed them, Arne offered the only praise he ever would. "You've a fisherman's blood," he said.

Odd would have known this without hearing it, but he blushed all the same, the color in his cheeks announcing not only his embarrassment but also his thanks for the chance.

Over the course of that summer Arne taught Odd everything: how the fish ran, what the wind meant, how to judge a lowering sky, how to mend a net. He taught him how to barter with the fishmonger and keep a ledger, how to sew oilskin and make gunnysack anchors. At the end of summer, after a long day on the water and in the fish house, as Arne cooked sausages and onions on the stove, he told Odd to sit down.

"We'll start building you a skiff this winter. There's plenty of work to do in winter without building a boat, too, but together we can manage. Next spring you'll get your first grounds. You'll use my fish house."

Odd nodded.

Arne stirred the sausages, forked an onion into his mouth.

"The grounds won't yield much. They'll be near the shoreline. And you'll still be apprenticing, but you'll be doing it in your own boat. The season after next you'll be on your own. Do you understand?"

"Yes, sir."

"Good. Now have some grub."

*T*he leaves were turning by the time Hosea fit the glass eye. Odd sat before a mirror in Hosea's examination room. Though his eye still pulsed and sometimes ached behind the patch, he could tolerate it. He hadn't seen the wound yet, and this fact alone worried him that morning.

"You look just like your mother, Odd," Hosea said.

Odd glanced up in the mirror. Hosea was standing behind him, his arms crossed.

"She'd be proud of the young man sitting here today. Even if he was fool enough to raid a bear den."

Odd smiled.

"Are you ready for this?"

"Where's Rebekah?"

"She's tending the store. You can show her when we're finished."

"All right."

"Okay?"

Odd nodded.

It took a few minutes for Odd to look into the mirror. When he did, all he saw was the sunken lids of his wounded eye. It dawned on him at once that the space where his eyeball once had been looked an awful lot like a miniature version of the cave entrance in which he had lost it. The eyebrow above the wound had grown back darker than the eyebrow above his good eye, and the effect was shadowy. It seemed to set the hole where his eye should have been deeper in his face.

He reached his hand up to the wound. The tips of his fingers dipped into the folds of his eyelids and he pulled them quickly back out.

"Let's see how it fits," Hosea said. "Tilt your head back."

Odd stared at himself for another moment before doing as Hosea said.

The sensation of having the glass eye inserted was a dull one, just the tugging and pinching of skin. It took only a minute.

"How does it feel?" Hosea asked.

Odd didn't say anything. In the years to come Odd had two eyes custom made, but that first was culled from Hosea's ready supply. And though it wasn't a perfect fit it wasn't bad either. Except for some tautness in the skin there was no sensation at all to having the glass eye in place.

"I believe this will suffice," Hosea said as he pressed the skin around the glass eye with his thumbs. "Are you ready to see it?"

"I am."

Odd sat up and looked at himself. He looked for a long time and didn't say anything. It was himself he saw, but it wasn't. He blinked and despite all his conviction he felt tears welling in his right eye—his good eye. He saw his right eye gloss over. The glass eye stared back brown and too large and dry as chalk.

"The skin around the glass eye will stretch a little. It's like breaking in a new pair of boots."

Odd's right eye was the color of wet blueberries, but the glass eye was brown. "I look like one of Danny's sled dogs," Odd said.

"You'll probably need to have new eyes fit as your skull grows. When you do, we'll have them made so they match your real eye."

Odd said nothing. He put his left hand in front of the glass eye and held it there. The tears welled again.

"It's temporary, lad."

"I heard you," Odd snapped. He used all his will to quell the tears. Blinked hard. And brought his face closer to the mirror.

"Listen to me, Odd: What the eye can't see, your heart will find."

Odd looked up quickly, met Hosea's eyes. "I don't understand," he said.

"Someday you will, son. Someday you will."

X

[August 1895]

*T*hea was nearly seventeen years old when she saw a tree for the first time, and then only from the rail of the topsail schooner *Nordsjøen*. The boat was bound for Tromsø, a day and a night out of Hammerfest, and those few on board were cold and tired. The captain and his three-man crew were busy at the rigging, dodging the skerries and shoals, slogging through frazil ice and fog. When the sun began its burn the high fjords and their plunging ridges on either side of the boat came into view.

At first she mistook the tree line for a lowering storm, some sharp front from the east. As the good boat slipped forward, though, she saw it was no storm at all. For all her short life she'd lived in Hammerfest, had never, before yesterday, been out of view of it. The hills in Hammerfest were gradual and bare—arctic desert—and what green there was came by way of the cloudberry boscage and lichen for a few summer months. Now a forest of spruce cascaded down the mountainsides, each minute the lifting of the fog revealed more forest. She'd been told of trees, but not these. No, the trees she'd heard of were still more than a month before her, in Amerika, on the shores of a lake said to equal any ocean.

Strictly speaking, the voyage between Hammerfest and Tromsø was the second leg of her journey. Early the morning before, she'd stood on the rocks while her papa had loaded her belongings into his fishing boat. They had an hour before the ferry would leave Hammerfest quay, and her mama was busy finding anything else she could send. They lived in a sod house on Muolkot, an island in plain sight of Hammerfest. Her papa had a few sheep and a potato garden. He had a skiff that was safe along the shore and in the harbor but not equipped for open water. He was a decent and pious man, a mostly quiet man. He played his *hardingfele* on Saturday nights and was capable of good humor, though not much recently. He knew he could not offer his daughter much. So he sold a sheep and half of his parcel of land and spent the rest of his life savings on passage to Amerika.

The voyage had been more than a year in the planning. A year of strict saving and hoarding, of frugal and meager living. Thea's belongings were paltry. In her carpetbag she carried only an extra dress, two scarves, her summer bonnet, a pair of stockings, and her mittens. It was cold enough passing through the fjord that she already wore her winter cloak and hat. She also had a basket of food, one meant to last her entire voyage. It contained three jars of soused herring, lefse, pickles, a pound of gjetost cheese, two jars of sheep's milk, two jars of cloudberry jam, and a small burlap sack of pears already bruised and mealy. Who could say where the pears had come from? Sewn into the skirt of her dress was a secret pocket, and in this she kept her purse. It held fifty American dollars and ten Norwegian kroner. When she got to Kristiania, she was going to put her papers in this same secret place. Last was her handbag, woven in the last days by her mother. It was filled with essentials: her Bible, diary, English phrasebook, and a hairbrush.

Slight as she was, Thea had no problem carrying her belongings. When the *Nordsjøen* reached the dock in Tromsø she had already retrieved her baggage from her bunk. She stood at the rail waiting for the gangplank to be dropped from the dock, first in a queue of ten weary travelers.

By the time she debarked and stopped in a harborside café for bread and cheese and coffee, it was already time to find her next boat, which would bring her to Kristiania. She boarded the *Port av Kristiania* at noon, two days of starts and stops along the western shore under steam ahead of her.

The *Port av Kristiania* arrived at her final destination in the middle of the night. Thea was sleeping in her bunk when she felt the ship's definitive stop. She found her bags and joined the crowd and by the time she reached the main deck she was wide awake and consumed by a new awe: Kristiania—even at night, perhaps especially at night—sprawled all around her. The gas streetlamps flickered near and far, those on the yonder hillside a kind of greasy mirage that might not have been light at all, might have been only an impossible reflection. There were warehouses on the waterfront three times larger than the ship she was now stepping off. Everywhere the sounds of harbor life thrummed: the grinding and shrieking of train and trolley tracks, the clatter of horses' hooves on the dock's planks, the moaning of loading cranes, and above and below all of it the sound of human voices.

Before then, Thea had never seen more than one hundred people gathered together. But even in the middle of the night there were thousands of people here. In the next slip two steamships, each twice as long as the *Port av Kristiania*, were loading, crowds of people tunneled into the shadowy quay. As Thea reached the gangplank, she noticed the taut ship lines crisscrossing the docks, the enormous nets hauling cargo onboard the steamships before her, and casks by the thousands ready to be loaded into ships' holds.

As soon as she was on the dock she was swept into a cordoned area where several nurses stood ready to examine and interrogate the passengers. One at a time they were led to tables. When it was Thea's turn, a grim-faced woman signaled her to come forward. Thea was asked to provide her ticket for passage. The nurse confirmed the ticket against a list in her passenger log and proceeded to ask a series of twenty-nine questions.

Aside from the routine questions regarding her final destination and place of birth and the promise of labor in America, she was also asked whether or not she was an anarchist or polygamist, if she was in any way crippled or had deformities, if she had ever been imprisoned. She spent fifteen minutes answering these and other questions, and when the interview was complete, the nurse took Thea into a curtained area and asked her to remove her cloak and hat.

The medical examination that followed was cursory. After the nurse listened to Thea's lungs with her stethoscope and checked her for a hunchback and diseases of the skin, she filled out a landing card and told Thea she could go aboard *Thingvalla*. As she ascended the steep gangplank, she could already feel the melancholy sea in the soles of her feet.

Thingvalla was a three-masted, single-stacked steamship already some twenty-five years old when Thea sailed across the North Atlantic. She had a third-class ticket and found her berth on the aft end of the tween deck. There were four canvas bunks in a six-by-eight-foot cabin, but it was late in the year and a ship made to carry nine hundred steerage passengers had only three hundred aboard. So she bunked with only one other passenger, a rawboned pregnant woman with a ghost's pallor and darting eyes. The woman's belongings were even more pathetic than Thea's: a filthy gunnysack not much filled and tied closed with a piece of balling twine. She had no foodstuffs and no purse and Thea, for all she'd seen, had never seen anything as sad as this.

Aside from the people aboard her, *Thingvalla* also held a cargo of barreled fish: brisling, anchovies, herring, cod. The casks must have leaked because the smell seeped through the interstices of the floor and on warmer days put a stink in the air impossible to ignore. The stench especially disagreed with Thea's bunkmate, who had trouble enough with the heavy seas and yawing vessel. Whole hours passed with a constant moan coming from the woman.

On their third day at sea Thea had had enough, and she ventured to the main deck for fresh air. The deck was slick and crowded and Thea could hardly bring herself to move. She stood on the threshold of the gangway, making a slow inspection of the panorama. Though *Thingvalla* was only forty nautical miles north of Scotland, there was nothing but the brumous sea and its slowly rising swells to see. Thea was used to long views, but this was otherworldly. In Hammerfest, the tundra was locked and still. Here the sea roiled and splashed and went on forever. It was the most beautiful thing she'd ever seen.

She spent an hour walking from one vacant spot along the railing to the next, finally able to believe she was gone. In all the time she'd spent wondering what it would be like, she'd never envisioned a world this vast.

She was standing at the prow when she noticed the western horizon. It was approaching with greater haste than the ship's steady ten knots might have warranted. The swells were growing, too, and a stiff breeze came from nowhere and started sheering the tops of the waves. The gulls that had been careening above took a quick and certain refuge in the tangle of lines connecting the masts. A moment later one of the ship's crew told her they were clearing the decks.

By the time she found her cabin the boat was already bucking. The pregnant woman had lit the lamp and the shadows it cast on the wall swayed as if in a breeze. "I've had enough of the dark," the woman said. The words surprised Thea, but she grabbed hold of them.

"There is a storm coming."

"You mean it's not already here?"

"I guess it most likely is. I saw the thunderheads up on deck. I went for the fresh air."

The woman merely nodded. In the lamplight her pallor looked even more pale than normal. "Would you like something to eat?" Thea asked. "Or to drink? I still have a little sheep's milk."

The woman hung her head. Embarrassed but eager.

Thea removed her food basket from beneath her bunk and set it on the floor between them. The ship's motion made each movement difficult, but she managed to get the basket open and remove the milk, which she offered right away to the woman.

She drank with gusto, finishing half the jar before she realized what she was doing. She capped the jar, and handed it back to Thea, who offered the cheese in turn. The woman took only a small bite.

"Please," Thea said. "Help yourself to all you want."

She took another bite.

"What's your name?" Thea asked.

"Ingeborg Svensrud."

"Is it very difficult with the child?" Thea gestured at the woman's belly.

She rested her hand on the unborn babe and took a deep breath. The ship had begun to complain, a sort of whining that accompanied the more violent waves. "This passage would be easier without the pregnancy, but I am blessed. I thank God every minute."

"I pray for you each night."

"Thank you."

"Where are you going?"

"To meet my husband in North Dakota. He left in April. He doesn't know about the child."

"He will be very pleased."

The woman smiled. "I hope so," she said.

*T*wo days the storm. The *Thingvalla* beating against the sea. Steer-age passengers had been ordered to stay in their berths, to keep their cabin doors shut and their belongings lashed. The stewards, instead of coming three times daily with their firkins of tepid water, came only once during the forty-hour blow. They ladled water into teapots and bowls and said they'd return when next the seas allowed. The general clamor had given over to a general moan, one heard even through the closed-up cabins.

Ingeborg Svensrud was at once miserable and rejuvenated, first by the storm and then by the food Thea shared with her. They didn't speak much, but whenever Thea removed the basket from under her bunk she offered some to her cabinmate.

In the middle of the second night of the storm, after thirty-six hours of the yawing *Thingvalla*, Ingeborg fell into a hollering fit. Thea asked Ingeborg what was the matter, but the woman only folded at the waist and let out another shriek. Thea somehow knew instinctively what had taken hold of Ingeborg, and she hurried into her cloak and set out down the gangway in search of the ship's surgeon.

It took Thea ten minutes to find her way up to the main deck and ten minutes more to find a crewman at his midnight watch. She told him her purpose, that her cabinmate was ill. Desperately ill and in need of a doctor. They spoke Norwegian.

"She's full of sick folk, your boat. Back down to your bunk, now. This deck's no place at a time like this." He spoke loudly, over the storm.

"Sir, I beg you. She's with child. She's in labor. She needs a doctor."

He removed his hat and pushed back his wet hair.

"Sir, she's desperate. She's alone down there."

He responded with an about-face, and Thea followed him up a staircase and into a dim, carpeted gangway. They walked nearly the full length of the ship and then climbed another staircase before stopping at a wooden door. The watchman knocked softly and then stepped back, elbowing Thea aside. He stood with his feet spread and his hands behind his back.

It took a full minute before the ship's surgeon answered the knock. He was dressed in his nightshirt, and as he swung the door open he was busy pinching his glasses on. Thea repeated the story of her desperate cabinmate and the surgeon, still more asleep than awake, reached behind the door for his bag and followed the watchman, Thea trailing the two men.

By the time they returned to the steerage cabin, Ingeborg had stopped screaming. The surgeon swayed from foot to foot with the ship, the watchman holding a lantern behind him. It cast a nauseating, blurry light on the cabin walls and ceiling.

"Well, now, what's this business?" the surgeon's voice boomed.

"Ingeborg, I've brought the surgeon. He's here to help you." Thea's voice was only a whisper, but it carried in that haunted cabin as much as the surgeon's. "Are you all right?"

The surgeon stepped to Ingeborg's bedside and put his hand on her forehead. "She's afire," he said. To the watchman he said, "Fetch my porter, quickly."

The watchman fixed the lantern to a hook on the wall and nodded and left.

Now the surgeon turned to Thea. "You say she is with child?"

"Yes."

To Ingeborg he said, again in a very loud voice, "We'll have a look now."

Ingeborg would not uncurl, her sorry blanket lay bunched around her.

"Come, now," the surgeon persisted, reaching for Ingeborg this time and pulling her onto her back.

She was indeed unconscious, though clearly breathing, her chest rising and falling with each labored breath.

"Your kind companion here has informed me you're with child. Let's have a look."

The surgeon removed his stethoscope from his bag and pressed it into the folds of her tunic. He listened closely, checked her forehead again, and stood erect with his hand on his chin regarding her.

"How long has she been unwell?" he asked Thea.

Thea explained how she woke to her wailing.

"Is she family?"

"No," Thea said. "I've only known her since we boarded."

"Then I'll have you step outside. For her privacy."

As he suggested Thea leave, Ingeborg stirred, a sudden and sharp movement that began and ended with her eyes. They were pouched, her eyes, and full of tears. She reached for Thea's hand and when she did the blanket fell from her lap. The woman's skirt pooled at her waist. In the folds of her dress her trembling hands held tight the lost child.

The boy was still attached to the umbilical cord, his pallor the color of rotten meat. His visage, in the slewing lantern light, looked restful.

In a voice altogether different than any he'd used so far, a voice far gentler, the surgeon said, "The child is lost, dear. Let's not lose you in the bargain."

He did save her, though from what Thea did not know. When the surgeon sliced the umbilical cord and removed the still child from its mother's lap, Ingeborg's cry was as sorrowful as a cold moon.

XI.

[*November* 1920]

*O*dd stared in wonder at the triptych of framed portraits of his mother. In the first photograph she stood outside the mess hall at the old logging camp up on the Burnt Wood River. A beldam and the handsome camp cook stood to either side of her. She wore an ankle-length dress beneath her apron and shawl, a man's wool hat, mittens. Her expression was clearest in this photograph, alert and flummoxed. Sad. The snow on the ground was glazed and dazzling, and it cast a light as keen from below as above. A pair of wolf pelts hung above the entry door to the mess hall.

In the second picture she sat up in bed, holding Odd himself in full swaddle. Her eyes rested on him, so her expression was less visible, but he could imagine how she felt. He thought it must be something like how he felt then, looking at those pictures. It was the first time he'd seen pictures of his mother, the first time he'd seen pictures of himself as a baby.

The third picture gave him the longest pause. It had been taken upon his mother's arrival in Gunflint in 1895. She rose in a blur behind the *Opportunity*'s mizzen shrouds. In the foreground, a sternline stretched taut to a cleat on the Lighthouse Road. In the background, the spanker flapped in the harbor breeze to accentuate the hoariness.

Her hands clenched the rail and her face, split by one of the shrouds, appeared to be going in opposite directions. She was bent at the waist, in the act of standing.

He closed his eyes, felt the urge to cry, and couldn't tell whether those almost-tears were for him or for her. He knew he felt her fear and sadness and loneliness vicariously, could glean her kindness and gentleness from the simple cast of her eyes.

"Was it a mistake? To give these to you?"

Odd looked up at Rebekah, who stood with her hand on the dining table. They were on the third floor of Grimm's, had just finished Thanksgiving dinner, the capon bones still cluttered a platter, the pot of congealed gravy sat on the middle of the table, the coffee cups were still warm. She had given him the pictures for a birthday gift.

"No," he said but heard the lack of conviction in his voice even if he didn't feel it.

"She was such a beautiful girl." Rebekah put her hand on Odd's arm, squeezed, then set to clearing the table.

Odd poured another ounce of whiskey into his coffee and took a sip. When Rebekah returned from the kitchen she brought a pecan pie and a bowl of whipped cream.

"I was an ugly runt," Odd said.

"Let's see." Rebekah stood above him, looked down at the picture of Odd and Thea.

"Look at that bunched nose. My head looks like a squash."

"Mmm," Rebekah said. She put her hand in Odd's hair. "Babies aren't usually born with hair like that. You came out looking like a young man. You were serious as one, too."

"Guess I foresaw my lot."

"That doesn't sound like you." Rebekah came around the table and sat opposite him.

"These pictures are a hell of a thing to see. I guess I'm feeling a little squirrelly is all." He folded the picture frame in thirds and smiled at her. "Thank you."

She smiled and took his hand. "Jesus," she whispered. She took a deep breath, shuddered.

"What is it?"

"Nothing," she said quickly. "Let's have some dessert." And she started to quarter the pie.

As she served it, Hosea came from the water closet, adjusting his suspenders, whistling, oblivious. Instead of coming back to the dining table, he detoured to the kitchen, where he packed his pipe and lit it with a wooden match. When he returned to the table he finished the dregs of his coffee and poured an ounce of whiskey in its place and lifted the pictures of Thea, of Odd's mother.

For a long time Hosea looked silently at the pictures, the smoke from his pipe clouding his face. When his pipe was finished he set the pictures down, put his pipe on his saucer, and lifted his cup of whiskey. "I've seen a lot of people arrive in this place. Lumberjacks and Lutheran pastors. Millers and petty con men. You name it. Not one of them impressed me the way your mother did, Odd. Not one of them."

Odd shifted his eyes from Hosea to Rebekah.

"She was impressive, Odd," Rebekah reiterated. "And such a cook!"

"The bread she pulled from the oven." Hosea said, almost a whisper, something wistful in his voice. He shifted the pictures in order to see them again. "Your mother, Odd," he began again, but stopped. Took another sip from his cup. "Your mother departed this world as innocently as she arrived in it. That should tell you everything you need to know about her."

The tone of Hosea's voice struck Odd as nostalgic. These holdings-forth were often easy to ignore, inflated as they usually were. But on that evening Odd sensed sincerity more than anything.

Odd said, "She couldn't have been all innocent. There's me to account for."

"Yes, well, if we spent all night accounting for you we'd need another barrel of Canada's finest to accompany our ciphering," Hosea said. "Let's take your place on this earth for granted. What say? Speaking of your place on earth, I have a birthday present for you as well." He stepped to the sideboard and brought back a large box wrapped in brown paper. He set the box before Odd, who had moved his coffee cup and plate aside. "Now, it's nothing like what Rebekah put together for you, but I hope you'll like it all the same."

Odd looked at the box.

"Go ahead, open it," Hosea said.

Odd, speaking to Rebekah, said, "You know what this is?"

"No doubt it's some foolishness," she said.

"Hush, now," Hosea said. "It's no foolishness at all. Open it. Go."

Odd removed his pocketknife and cut away the wrapping paper. He cut open the box and flipped it open. He pulled out a boat's bell, about six inches round. Circling the bell's waist, a series of fish had been engraved in the bronze. Thirty, perhaps forty fish.

"Goddamn," Odd said.

Hosea fairly beamed. "I ordered it from a bell founder in Bremerhaven, Germany. I thought, perhaps, after the motor went in. The last touch, you know?"

Odd was speechless. He flipped the bell over, felt the smooth interior, the clapper hanging by a leather strap. Sure enough, the words BREMERHAVEN DEUTSCHLAND were engraved on the inside lip of the bell. And the date.

"My goodness," Rebekah said.

"This is something else," Odd said.

"Hang it from the cockpit, lad."

"I will. You bet."

"And now it's fair to ask: What are we going to do with that crated-up engine out back?"

"I'll get Danny over here."

Rebekah put a piece of pie in front of Hosea, who tucked his napkin back into his shirt collar and took his first bite of pie. He said, "Rebekah, have you been over to see Odd's boat?"

Her breath caught. "No."

"You should come over and have a look," Odd said. He winked at her.

"His motor arrived yesterday. From the looks of things, just in time. Winter has arrived." And Hosea pointed out the window. The winds had finally come down from the north, bringing cold and snow. It came in curtains now. The season was changing.

Hosea continued, "I'd venture to guess we've seen the last of our ferrying friends up shore. We'll be set in harbor ice soon."

Rebekah asked Odd, "Would you tell me about the motor?"

"It's a Buda four-stroke. I bought it because the catalog said, 'Buda marine engines embody no freakish ideas or experiments.' Guess I figured there was enough freakishness already laid into her curves and lines."

"What in the world does that mean?" she said.

Odd tipped another finger of whiskey into his cup, filled it with coffee.

"I think what Odd means," Hosea said, "is that he is building an unconventional vessel. He's taking risks in the interest of satisfying his curiosity."

Odd couldn't help but smile. "I'm taking risks, all right." From the corner of his eye, he could see Rebekah press the blush from her cheeks.

"How fast will she go?" Hosea asked.

"Not more than fifteen knots," Odd said, sipping his coffee. "Not more than fifteen knots with a stiff breeze on her tail." He set his cup down. "But I didn't build her for speed."

"When will she be finished?" Hosea asked.

Odd gave the question serious consideration. "All that's left is the motor. And a last coat of varnish. If it came down to it I could launch her in a couple weeks but I'll let her set the season in the fish house. I'll put in the water come ice-out. I'll set my first nets next spring over her side."

"That's exciting," Rebekah said. "Will you take me on her maiden voyage?"

"Does that not go without saying?" Odd said.

They finished their pie and digestifs and Hosea adjourned to his sitting chair beside the fireplace in the parlor. Rebekah and Odd cleared the table and washed the bone-china plates and cups and saucers. As they replaced them in the sideboard, Odd said, "Come over. Tell him you want to have a look."

"Okay," she said

Odd walked to the water closet.

In the kitchen Rebekah hung her apron behind the door, hung the dishrag over the faucet, and pushed her hair behind her ears. She walked into the parlor. "You look like you're about to fall asleep," she said.

Hosea was indeed drowsy. He set the book he was reading on his lap. "You prepared a wonderful feast this Thanksgiving."

"I'm going to see Odd's boat," she said.

"I would join you, but I'm well spent."

"We'll be busy tomorrow. You should go to bed."

Hosea closed the book on his lap. "You're right."

Rebekah hated these conversations, hated that the two of them could fall into the trappings of domesticity like this, hated that they could seem fond of each other. "Odd will walk me back, I'm sure."

Odd came through the house holding the picture frames and the bell. He went to the top of the staircase and said, "Thanks for the eats. Thanks for remembering my birthday. I guess Rebekah's going to have a look at the boat."

"Happy birthday, lad. I hope you and Danny can get to the motor soon."

"We will. Tomorrow, if I can get the truck through the snow."

Hosea nodded approvingly. "Wait for Rebekah downstairs. I'd like a word with her."

"Good night, then," Odd said, and walked down the stairs.

When Hosea was sure Odd had descended the second staircase, he looked at Rebekah. "Your gift to Odd, it was wonderful. Thank you for talking me into finding those old pictures."

"I'm glad he was pleased."

"And the bell? You think he liked it?"

"It pains me to say it, but yes, I believe he liked the bell."

"Pains you?"

"Oh, never mind." She took her cloak from the front closet. She sat on the divan and laced her boots, then stood to leave. "Good night," she said and turned to leave.

"Rebekah?"

She turned again. "What is it?"

"Your innocence is not unlike Thea Eide's ever was. I meant to say that over dessert."

"I've never been innocent a day in my life, you've seen to that."

Hosea sat up in his chair. "Don't bare your teeth at me like that. I was feeling generous. Be grateful."

She said, "I'm sorry."

Hosea stared at her for a long moment. "Very good. Go ahead over to Odd's."

*T*hey walked up the Lighthouse Road, the hypnotic sound of the waves on the breakwater in the distance. The snow fell slantwise. They passed the hotel and turned up the alleyway and found the lakeside trail that led to Odd's fish house. There were already four inches of snow on the ground—the first real snow of the season—and Odd kicked a path clear for Rebekah as he went along.

When they came to the gravel beach on the cove, Odd walked to the water's edge and stood looking out at the lake beyond the point. Rebekah waited up on the knoll, shivering from the wind. She wanted to go inside, had so much to tell Odd. After a minute she said, "Come up, Odd. Let's go inside. I'm cold."

He turned to her. "You go in. I'll be there in a second. Rekindle the fire in the stove." And then he turned back to look at the water.

The pictures of his mother, now tucked inside his coat, held in place by his hand in his coat pocket and the waistband of his trousers, had awakened something inside him. Was it sadness? Surely the look on her face in those pictures conveyed nothing if not sadness, even the picture in which she held him. Was there another word for this feeling? If he dove into the winter water, would it wash away? He shuddered at the thought of the lake and turned to look up at the fish house, the window in the door now glowing amber from the table lamp she'd lit inside. A kind of beacon. *Follow it on in*, he thought.

She was unlacing her boots by the warmth of the woodstove. She looked up at him. "My boots are full of snow."

"I guess winter decided to come after all." He set the bell by the door, took off his coat, and crossed the fish house. From its hook on the wall he took down the lantern and lit it. He set the pictures on the ledge above his bunk and looked at them for a moment before he turned.

She was crying.

He walked quickly to her, knelt, and said, "Hey, hey, now. What is it?"

"I have to show you something, Odd. Another picture. I have to show you this and then I have to tell you something. You have to listen and I don't want you to say anything. Do you understand?"

Odd nodded. He pulled his three-legged stool from beneath the boat, which sat in its bracings.

She reached into the pocket of her skirt and withdrew a postcard that she kept palmed in her hand. He could tell she was steadying herself. Steeling herself. Though for what reason he could not fathom.

"I'm showing you this because I want you to know everything. Because what I have to tell you will change a whole lot, and you need to know this in order for that to happen."

"What in the world are you talking about?"

"Shh," she snapped. "I said I want you to listen. I don't want you to say anything until I'm finished."

Now she stood and put the postcard to her lips. Then, as though pushed, she reached between them and handed him the postcard and turned away. She did this in one motion and stood with her back to him, her hands at her mouth.

"Don't say anything. Do you understand? Do not say anything. Let me figure this out."

Odd looked up from the postcard and waited for her to turn around. He waited three full minutes, his mind clamoring for a clear thought.

"Hosea rescued me, in a way. And he was always—*always*— perfectly honest with me. Before we left Chicago he told me exactly what would be expected of me." Now she turned to face Odd. "That," she said, pointing at the postcard, "is the price I have had to pay. A small price compared to the one I might have. The price I would have."

She walked back over to Odd. "I know he can be a brute. And I wish he wasn't. But if I'd stayed in Chicago it would have been much worse for me. Sometimes Hosea is as kind as a preacher. Others, well, he's got his ways." She paused, looked down at him. "I guess you know all about him."

She shook her head and closed her eyes. "Dear God, how am I supposed to tell you this?"

"Tell me what?"

She reached down, took the postcard from his hand, and walked to the woodstove. She opened the door and put the postcard in the flames, closed the door, and walked back to him. She knelt before him and took his hands. "I'm pregnant, Odd."

Rather than some emotion rising in him, Odd saw instantly his own bunched face in the photograph with his mother. He saw his eyes, just slits then, the old-man lines coming off his baby's eyes. He would have given anything to know how he'd felt when that picture had been taken, in his mother's arms. Maybe that was what it was, the feeling that had been plaguing him since he'd left Grimm's. He reached up and felt the lines coming off his eyes, he closed them, regained the moment, and looked at her. At her waiting face. He saw only his love for her in what looked back.

"I don't know what to do," she said, her voice hardly audible.

"Rebekah," he whispered. "Baby." And he reached down and picked her up and held her on his lap.

"I'm too old to have a baby," she said into his shoulder. "I'm nearly twice as old as you."

"I guess this is the first moment that ever mattered."

"It matters because I'm pregnant."

"I can't tell you whether or not you're too old to have a baby. But it seems to me if you're young enough to get that way, you're young enough to see it through."

"We were like a brother and sister, Odd."

"We sure were, right up till that day at the farm. Right up till that day up in the flat."

She took a deep breath. "What have I done?"

"I guess we did it together."

She ran her hand through his hair. "Hosea will be so upset if he finds out."

"This ain't Hosea's business, it's ours."

"That's easy for you to say, Odd. But I live with him. That's my life over there at the apothecary."

"Not anymore," Odd protested. "Now it's you and me. And our baby."

She sat up, looked at him. "What? We're to live in a fish house? On what you make fishing? We'll be *disgraced*. No one in town will so much as glance our way. For that matter, who will deliver the baby? Hosea?"

"We'll get out of here, then," he said. He could hear desperation in his voice.

"And go where?" she asked. "And live how?"

"We can go wherever the hell we please," he said. "We can live however we want."

She looked at him now and smiled, though her face was full of sadness. "There's not a way I don't love you, but I don't think I can have this baby."

"What are you talking about, not have the baby?" He set her down, stood up, paced a few steps. "You think I didn't know about the post-cards?" Now he felt helpless. "Why'd you show me the postcard, any-way? If you're going to get rid of the baby, why'd you feel the need to put that under my nose?" He pulled his tobacco and papers from his shirt pocket and rolled a cigarette over the counter. The snow was spitting against the window.

"How did you know about the postcards, Odd?"

He turned to face her. "You think I just sat on my hands all those years? While you and Hosea were downstairs tending to the shop, I was supposed to practice my grammar lessons up in that house of se-crets? Honestly?" He ran his hands through his hair, took a long drag on his cigarette, looked out the window onto the darkness of night, the lightness of falling snow. "You have me pegged a fool, don't you?"

Now her voice rose. "You've known all this time and never said anything?"

"What in the world was I supposed to say?"

There was no answer to that question, and they both knew it. He stood at the window trying to think this whole thing straight. But he couldn't. Something was nagging him. "He's still taking pictures?"

"Oh, Odd. He hasn't taken a picture of me in years." She stood up, walked over to him. "I'm forty-one years old. Too old for just about anything. Too old to have a baby."

He turned to face her, there were tears streaming down his cheeks but his voice was perfectly calm. "Don't you see? Your whole life you've been his captive. He ain't got rights. You've paid your dues."

"He was as much a father as I ever had, Odd. He gave me a place to live. He bought me nice clothes. He taught me how to read."

Odd swung around. "I've got to think," he said. "Give me a minute to think."

And so he did, as he marched around his boat, into the dark reaches of the fish house and back into the lamp and lantern light. Rebekah sat with her head in her hands, unable to face the young man she had loved from the first moment of his life. This man she had loved in ways she hadn't known were possible.

He must have made ten laps around the boat. After five minutes he stopped and rolled another cigarette and lit it and took a coffee can from under the fish counter before he resumed the stool in front of Rebekah. "When will the baby be born?"

"I suppose the baby would come sometime next summer."

"Okay. All right." He flicked the cigarette ash. "I ain't gonna beg you. I ain't gonna tell you the hundred reasons Hosea ought to be shot for the way he keeps you under his thumb. But I will tell you what we're gonna do."

She shook her head sadly, said, "Oh, Odd."

"I listened to you when you asked. You do the same for me." He pulled a bunch of twine from the coffee can, under which lay a wad of cash, which he also withdrew. "I got upwards of a thousand dollars here. I got a boat that only needs the motor put in it." He put the money back in the can.

"We'll leave as soon as the ice-out—"

"I'll be five months pregnant by then. My belly will be out to here," she interrupted. She held her hand six inches in front of her stomach.

"All right. Hold on, now," Odd said. He took another lap around the boat, looked in at the motor box, did a little figuring. Then he looked back across the fish house at her. "Then we'll leave next week. Before the cove freezes. Danny and I will get to work on the motor first thing tomorrow morning." He nodded, felt sure of himself.

He walked over to her. "We have to get out of here. Start fresh. Give this baby a chance." Now he put his hand on her stomach.

"Where would we go. Odd? How?" Her voice was full of doubt.

"We'll take my boat. We could go up to Duluth. Or on down to Canada. Cross the lake to Michigan. We could go all the way down to the Soo, and then anywhere in the world from there. I'm a young man. I can get a job anywhere." He took her chin in his hand and raised her face to his. "Haven't we talked about this? Ain't it true that you've asked me a hundred times to get you out of this place?"

She smiled another of those sad smiles and felt the tears welling in her eyes. "What about the fish house, Odd? What about the farm?"

"They ain't going anywhere. I'll see if Danny wants to live here. He can look after it. Maybe buy it from me. I'll talk to Mayfair. See about selling the farm. None of that's important anyway." He was talking faster than he could think.

She shuddered, did not know what to say, much less what to think.

"What do you say, Rebekah? We could make a start of it."

XII.

[January 1896]

*T*rond urged his horse across the shallow, half-frozen Burnt Wood River. The horse was as weary as the rest of the world, and he moved through the snow and brittle boscage with complete resignation. The steam blowing from his nostrils blended with the fog blowing in off the lake.

Trond had his collar turned up against the wind, his chin tucked to the shoreward side of the trail. He'd never been to the wigwam village and was frankly daunted by his errand. He knew Joseph Riverfish, knew him as a fine and good man, a family man, a superb woodsman and fisherman. What Trond didn't know, among a hundred such details, was how one called out in greeting, how one would sit in the wigwam, whether the settlers were even allowed in the wigwam, for that matter. Upon Hosea Grimm's suggestion, he carried in his saddle-bags a sack of candies for the children and a warm pint of Canadian whiskey for Riverfish himself.

When Riverfish's dogs caught the horse's scent they sent up a randy yammer. The village was in a crescent-shaped meadow, bordered on the north by a forest of spruce and on the south by the lake. The dogs were staked in a line along the western edge of the village, and as

Trond passed them on his horse, they lunged playfully, pulling their chains to their limits. There were a dozen of them, Spitz breeds from some arctic part of the world.

The village was six wigwams. A plume of gentle smoke rising from each. Four canoes were tipped over, half covered with snowdrifts. The dogs must have alerted Joseph Riverfish because he stood at the entrance of the nearest wigwam, a bear pelt over his shoulders like a shawl.

"Hello!" he shouted and waved. "Hello, there!"

Trond raised a hand in greeting and rode the last hundred feet and swung off the horse, which he patted on the withers. "Hello, Joseph," he said.

Riverfish spoke three or four languages—among them German and English—but each with the heavy accent of his native Ojibwa. "It be a cold day for horseback riding, no?" he asked.

"A cold day indeed," Trond said, taking off his mitten and extending his hand.

Riverfish pulled his own hand from his bearskin and the two men shook. "Come inside, the fire is warm and there's plenty to smoke."

"All right," Trond said. He stepped to his saddlebag and removed the candies and hooch and then bent to hobble the horse.

Inside, a fire built on a plush bed of glowing embers warmed the conical room. The fire was circled not with rocks, as Trond was accustomed to, but with lengths of birch logs. Riverfish's wife sat to the left of the buckskin entrance, her feet tucked beneath her, her hands busy with beadwork, her belly full with her tenth child. Four of her youngsters sat in the circle, the girls playing with dolls made of willow withes, the boys whittling sticks.

Riverfish unrolled a rush mat and suggested Trond sit. Before Joseph sat himself, he found his pipe and packed it with kinnikinnick and lit it with a twig pulled from the fire. He offered the pipe to Trond, who knew enough to take a puff. The pipestone lit up like a firefly.

Trond handed the pipe back to Riverfish, who took a smoke.

"The stem is from a hazel tree. We split it and hollow it and glue it together again." He smiled broadly. "Our glue is from the backbone of the *namé*, what you call the sturgeon fish."

Trond took another smoke, then offered Riverfish the bottle of whiskey. "I brought this for you. And this for the children." Now he extended the candies.

The children stopped their play and giggled and came around the fire. Joseph gave them each a candy.

The walls of the wigwam were covered with birch bark. The poles were cedar. With the fire burning and the kinnikinnick wafting and the hooch now passing between them, Trond couldn't even smell the pot of squash soup cooking in the kettle over the fire.

"I've come with an offer of work, Joseph. I need a favor and thought you were the man for the job."

"Very good."

"There's a fellow up the shore, near Castle River, the name of Olli Odegaard."

"Olli One Foot," Riverfish said, and smiled his infectious smile. "I know Olli well."

"He's selling these dogs, calls them Ovcharkas."

"I have seen them. Big dogs."

"That's what I understand. I want two of them. For the camp. To watch over the camp."

Riverfish took a long smoke. "You need me to deliver these dogs?"

"I'll pay you twenty dollars. I need them right away. I thought if not you, then your son. Where is the boy?"

"Samuel is working the line. Up the Wisakode-zibe."

"The Wisakode . . ."

"Your Burnt Wood River. Samuel will go tomorrow to deliver the dogs."

"Excellent. Thank you."

"Now," Riverfish said expansively, "you will stay and eat."

"I will, thank you."

Together they ate the squash soup. They ate dried berries and deer tallow, smoked trout with maple sugar. The children, when they were finished with their lunch, were each given another piece of candy. When all were fed, and Joseph's wife content that Trond had had enough, they shared a final pipe. As Trond straddled his horse and put on his mitts, Riverfish sent his good wishes. The horse stepped without enthusiasm. An hour later Trond was back at the lumber camp on the Burnt Wood River.

Samuel Riverfish left the following morning before first light, his dogs hysterical in their traces, eager to run despite the sound of open water not a half mile over their lakeward shoulders. He packed lightly, only food for the dogs, a canvas tarpaulin to sleep under, snowshoes newly bent and twined from birch wood. Trond had offered him five extra dollars if he could deliver the Ovcharkas in three days. His only chance was to run the shore, something he'd never done before the first week in February, something nobody did before then.

He was dressed in fur: a beaver-skin hat, moose-hide coat, pants quilted together from equal parts marten and fox and lynx, mukluks and mittens sewn from a black bear's hindquarters—a madman's attire, but warm. He'd trapped or killed every inch of hide on his body.

Just fourteen years old and built like a girl, with a face—as his father said—fresh as a baby's ass, Samuel was already known for his temerity, a quality not to be confused with bravery. There were rumors among the townspeople that he had faced a bull moose with nothing but an eight-inch bowie knife between himself and five feet of spanning antlers. Though foolhardy, he was also trusted. For two years he'd been helping his father with the winter mail route, a job some said was the worst in America.

He reached the Chinook River before lunchtime. The ice along the shore was firm, even at the mouths of streams and rivers, but the farther south and west he went the closer attention he paid to its tempers. He had seen his father's sled break through the ice not far from where he stood.

He would feed the dogs and test the ice at the mouth of the river. The vapor rising from the open water had disappeared, but now he could actually see the line demarcating the ice and water. He set the snow hook and parceled out the dogs' chow. Two fist-sized chunks of venison each. They ate as though their last meal had been a month ago.

Samuel took stock as the dogs ate. There were veins in the ice at the mouth of the river, but still it felt firm beneath him. He walked a quarter mile past the river, checking for cracks or ridges or undulations of any sort, none of which he found. By the time he returned to the sled the dull sun was already dropping. The dogs had finished their venison and each had dug a sizable chunk of snow and ice to suffice as drink. The lead dog, a bi-eyed husky Samuel called Nord, had dug a hole eight inches deep and a foot wide. When Samuel stabbed at the ice with his bowie knife, he was able to sink the blade to the hilt without tapping water. A good sign. He would run easy for an hour.

The dogs finished their snow. Alert now and ready. Samuel stepped onto the runners and had a good grip on the handlebar when he took the snow hook up with his free hand. The dogs were gone with the absence of the tension.

There was not much wind. But what did blow came from the northeast, helping his cause even as it foretold more cold. He wondered about the dogs he was fetching. Erlandson had told him about the bear, had given him two lengths of chain in the event they would not run with the team. This thought was unfathomable to Samuel, dogs that would not run.

He fed the dogs again before sunset and passed the settlement at Misquah in a dusk smoking with cold. The lake was holding up, but he ran very near the shore. On the beaches when he passed rivers and creeks. He heard wolves howling on Bear or Gull island. The dogs answered back.

By the light of stars he passed Copper Bay, then Otter Bay. When the sun rose he rested the dogs and lit a fire at Big Rock Bay, sitting on the beach in the lee of the towering cliff. The dogs stopped on command and collapsed, curling into themselves. Danny set the snow hook and slept on top of the sled without the comfort of the tarpaulin. He woke two hours later and fed the dogs again.

In the light of day he saw how precarious the ice was, even in the bay, so he ran up the Big Rock River until he crossed the trail, where he turned south again toward Castle River. He was there by lunchtime.

*T*he Ovcharkas were kept like thieves, each in its own cage of metal bars, a floor spread with hay. At first glance Samuel mistook them for slumbering bears. Four of the six advertised dogs remained, each one black as onyx and measurably circumspect as Samuel approached them. In less than five minutes he had decided which were best suited for the task at hand. By the time the Laplander limped up the path from his cabin, Riverfish had begun talking to the dogs like he would a sweetheart.

"I heard your team yelping. Glad you left them down on the river shore," the one-legged man said. "Your father is good?"

Samuel extended his hand and said, "He sends his greetings."

"You running the mail?"

Samuel reached inside his coat and withdrew the sealed envelope Trond Erlandson had sent with him. He handed it to the Laplander. "The foreman up at Burnt Wood River has sent me for two of the dogs."

The Laplander took off his mitts and opened the envelope. "What for?"

"Wolves."

"To hunt wolves?"

"To guard the logging camp."

The Laplander shook his head. He lifted his peg leg from the spot where it had sunk and rested more lightly on it. He put the envelope in a pocket before replacing his mitts. "They'll guard against wolves. I'd put two of them up against a small pack."

Samuel was again eyeing the dogs. "I like the two with white ears. The one atop the kennel, she's a bitch?"

The Laplander nodded. "The other's just about the meanest dog I've ever met."

"Will they run with my team?"

"No, not all the way up to Gunflint. How big is your sled?"

"They'll fit on my sled." He looked at the dogs again. "Will they stand the ride?"

"We'll crate them, muzzle them. They might moan about it, but you'll get them home."

Samuel studied the dogs again. "Where did they come from?" he said.

The Laplander told him about his homeland, of the wolves that had nearly extinguished the sheep herd the year before he'd come to America. About a Russian who lived just across the border in Alakurtti, and how he had obtained from him three of the dogs. He told a summary version of his breeding the dogs and a yarn or two about their bravery, including the much-rumored treeing of the bear. A true story, he assured Samuel.

An hour after he'd arrived at the Laplander's, Samuel had the Ovcharkas loaded on his sled. His own dogs were uneasy in the behemoths' company, but he soothed his team and fed them before they started home. The Ovcharkas, in their leather muzzles, housed in chicken-wire crates, were magisterial in their silence, tolerant—Samuel thought—to the point of spookiness.

The Laplander sent twenty pounds of dried coho salmon with Samuel, and the boy stopped at sunset to feed the dogs. He built a fire at the mouth of the Big Rock River and melted snow. The frozen fish cooled the boiling water promptly. Samuel lifted the tops from the crates and lowered a bowl of potage into each. When he removed their muzzles and watched the Ovcharkas eat, he could hardly believe their voracity. They slobbered the water up even as they chewed the fish so that in no more than two minutes the black dogs had finished their feast. And as quickly as they ate they curled back up, in unison, to hold in silent abeyance a ferocity Riverfish could as much as feel in his hands and feet. When the huskies were done with their own hunks of venison, Samuel clucked his tongue and drove out onto the lake.

He ran all night and all day and with his spent team passed through Gunflint and turned up the ice road an hour before sunset. As Samuel pulled into camp and let the Ovcharkas out of their crates one at a time, each laid an enormous turd that stank of fish. It took all of Samuel's strength to hold the dogs steady on their leads. One by one and according to their rank, his own dogs took turns stretching their traces taut in order to sniff the piles of shit.

Despite the frigid evening, Trond Erlandson hurried from the wanigan when he saw Samuel Riverfish. As he crossed the open commons of the camp, he met the bull cook, whom he directed to the stable. By the time Trond reached the dogs he had already pulled two twenty-dollar banknotes from his pocket and offered them to Samuel.

"You said twenty dollars, plus five if I met your deadline. This is too much," Samuel said.

Trond didn't respond, only went to the bitch and offered the back of his hand. He had no fear of the dogs. Satisfied she would allow it, Trond tousled the scruff of black-and-white fur behind her ear. He repeated the same greeting with the other dog. Finally he stood and turned to Samuel.

"Lord Christ, they are small mountains."

Samuel agreed.

"How was it with them?"

"They rode on that sled as if bred for it," Samuel said. "They never made a sound."

Trond's eyes widened as if he understood perfectly. He returned again to the bitch and knelt before her. He offered his hand for the second time but she did not so much as sniff it. Instead she lowered her head and leaned toward him. He ran his hands up and down her ribs, felt the muscle in her forelegs, lifted her face by the chin so he could see into her black eyes. She held his gaze for a moment, then cowered. Trond slowly removed the leather muzzle from her snout and let her lick the back of his hand.

He walked over to the other dog. When he removed his muzzle the dog's lips quivered and he began to bare his teeth, but Trond clubbed him on the nose and the dog put his head down. The foreman knelt before the dog and raised its face to meet his own and said out loud, "You stay mean when you're staked out there. You let me know when the wolves are coming."

By then the bull cook and stable keeper were crossing the open yard. Each of them carried a length of chain over their shoulders, and when they reached Trond and Samuel they stopped short to take in the Ovcharkas.

"We could use those dogs to rest the horses," the stable keeper said. "If it came to that."

Trond smiled. "I want this cur out in the paddock. Stake him under the ridge. And make sure his kennel door is turned away from the wind. Keep her near the stable. And feed them."

"Feed them what?" the bull cook asked.

Trond looked down at the Ovcharkas. He fed his St. Bernard scraps from the kitchen. These dogs needed square meals, though. This he could see. "Ask the ladies in the kitchen for whatever they've got leftover. I reckon these dogs aren't particular." He turned to the stable keeper, "Tell the teamsters to carry rifles tomorrow. See what they can hunt."

Trond turned to Samuel Riverfish. "You've done well," he said. "Those extra dollars are a gratuity. Your father will hear about this. Now, go get some rest. I can see you need it."

Samuel thanked him and left with his dogs.

So the dogs stood sentinel in the dark—the bitch on twelve feet of chain near the horse barn, the dog staked out at the end of the paddock—each of them full on a gallon of sowbelly stew. That night, for the first time in a week, there was no wolf song to serenade the jacks. Thea, waiting for the howl, could not sleep in its absence.

XIII.

[*November* 1920]

*T*he snow had stopped but for those drifting flakes that rose as much as fell, and the silver light of the headlamps caught the flurries' glimmer. The trail was cut for dogsleds, not pickup trucks, but it was the only way to the wigwam village. So Odd drove slowly, the soft boughs of the spruce trees sweeping the canvas canopy that covered the cab.

Rebekah sat next to him. He could see she was tired but couldn't judge whether the exhaustion on her face was masking happiness or dread. He wished like hell he knew. She hadn't said much since midnight, even with all there was to discuss.

"Danny's gonna be rightly peeved, me showing up like this," Odd said.

"Hmm."

Odd looked at her. "Every hour counts now, Rebekah."

She reached up and touched his whiskered face with her cold fingertips.

Odd grabbed her hand and kissed it.

The wigwam village was more properly a town unto itself those days. The wigwams themselves had become squat cabins with horse barns beside the smokehouses and woodsheds. There were bicycles leaning against some of the cabins, a motorcycle and sidecar outside Danny's folks' place. Danny had his own cabin, and smoke streamed from the tin chimney. Odd stopped the truck and drummed his fingers on the steering wheel.

"In two days I'm gonna have that boat floating in the water. We're going to leave Sunday morning, before the sun. Come hell or high water, we're gone. You understand? Pack whatever you need. Dress warm. As warm as you can. Danny will be out back of Grimm's to help you with your bags. I'll be at the end of the Lighthouse Road. We'll be free." He reached for her hand and held it tight. "Just you and me. Okay?"

She nodded, said nothing.

Now he reached up and caressed her face. "Sit tight for a minute, all right? I'm gonna rouse Danny."

Rebekah buried her hands in her lynx muff and lowered her chin into the collar of her cape.

Danny's cabin made Odd's fish house seem opulent. It was dug into a hill with a low ceiling, plank walls and floors, just enough room for his traps and hunting gear and a bunk. He warmed it with a wood-stove that, as Odd entered, was glowing. Danny had heard the truck pull up and was already out of bed, standing there in his long johns, wiping the sleep from his eyes, a lantern lit at his bedside. "Christ, it's early," he said.

"I need help," Odd said.

Without pause Danny was sliding into his dungarees, into his chamois shirt and wool socks. As he sat on his bunk to lace his boots, Danny said, "You got a mind to tell me more?"

Odd had rolled a cigarette and he lit it and offered it to Danny. He started rolling one for himself, said, "I gotta get the motor on the boat."

Danny looked up. "At six o'clock in the morning?"

Odd lit his own cigarette. "It's Rebekah."

"What's Rebekah got to do with the boat?"

"We're gone, Danny."

"You're gone?" He nodded, arched his eyebrows. "This ain't the best time of year to set sail."

"I know that."

Danny tied his second boot and stood up. He took his coat from a hook on the wall and put it on and said, "All right. Let's get the motor."

They stepped outside and Danny threw the latch on the cabin door, then climbed onto the bed of the truck.

By the time they got to Grimm's the first sign of day was up on the eastern horizon. Odd parked behind the apothecary and Danny jumped out. Odd grabbed Rebekah's arm before she could do the same.

"Are you okay?" he asked.

"No."

"What's wrong?"

"I'm scared and confused. I've seen enough women deliver their babies to know to be scared."

"But you've seen enough to know it usually turns out all right."

"Usually," she said. She bit her lip. "It's not just the baby, Odd. It's leaving all this." She gestured up at the apothecary, out at the town. "I've lived here for twenty-five years. This is home. There's Hosea."

He took a deep breath, squeezed the steering wheel until his knuckles turned white. "We're done with him now. We don't need him. I'll take care of you. You and our baby." He put his hand to her face, caressed it gently. "You're going to be there on Sunday morning."

She turned her head slowly and looked at him. There was just enough morning light that she could see the wet in his good eye, could see the hard, cold, empty stare of his glass eye. She was grateful for that look, relieved that somewhere in her own fraying thoughts a voice told her yes. So she said, "Of course I am." And then she slid from the truck and walked in the back door of the apothecary.

One of the first things Odd had done when he'd started on the boat was build a davit that could be attached to either of two posts he had set in the floor. From the davit he hung a three-pulley block and tackle and used it to hoist the keel onto the strongback. He'd used it for a dozen things since, and in the hazy light of that morning they rigged the largest of the motor crates with two twenty-foot lengths of chain and attached the chain to the hook of the block and tackle and pulled the crate up onto the boat's deck.

Danny shouldered one of the smaller crates over the gunwale and then peered into the boat. It had been a while since he'd seen it. "You're gonna have this thing in the water in two days?" he said.

Odd didn't stop working. "Yup. That's my plan."

"It's been an awful warm November, I'll give you that. You've got time before the ice sets."

"The main thing, besides the motor, is another coat of varnish." Now he paused, stood with his hands on the gunwale looking over the edge at Danny. "I'll pay you twenty dollars to do the painting."

"Like I'd take your goddamn money."

"Well, I ain't gonna let you do it for free. I know you've got better things to do."

"I got a couple days to spare. I'm here to help."

"I ain't asking you to do this," Odd said. "I wouldn't ever expect it."

"I know that."

Odd reached into the pocket of his trousers and pulled out his wad of cash. He peeled back a five-dollar bill and handed it to Danny. "For turpentine. Klaus Hakonsson sells it out of his shop." Odd checked his watch, peeled another fiver from his roll. "He must be open by now. Take the truck. Get the turpentine, then stop at the dry goods and buy us some things to eat for the next couple days. We're gonna be a couple of hungry sons of bitches. Make sure you get coffee. And braunshweiger."

"And onions, in that case."

"We'll be some fine-smelling soldiers."

Danny was gone for two hours. When he returned Odd was out front of the fish house standing over an open fire. A charred pot hung from a cast-iron tripod over the flames. He had sawhorses set up off to the side, and on the plank that spanned the sawhorses buckets of pine tar and Japan drier sat ready. Danny put the cans of turpentine on the makeshift table and went back to the truck for the groceries. When he was done unloading he came and stood beside Odd.

"Some sort of witches' brew?" Danny said.

"It's linseed oil." Odd pointed at the cans and buckets behind him. "That's our varnish. It's time to get the brushes going." He looked up at the dull morning sky, judged the sun's spot behind the clouds. "Must be about eleven. I'll be sleepless these days."

"I'll keep you company. Got us a little something extra."

"Something extra?"

"A case of Hakonsson's home brew."

"Maybe I ought to be stealing you away, Riverfish," Odd said, a wry smile creeping.

"I don't put out the way your gal does, be clear on that."

Odd's smile went full. "Not many do, brother. Not many do."

By noon the boat was wiped down, the varnish brewed and cooling in an empty whiskey barrel. They worked in unison, Danny painting the hull while Odd puzzled out the motor. It came with a twenty-page manual that Odd had all but memorized over the previous days, and by suppertime of their first day working he had the main engine mounted in the motor box and the vanadium-steel shaft threaded through the skeg and coupled to the engine.

The fish house smelled of the varnish, pitchy and fresh but strong, so they opened windows and the big barn doors. At midnight they broke to eat and crack beers.

"When are you going to fill me in?" Danny said.

Odd had a mouthful of braunschweiger and onions so he finished chewing and took a long pull from the home brew and said, "Well, Rebekah's in the family way."

"Oh, hell."

"Naw, it's a good thing. It's getting us out of here."

"Rebekah wants out of here?"

Odd took another pull on his beer. "She's scared."

Danny shook his head. "Careful, making a lady do what she don't want to."

"Who said that?"

"Never mind. Where are you taking her?"

Odd nodded. "We'll go to Duluth first. See what I can shake out. See what happens in the springtime."

Danny nodded. "You better hope for no wind come Sunday and Monday."

"I'm hoping."

They ate in silence, popped a couple more beers. When Odd finished his sandwich he rolled a cigarette and pushed himself off the counter. He took a long drag on his smoke.

"I guess it goes without saying this stays between you and me?"

"If you insult me one more time, I'll kick your lily-white ass."

"I'm a bundle of nerves. You can forgive me," Odd said.

"One last time." Danny finished his sandwich. "Anyway, most folks around here got their own secrets. They don't need yours any sooner than they need another month of winter."

Odd smiled.

Danny said, "I got no idea where you went, brother."

"Then I've got one more favor to ask."

"Shoot."

"How'd you like to squat here? Keep an eye on the place till I can figure out what to do with it?"

Danny looked appraisingly into the four dark corners of the fish house. "I wouldn't know what to do with all this luxury."

"Hey, now," Odd snapped. He smiled. "This is your chance to move to the big city. This place makes your bear's den look worse than it is."

"You'd know about bears' dens, wouldn't you?"

"I guess I would. I guess I would."

Danny smirked. "What are you going to do with this place?"

"I reckon I'll have to sell it. The farm, too. Maybe not. I don't know. Maybe we'll come back. Hopefully we will. I'm gonna talk to Mayfair before I leave." Odd finished his cigarette and stubbed it out. "I don't want to leave the fish house sitting here in the meantime, though. What if I said it's yours to keep if I don't have it figured out next year at this time? I could have Mayfair draw up some papers."

"What in the hell is with you? I don't need goddamn papers drawn up or money from your pocket."

"I'm sorry, Danny. I guess life seems a little more official the last couple of days."

Danny stood up. He looked again into the dark corners. "Hell, yes, I'll squat here. And you take all the time you need to decide what to do."

Odd offered his hand, which Danny shook firmly.

*T*hey worked through the night, Odd on his back under the boat, fumbling the propeller into place, caulking everything. Danny finished with the varnish. They'd switched from Hakonsson's home brew to coffee sometime in the middle of the night and between the fumes of the varnish and the caffeine both were jittery and twitchy.

As dawn neared Danny broke for a couple hours' sleep. Odd stoked the stove and closed the doors, hoping to warm the place up and hasten the drying of the varnish. He spent the time Danny slept working on the engine. He installed the ignition and battery, the twelve-volt generator, the starter. He double-checked everything against the manual, sealed for a second time the propeller shaft. Finally he poured a couple gallons of fuel into the fifty-gallon tank. He added the motor oil and primed the engine and stood in the cockpit, his hand on the ignition. The smell of varnish was still heavy in the air, but he'd moved all the rags and brushes outside, hefted the whiskey barrel out back and covered it. He thought he was safe. Thought there wasn't much to worry about.

He started her up, let her run for thirty seconds. The Buda coughed and sputtered but caught and ran smooth. Odd knelt at the motor box and adjusted the choke. Despite her purring he was full of doubt. He saw himself rowing the last ninety miles up to Duluth, or worse. But he also believed more than ever in his sense of urgency. Believed that leaving before the next daybreak was essential in a way that he never could have figured. Thought if they didn't he'd lose Rebekah forever.

The engine woke Danny and he stepped to the boat, his hair mat-
ted and damp from the heat of the stove. "You trying to cook me
alive?" he said.

Odd had a distant and pleased look on his face. "It's time to put this
thing in the water. I'll lay the ways, you get your brothers."

Danny donned his coat and left to fetch his four older brothers.
Odd threw open the barn doors on Danny's heels. It was a gentle
thirty-foot slope from the fish house to the boat slide. Between what
was left of the Thanksgiving snow and the overgrown grass the ways
sat up high. He had twenty cedar logs piled on the north side of the
fish house, and he spaced them a foot apart. His original plan had in-
cluded building a custom set of rails to winch the boat down to the
water. But building such a contraption would have taken a full day and
he didn't have the lumber for it anyway.

When Danny returned with his brothers they got right to work. As
he removed the braces, Odd explained how they'd go three men on
either side of the boat, shoulder it off the strongback and out the barn
doors, then set the starboard hull onto the ways. Once they had it resting there, they'd tie lines fore and aft and use the winch to lower it
down to the water. The hard part would be getting it onto the ways.
He asked were they ready and lined them up under the boat and said,
"Once we get this thing off the strongback, there's no setting it down
until we have it on the ways, got it?" They all grunted and Odd said,
"All right, on the count of three."

It was a hell of a load, even for six brawny men, but they inched her
out the barn doors and the six snow-covered feet to the first of the
ways and laid her gently on her side. The Riverfish boys rolled smokes
while Odd rigged two lines around the boat, spliced them, and fixed
the rope to the winch. The winch was fastened to one of the support-
ing pillars in the fish house.

"Danny, you winch her down. You boys help me guide her. We have to keep the skeg and rudder up off the ways. Something happens with the line and she starts sliding, you lay your goddamn lives down for her."

So Odd stepped backward between the ways as Danny cranked the winch and Danny's brothers stood ready fore and aft. When the boat reached the last of the ways Odd hollered, "Wait!" and he and the Riverfish boys inched her up onto the boat slide. He walked backward down the slide, into the freezing water. When the port-side gunwale reached the shoreline he summoned the brothers again and asked them to hold her steady while he removed the lines.

He was waist-deep in water when he got the rigging free. "All right, boys. This is it. Gently, now, slide her the last yard."

There were ten Riverfish hands on the port-side gunwale as they lowered her into the water and ten wet boots when they were done. The boat bobbed for a moment and found her balance. Odd was by then in water up to his chest, his hands on the starboard hull. He walked through the water around the aft end of her. In knee-deep water he walked along her port side up to the prow. She looked even better in the water than he'd thought she would. He stepped aboard, whipped a line on the belaying cleat, and tossed it to Danny onshore. "Tie this to one of those gunnysacks." For good measure he fixed another line to another cleat and tossed it ashore, told Danny to tie it to the other gunnysack.

He lifted the sole and checked to see if water was leaking into the bilge. It was as dry as it had been on the strongback. He walked around the cockpit and checked the bilge up front. All was sound. He went to the cockpit, punched the ignition, and felt the engine hum on. He stood there on the keel line, put his hands out to either side, shifted his weight from one foot to the other, felt the nearly imperceptible teetering, and whispered aloud for only himself to hear, "Goddamn, she's gonna float."

He killed the engine, stepped ashore, and walked up the boat slide to where the Riverfish boys were stomping their cold feet.

Danny said, "She taking any water?"

"Not yet."

"She looks good."

Odd said, "She does, don't she?"

And she did. Her sheer was gorgeous, rising gently from the cockpit. She had five feet of freeboard at her bow, three feet at the transom. The homemade varnish had dried almost black, a color to match the water at this time of day. He'd never thought for one minute he'd be using her to go on the lam, but she looked up for it, sleek and sharp, ready to run.

*S*aturday afternoons usually found Curtis Mayfair receiving visitors. Odd arrived at twilight and saw the lamp glowing in Mayfair's office, one of the townsfolk sitting across from the magistrate. Odd sat on the steps outside and rolled a smoke while he waited his turn.

He looked up and down the Lighthouse Road, taking stock of the only place he'd ever really been, realizing he might not be coming back. This thought filled him with gloom. He looked out at the harbor, at the breakwater and the wild waters beyond. *I was goddamn born here*, he thought. *I got rights to it.* But then he thought of how complicated everything would be. He thought of Hosea's sense of entitlement, knew that Hosea believed he'd saved Odd and Rebekah from lives of deprivation that only he could imagine. Odd wanted his child to come into the world free of such nonsense, free of Hosea's strange grip. Odd looked up at the fat skies, shook his head in sadness and disgust, and stubbed out his cigarette.

It wasn't long before Mayfair stepped outside. He bade Will Halvard good evening and turned to Odd. "There's a fellow I don't see often enough. How goes it, Mister Eide?"

Odd stood and offered his hand and said, "I'm getting by, Curtis."

"You're here to see me?"

"Was hoping for a word or two. You have a minute to spare?"

"I've always got time for the good people. Come on up."

They climbed the stairs side by side and walked into Mayfair's office. Curtis stepped behind his desk and plopped into the big leather chair. He leaned forward, put his elbows on his desk, and said, "Aren't these your halcyon days, Odd? Days you sit around mending nets and chasing skirts? You look like you've not slept in a fortnight."

"I've missed some sleep the last few days. It's true. Finished my boat. It's anchored in my cove as we speak."

"It's a strange time to be launching her, isn't it?"

"Something's come up."

Mayfair sat back in his chair, looked over the tops of his glasses, and said, "All right. I'm listening."

"I'm leaving town."

"Where are you going?"

"I can't say."

Now Mayfair removed his glasses. "How long will you be gone?"

"That I don't know."

"Are you in trouble, son?"

"A kind of trouble, I suppose."

"Trouble with the law? Something I don't know about?"

"Nothing like that, no."

"All right."

Odd sat up in the chair. "I need to know what I've got with my fish house and the farm."

"You mean what it's worth? How much equity?"

"That's what I'm wondering."

Mayfair nodded sagely. "I see. Well. Roughly speaking, taken together, your holdings are worth some four or five thousand dollars, I suppose. Are you looking to sell?"

"Not now. Dan Riverfish is going to squat in the fish house until I figure things out. I'd like to make it so anything needs doing, Dan's in charge."

"It sounds like you're talking about power of attorney. What about Hosea? Why not leave Mister Grimm control?"

Odd arched his eyebrows the way Danny always did. He couldn't help but smile. "I don't think Hosea's gonna be happy about my leaving."

"Odd, you're being cagey."

"I don't mean to be. It's just complicated."

"If you insist on making Daniel Riverfish your attorney-in-fact, that's easy enough to do. And of course, I've always got your best interests at heart."

"I've never doubted that for one minute."

The magistrate pulled open one of his desk drawers and withdrew a piece of letterhead. "I gather that time is of the essence?"

"It is."

He took a fountain pen from another desk drawer and put his glasses back on and began writing. He spoke as he wrote. "This letter declares that Daniel Riverfish is your attorney-in-fact and as such able to conduct legal and fiduciary matters on your behalf. It takes for granted Mister Riverfish's willingness to act as such. It will expire in one year, at which time you'll need to renew the agreement." He finished writing and slid the letter across his desk, offered Odd the pen. "Sign across the bottom."

Odd did so without reading the letter. He slid it back across the desk. "Let's say something happened to me, would my property go to Danny?"

"No. Nor would he be able to execute your estate. The power of attorney terminates upon the death of the principal. If you want your estate to go to Mister Riverfish, we'd need to write a will and testament. Do you wish to make Riverfish your beneficiary?"

"No. Anything happens to me, I'd like everything to go to Rebekah."

Again Mayfair took off his glasses. "Mister Eide, I'd be remiss if I didn't ask if there's something I can do. You have my confidence, you understand?"

"I appreciate it, but no help's needed, not beyond what we're writing up here."

Mayfair took a long, deep breath, withdrew another piece of letterhead from the drawer, and wrote Odd's will.

After Odd signed the will the two men stood and walked together outside. The town was hushed, the harbor water bristling. It was too warm for the end of November. Odd thought of the weather as cautionary.

Mayfair put his hand on Odd's shoulder.

"Sometimes I look at this place and wonder why I don't leave myself," he said.

"This town would fall into the water if you left."

"Aw, hell, don't tell an old man stories. I've heard them all."

They walked down the steps and stood on the Lighthouse Road. Mayfair said, "I still remember the day your mother landed here. She came walking up that road the prettiest thing this town ever saw. Could have been carried away by any old breeze, she was so lithesome, but my goodness. Even Missus Mayfair said so." Curtis turned and looked the opposite direction, toward the apothecary. "Was Hosea that took her in. Was Hosea that found her a life here. Hell, was Hosea that brought you into the world. Just remember that."

"With all due respect, was my mother that did the bringing. Besides, since when are you in the Saint Hosea Society?"

"Listen, Odd. I know Hosea's got his eccentricities. We all do. But that man raised his daughter without help. He as much as raised you."

Curtis Mayfair led Odd to the railing on the other side of the Lighthouse Road. They stood there on the water's edge. "Hosea Grimm arrived on the first boat in the spring of ninety-three. He stood over there on the beach with his hand shielding the sun, watching the tender go. He was wearing orange jodhpurs and knee-high boots, one of his damn hats. He looked even then like both a clown and a high prince. He gives us folks watching from here a wave, then gets to work. Raised a big canvas tent, gathered firewood, hung his foodstuffs in a tree. He dug two fire pits, fashioned a rotisserie of green spruce limbs over one of them, built a strange cairn five feet tall that looked for all the world like some troll's quaint hovel over the second. In two hours he had a campsite that would last the season.

"The next morning he tramped into the woods, a pack over his shoulders, a Winchester in his hand. Newcomers always aroused interest around here, but this man come ashore in orange pants and circus hat the day before set a new standard for strangeness. We couldn't stop wondering about him. Anyway, it was hardly past lunchtime when he walks out of the forest, a tumpline around his forehead, trailing a travois. Tied to the travois was a field-dressed caribou. Two hundred pounds. He brought it to his camp, inverted the travois, and tied it off on a boulder and two trees. Hung the buck from up high.

Before he butchered it, he started driftwood fires in both the pit and the cairn. He spent an hour skinning and the time before supper carving the meat off the bones.

"All night he stayed up, stoking his cairn with the green birch wood, smoking the venison. The next morning he walked into the Traveler's, doffed his hat, and went from table to table introducing himself. Charmed the hell out of a bunch of people not easily charmed. Then he invited us all to his campsite that evening.

"You've got to understand, we weren't much more than a dozen fishing families back then. The Indians living up in the wigwam village. A hundred people in all. Every single one of us gathered at Hosea Grimm's campsite for his proffered feast. A giant vat of pemmican. We stood there, spooning the grub, listening to Grimm.

"He told us the Minnesota and Dakota Lumber Company had procured twenty thousand acres of land up along the Burnt Wood. Said the next year a hundred lumberjacks, thirty men to run a mill, thirty more to oversee distribution of the lumber, they'd all be moving into Gunflint come springtime. They'd bring their families and build houses and schools and bibelot shops to sell whatever people would buy. He reckoned the town would quadruple in size. It would take some years to fell the forests. Then the same interests would mine the ore and copper in the hills to the west. They'd build railroads and highways. A harbor breakwater would be needed, and a quay to accommodate the great ships soon to arrive. If necessary, the harbor would be dredged so those ships might sail right to the shore. Times were changing, he said, and he was there to help usher in that change. All he asked for in return was a place among us.

"So, sure, he's got a lot of pots on the fire. And it's true some of what he cooks up stinks bad as moose shit. But he was true to his word. He never took more than was his, and he got us all ahead of the robber barons. We still own this town. We always will. He had something to do with that. He had a lot to do with that."

Odd had listened to Curtis with both ears. It was a story he'd never heard before and since it came from Mayfair's mouth, he had no reason to doubt it. But then he thought of Rebekah, of her life in chains, of the things Hosea had made her do. Odd spit. "I appreciate hearing the story. No doubt it's a testament to something. But I have my reasons for feeling suspect."

"I've never known you as anything but a straight shooter, son. I believe you've your reasons." He turned to face Odd. "Curious as I am, I honestly don't want to know what they are. I'm happier to live in ignorance."

Odd smiled, though nothing was funny. The blind eye was a bad disease in this town. They shook hands and parted without another word.

XIV.

[February 1896*]*

*E*ven as the hours of daylight lengthened in the first week of February, that winter persisted. Thea fed the dogs those days. Each morning and again each evening, after the jacks took their breakfast and supper, she would haul two wooden pails from the mess. Often as not they were brimming with bread crusts and beans, fatback and milk, but the hounds did not seem to miss their fish. They ate with zeal. By the time she crossed the paddock to drop food for the dog staked under the ridge, the bitch had always finished her slop and would be sitting queenlike in the snow. Thea thought their demeanor was suspect and restful, as though their greater, graver purpose required stores of energy and emotion better not wasted.

The sled drivers had taken to carrying rifles in the woods, but each night for a week they returned to camp without game. In the early days of winter, it would not have been uncommon for the teamsters to see a hundred caribou during the hauling hours, so their sudden and complete absence was yet another harbinger of doom: That winter had become its own disease, the woodland creatures had vanished in the sickness.

Even in their mounting despair the jacks still toiled. Each day sled upon sled descended the ice road and pulled into the mill in Gunflint, where the millworkers unloaded the cut. On February twelfth one of the great horses was killed on the ice road, crushed by a careening load of timber. In the same mishap a teamster lost a hand. Soon after one of the crews had a man beheaded on the northern parcel and two days later one of the sawyers passed through camp minus a leg. These were known hazards, though, and the general comportment of the men in the shadows of such calamities was not much changed.

For her part, Thea steadied during those weeks. She became a dynamo in the kitchen, in charge by then of the suppers as well as the baking. Her favorite job was of course feeding the dogs, those two chances each day to stretch her legs and breathe fresh air. Cold as it was. The dogs greeted her and the pails of food and the three of them formed a sort of congregation of lonesome souls.

In the two weeks since the Ovcharkas had arrived there had been no wolf song. Groups of men visited the dogs each night after supper, offering busted ax handles in lieu of rawhide, bringing in their pockets crusts of bread and hunks of meat to reward the dogs. The jacks, after paying the dogs, would stand against the paddock fence smoking their pipes or cigars, offering woodsmen's philosophies on the nature of such beasts, on the likeliest source of their lineage. One of the men went so far as to offer the great bears of the Yukon as the most likely origin of the breed. None of the others gathered that evening—though preternaturally inclined to ribbing and chiding—would even dispute the possibility. If that winter would not relent, if the men suffered their frozen flesh and injured limbs, if they were reminded daily of the perils of their labor, they were at least more calm in their few hours of leisure each evening, and certainly more comfortable in their slumber.

On the first morning of the third week more snow came. After

breakfast Thea hauled her buckets to the horse barn. She dropped the
first before the bitch, hammered her water free of ice with a hatchet,
then followed the fence line around the paddock to the kennel of the
dog. She had named the dog Lodden for his long strands of wiry black
hair, and each morning now she would call his name as she crossed the
paddock. As she approached his kennel, calling him, she saw that a
wide swath of snow trailed away from his roost. She saw also the frozen earth cratered around the spot his stake should have been, saw his
leather collar and the length of chain tangled atop the packed snow.
She hollered his name into the wilderness, dropped the pail at the opening of his kennel, and hurried back toward the mess.

She was almost jogging as she headed on to the camp office. As she
entered, a young man she recognized from the chow line peered over
his glasses and onto an open ledger. He looked, no doubt surprised to
see her. Before he could greet her she said, "Lodden, Lodden. *Hund!*
Hund!" He came from behind the counter and went straight to the
door. He opened it, a whirl of snow came in at his boots. "The dog?"
he said. "The new dog? What?" He stepped back in, closed the door.
While he donned his coat and hat he asked again, "Did something
happen to the dogs? Is that what you're saying?"

He flew out the door and was gone in the snow before he reached
the paddock fence.

Within an hour what few men remained in camp were scattering
into the passel of white pine. The bull cook, the brothers Meltmen,
the clerk, they all set out into the wilderness, calling for the dog. By
the time the jacks returned from their parcels, word of the missing dog
had already spread. Whispers above the evening's stew ranged over the
possibilities.

One of the men said, "That weren't a godly beast. Likely he's in the
Devil's Maw, making fast with Beelzebub."

When the searchers returned with lanterns aglow and no word on the hound, the rest of the camp retired with a new set of misgivings.

But sunup found the dog back in camp, blood staining his muzzle and the snow outside his kennel. Only the hide and bones of a caribou fawn remained. The same scene played at the bitch's stake, for the dog must have rent the fawn and left the hindquarters for his sister. The Ovcharkas found a new and holier place in the minds of the men. Lodden was left to his duties without the hindrance of stake or chain. For the rest of the cold spell he roamed the camp's perimeter with a beautiful arrogance.

*F*or three weeks during February the temperature still had not climbed above zero, two feet of snow had fallen, the horses had grown coats like bears, but still the camp trundled on. Hosea visited camp often. His leather satchel over his shoulder. He set up a makeshift examining room in the wanigan. Several men had frostbitten fingers or toes or both amputated. Others had black scabs of dead flesh removed from their upper cheeks. Two men had even died by way of the cold; the first of hypothermia, the other of a heart failure way up the northern parcel. Their deaths inspired more dread than sadness, as most of the men knew the calendar well enough to note how much more winter was in the offing.

There were nights during that interminable stretch when the woods above Gunflint on up to Canada were the coldest place on earth. One such dawn broke minus fifty-two degrees. So it was properly strange when Thea woke on the last morning of February to the sound of dripping water. She kicked her eiderdown away and lit a candle in the kitchen. She stoked the scullery fire. Before commencing her morning chores she poked her head out the mess-hall door. For the first time since the ides of January she could smell the horseshit under the snow. During the night a fog had risen, fey and reeking.

In the root cellar Thea collected the morning's fare: the oats, the buttermilk, the bacon. There were bushels of sprouted potatoes and overripe onions and twenty pumpkins ready to be made into pie. She gathered fifty pounds of potatoes and five pounds of oleo. She had baked the bread the night before, and she removed twenty loaves from the wooden breadbox. She thought if the men were anything like herself, the warm weather on the heels of such cold would induce their greatest appetites.

Indeed, when the men arrived after reveille, they found their seats quickly and ate with gusto. Each was served a rasher of bacon, four slices of bread and oleo, boiled and salted potatoes, a heap of steaming oats, and coffee to wash it down. Fifteen minutes after taking their places at the tables they rose and marched out of the mess hall, their mittens and hats in their hands, their coats and shirt collars unbuttoned. Under a dull sun they climbed aboard the empty hauling sleds and lit their pipes or cigars. Thea went to the door and watched as the horses pulled onto the ice road. She could see the runners plowing through the soft snow. Lodden followed the sleigh to the first bend before reversing his enormous stride and backing toward camp.

She had only finished her tea when the supply sleigh arrived, hauled by two horses worse for the season. The same company that owned the mill owned the timber and two camps—the Burnt Wood River Camp and another in the Cloquet Valley—and the sleigh ran a regular loop between the two, stopping at the commissary in Duluth to reload with each pass. Twice each week the same drivers dropped the stores, both the usual fare and, on Fridays, what passed for Sunday dinner. Oftenest this was herring but on that day it was one hundred pounds of pork chops, a cask of fresh apples, and three gunnysacks of butternut squash. Thea pinched two of the apples while the brothers Melt-men unloaded the sleigh.

While they worked, Thea took the apples from her apron pocket and fed one to each of the horses.

She was paring the squash on a bench outside the mess hall, the warm sun still hazy above the clouds, when she saw Joshua Smith steer his fine hickory sleigh around the last bend on the ice road. He sat on a seat of crushed purple velvet and wore a mink coat and beaver skin hat. His boots were Anishinabe-style moccasins, covered in bead-work and quills and lined with sheep's wool. His mittens hung from the cuffs of his sleeves.

"Good afternoon," he said, then pulled his watch from its pocket and corrected himself. "I should say good morning. Is Trond about?"

Thea understood he was asking for the foreman and shrugged to suggest she did not know.

"Have you got coffee in there?" He pointed at the mess-hall door.

She understood this query, too, and nodded and hurried in. At the stove Thea poured coffee and offered him a cup.

"I thank you," he said and took a long drink.

She noticed that one of his front teeth was dead.

"I've heard rumors of women working the Burnt Wood Camp." He took another drink. "But I didn't believe it." He looked at her directly, his dead tooth dividing an impish smile. "A man could sure use a bowl of that stew boiling up yonder."

Thea looked down.

He smiled his dead-tooth smile. He said, "You've got a thing for quiet, eh? Where are you from, darling?" He cocked his head as if to take stock. "Those cheeks and blond locks, I suppose you ain't from Africa." He laughed at his joke. "Norway," he ventured, "Norge?"

Her eyes widened and she replied in Norwegian, "I am from Norway." And then, recalling her English lesson upon leaving Hammerfest, she continued in English, "I am new in America."

To her surprise and relief he responded in Norwegian, introducing himself as the watch salesman Joshua Smith, down from Duluth. He informed her that Trond expected him and repeated his request for a bowl of stew. She moved slowly to the pot on the stove and fetched the stew, deciding as she crossed the hall that despite his dead tooth, Smith was handsome in a way none of the jacks was. His handlebar mustache exaggerated a rakish smile and those eyes of his were wide and devilish enough to cast spells.

He ate standing, loosening the buttons on his shirt. She was used to the jacks and their absence of manners and Smith cut a marked contrast. He dabbed the corners of his mouth with a handkerchief after each bite, there was no slurping, no licking the bowl once the meat and vegetables were eaten. He did not belch when he set the bowl on the tabletop. Without asking, he took a tin cup and went to the cistern and dipped a cup of water. When he finished drinking he used the ladle hanging from the lip and dipped himself another. With every movement he became more at ease in the room.

When he said, "The cold will be coming right back," again in Norwegian, Thea could not help herself and asked, "How do you know?"

Smith replied, "The winds are already bringing it."

*A*fter dinner he set out his wares: watches and knives and small canisters of curatives and powders. He offered cigars, advertised as finer than the rolled-up dogshit they were peddling in the wanigan, and pipe tobacco imported from Zanzibar. He laid out boxes of chocolates and horehounds. When the jacks leaned in and whispered about hooch, he pulled his coat aside to show pockets with hidden half pints. He passed the bottles with a magician's sleight of hand, recouping quarters and dollars with equal cleverness. Standing behind a table in the mess hall, a green felt cloth covering the pine boards, sporting a suit of worsted wool and having traded his beaver-skin hat for a black stovepipe, his mustache styled with bear-fat pomade, his pince-nez magnifying his huge brown eyes, he looked like he could have sold a whip to an ox.

Clearly the jacks were in a buying mood, and Smith did a steady business. Even as he haggled in four different languages, even as he extolled the virtues of his fine Spanish blades and Swiss timepieces and pocketed the loggers' earnings, Smith managed to keep an eye on Thea. In her own way Thea made a sly study of Smith, too.

After Trond bought the last pocket watch, after Smith loaded his unsold goods back into his haversacks, after the jacks adjourned to the bunkhouse, Smith and the foreman and the bull cook and a pair of company men up for the weekend dealt their first game of seven-card stud. They uncorked a bottle of Canadian rye and passed it around the table

*A*bigail Sterle's croup had worsened, so after supper the Meltmen brothers brought her to Hosea Grimm's for care. Thea worked all through the evening hours, doing the job of four herself.

Thea's hands were wet to the wrist in beaten eggs when she drenched the last of a hundred pork chops in the wash and rolled them in cornmeal. She could hear the Saturday-night accordion and merrymaking from the bunkhouse. The poker game was winding down. Smith's back was to her, but every other hand he'd turn and leer. A second bottle was being passed around, and a cloud of cigar smoke hung over the table.

Thea wedged the last pair of pork chops onto the baking sheet— the sixth sheet, each of them loaded—and wiped her hands on her apron. As she did, the card game concluded and the players donned their coats and hats. Smith, his mustache losing its shape, gave her a last drunken grin as the men filed out. She stored the pork chops and stood alone in the mess hall. Exhausted, she thought about retiring for the night but then thought better of it and decided to make the next day's pies. So she boiled water for tea and kept working.

She had already spread the dough and lined the pie tins and mixed the apples and brown sugar and cinnamon when she stepped outside for a breath of fresh air an hour later. The snow had stopped and a full, bright moon hung on the edge of the sky. The bunkhouse had grown quiet but for a few last revelers skylarking outside the door. Smith was right, that hell of cold had blown back in. She hugged herself and turned to go in for the night when she saw a strange sight.

One of the draft horses was being led into the middle of the pad-dock, snorting plumes of cloudy breath into the night. The handler was nearly invisible in the shadow of the horse, but it was not the barn boss, she knew, for the man pulling the bridle stood at the horse's shoulder and the barn boss was no more than five and a half feet tall. When the man and horse reached the trough, the handler turned to leave, but only after hobbling the horse. Satisfied, the man loped back to the barn.

Thea noted what she had seen but thought little more of it until an hour later, when the horse began to scream.

No longer filtered by the cold and dark, the wolves' howls came over the ridge, near and frightening, as though each element of that night—the coldness and darkness and stillness, the moon's bright luster—had its own voice in the discordant choir of the pack. In camp, the jacks stirred. Some came outside for a smoke or to stare up at the sound as though it could be seen. Thea had been readying herself for bed but lit another lantern in the kitchen when she heard the wolves.

They wailed for what seemed an hour. The jacks returned to their bunks and a silence spilled over the night, eerier in its way than the close song of the pack. It was in that interval of calm that the wolves emerged from the ridgetop pines. The dog, Lodden, greeted the pack even as he retreated to the horse hobbled in the paddock, his hackles and slaver evidence of an outrage a thousand years in the breeding. Lodden moved silently, though, even as the draft horse screamed and snorted and finally collapsed onto the trampled snow.

Though terrified, Thea could not help but be drawn to the commotion. Against her instincts and better judgment, she hurried to the door of the mess hall with a lantern. As she shouldered the door open, the watch salesman Smith met her. In Norwegian he said, "The wolves have come."

He still smelled of hooch even in all that cold and in that first moment of recognition she was actually happy to see him. She felt her spirits rise. But then he took the lantern from her hand and made a great show of extinguishing the light. He set the lantern on the floor and approached her as if inviting her to dance, took her hard by the wrist and ushered her into the kitchen. He pushed her onto the kitchen table, piecrusts scattering, the horrible screaming horse and growling dogs in the paddock a befitting accompaniment to his meanness.

She tried to kick him as he came toward her, but he grabbed her boot and twisted it off. She opened her eyes and saw his limp face and fierce eyes and that dead tooth. Then she closed her eyes and felt Smith's hot breath on her neck.

Now there were men yelling in the bunkhouse and barn. The barn boss had set free the bitch and the Ovcharkas circled the horse as eight wolves whirled about the paddock. They moved to their own ancient choreography, their red eyes in the darkness, their thick pelts shimmering like tinsel under the moon. They were silent, but the dogs understood their intentions. Lodden charged a closing wolf, swatted it with his massive forepaw, and bit with two-inch fangs and the wolf wheeled and growled and circled back into the ranks. In the barn, rifles were loaded with shivering hands.

And in the mess hall Thea could not breathe under the drunkard, who held her neck with one hand while he pulled up her skirts with the other. She wanted to cry out but could not, neither for his hand around her neck nor her great confusion. He pressed his hips against her and removed his hand from her neck. As if she had just come up from underwater, she took a gulping breath. But then he ripped her stockings off and she was drowning again.

A desperate yelp came from the night. Lodden chased one of the wolves to the edge of the paddock and broke its hind leg as it attempted to jump the fence. The other wolves continued to circle. At the fence, Lodden set his jaws into the ruff of the injured wolf and sawed into its veins until the blood poured onto the snow. The dog lifted the dead wolf as if it were a pup of his own and carried it across the paddock and tossed it at a trio of its packmates. A warning and boast both. The next wolf Lodden had in his fangs merely rolled over. The dog eviscerated the wolf's pink belly in a single chomp.

Then the horse was up and bucking, the hobble kicked free. And the jacks came out of the bunkhouse and barn and started firing at the pack, who would not retreat but seemed unwilling to blitz again despite their hunger.

Thea thought she might faint but was astonished to feel Smith's wet lips on her ear, to feel the gale of his breath. He clutched her breasts violently, and in that same moment she felt a world of fire in her belly. He grunted with each thrust of his hips, and with each thrust she felt a part of her body leaving her. Like the steam that had earlier that season risen from the jacks in the mess.

In the paddock the wolves were suddenly wise. As another shot rang from the direction of the barn, they turned and ran for the trees on the ridge. Lodden and Freya chased, and before the pack reached the trees the dogs tackled the last straggling wolf and sank their fangs into his throat.

Smith's end came with a sobering shudder and he looked at Thea for the first time since meeting her at the door. For a moment he seemed confused, as though he did not know where he was, but then he pushed himself up off his elbows and buttoned his trousers. Three more rifle shots hollered through the night.

As he ran out the door, Thea fell from the table onto her knees. She opened her eyes and saw only the darkness of that unholy night.

XV.

[*November* 1920]

*A*s he motored out of the cove, as his boat rode the gentle swells, he knew he was crossing seiches, knew because there'd been no wind for two full days, knew because the pressure was falling, had been falling all day, the pulsing behind his glass eye his barometer. He was glad of the seiches, they allowed him to feel the water under his boat, feel it come up through his feet and into his legs.

She moved nicely, his boat. Heavy in the bottom, firm up front. The wheel quick to the rudder. And even as slowly as he went, the boat came out of turns smoothly, found her level quickly. He was dancing with her, learning her manners and mien.

He straightened, headed due east, pushed the throttle to three-quarters. The lake was barely rippling and the boat planed out as quickly as she accelerated. He turned her full left, north, came back across his wake and then full right. The water churned up around him as he throttled down, let her bob there in the mess of the wake. He was a quarter mile offshore, facing town. By God, he was about to be gone.

In the Gunflint harbor he went first to the fuel dock and filled his tank. He put payment and a note in an envelope and dropped it into the harbormaster's mailbox and climbed back aboard the boat, untied her from the dock, and crossed the harbor to the Lighthouse Road, where he tied up again and waited for Rebekah. The moon was over the hills above town, nearly full and heavy with light. He remembered what Hosea had told him once about how the moon tugged the waters of the oceans of the world. Tides, he called them. Like seiches but without need of wind or pressure. Odd wondered was the moon really capable of that. All he wanted now was the light of the moon to show him Rebekah walking up the Lighthouse Road.

And it wasn't long before he saw just that. Saw her silhouette backlit by the moon, as if she were the tide itself, the moon pulling her toward him. Saw Danny laden like a pack mule next to her. Saw her coat flaring out not from a wind but from how fast she was walking. Then saw her face as she stood on the Lighthouse Road above his boat. Saw a look something like pity cast his way, a look cast by the moonlight.

Odd reached his hand up and helped her into the boat. He escorted her to the bench in the cockpit, told her to sit down, offered a woolen blanket for her lap, knelt before her and tucked the blanket around her legs. He whispered that he loved her. In return she gave him a smile, a faint smile, to be sure, but a smile all the same.

Then Odd took her belongings from Danny. Two bags stuffed to bursting. A chest that must have weighed eighty pounds, a hatbox, a pillowcase full of foodstuffs. He stowed the bags in the lockers on either side of the cockpit, stashed the chest behind the motor box and lashed it and covered it with a canvas tarp. He asked Rebekah to hold on for a minute and then climbed from the boat onto the Lighthouse Road.

He looked steadily at Danny. "I set it up with Mayfair that you're in charge of my property. If anything happens to me, it goes to Rebekah. I'll be in touch once we're settled in Duluth, if Duluth is where we end up staying. I'll send news through Mayfair."

"I'll be careful not to burn the place down."

"Hosea's first stop is going to be my front door."

"I'll have him in for tea," Danny said, and smiled.

"He's a wily old prick."

"And I ain't no northwoods rube. Don't worry." ·

Odd looked up the Lighthouse Road, over Danny's shoulder, at the moon now resting on the hilltop. He looked behind him, out over the lake and onto the eastern horizon. The first inkling of light showed clouds. He looked back at Danny.

Danny said, "There's safe water in Otter Bay. That's halfway up the shore. Safe water again in Two Harbors."

"You reckon the weather will hold? I got that feeling in my eye."

"Get on the water. You'll find out."

"Danny, thanks, brother."

Danny clapped him on the shoulder. "The world's waiting."

Odd climbed back aboard his boat. He untied the sternline while Danny untied the bowline and held them to the quay. Odd punched the ignition and the Buda rumbled to life. He was already growing attuned to the sound of it, was already learning the way the vibrations felt in his feet. He was ready to go.

Odd throttled the boat forward and turned her left and headed along the Lighthouse Road out past the breakwater. He turned south and west and got her up to speed and they were on their way.

See the sun coming up?" Odd said. They'd been a half hour in the boat and off the portside bow the sun shone dull, half above the horizon, above the water.

"Hmm," Rebekah said.

"We're on our way, Rebekah. The rest of our lives—" he gestured to the wide-open waters before them "—it's right out there."

She looked up through the cockpit window but didn't say anything.

"Are you happy?" he asked.

"I'm here," she said.

*I*n two hours they motored past the settlement at Misquah, past the mouth of the Birch River and the looming hills through which it ran. There were half-a-dozen fish houses dotting the craggy shoreline, half-a-dozen skiffs upturned for the season. This was as far south as Odd had ever been, and then only once, the summer before, when he had delivered a barrel of whiskey to the Lutheran pastor whose church stood stark white on the hillside.

They were a mile offshore, nosing into a quartering wind, the lake not much agitated by the southwesterly breeze. The boat ran like she was on a rail, and Odd felt capable of anything.

He'd piled some of their bags in the cockpit and Rebekah lay on them, her legs under her like a cat, a blanket tucked around her, sleeping. How could anyone sleep on a day like this, Odd wondered. He looked down at her. So lovely, wisps of hair streaming from under her hat, her eyes impervious to the wind and the dull, throbbing sky. He reached down and pulled the blanket over her shoulder. He tucked her hair behind her ear.

The world through the cockpit window was all lake. Like it was carved from an infinite slab of granite. The feel of his boat beneath him would have been enough at any moment of his life before now, but here she was, sleeping at his leg, with a child in her belly. His child. He could see their life shining back at him, reflected off the water, could see the child coming toward him every bit as real as the next swell. Again he reached down and adjusted the blanket. Until five days ago he'd never once thought of having a child, now the lake wasn't even big enough to contain the promise of it, the promise of the life he saw taking shape.

At noontime, six hours up the shore, the sky finally broke above them. They were passing the town of Otter Bay when Rebekah woke without a word. She went to the transom and hiked her skirt up and peed over the back of the boat. She came back to the cockpit and still without a word fetched the bag of foodstuffs. She took a sandwich wrapped in wax paper and passed it to Odd, who smiled and took it. She poured two mugs of milk and brought two apples from the bag and arranged it all on the cockpit dash before sitting back down on the pile of bags.

Finally she said, "Where are we?"

"We just passed Otter Bay. We're halfway gone."

She took a bite of her own sandwich and settled back against the cockpit wall. She trained her eyes on Odd's face for a moment and then shifted them to their wake. She ate her sandwich and Odd ate his and when they were both finished he took the apples from the dash and handed one to her.

"Another six hours," he said. "We'll be getting there in the dark."

"That sounds about right."

Odd looked down at her. He shook his head.

"Six hours up the shore and it looks exactly like Gunflint. It's all the same place."

"It ain't the same place," Odd said. "I can tell from way out here there's less bullshit in those woods." He nodded up at the shore.

She smiled, so he did too.

"And Duluth is a real city, Rebekah. They've got more than trees and fish down there. We can buy a brick house and a Model-T. We'd even have proper roads to drive on."

She looked at him for a long time, could see in his face all the faces of his childhood. She could see all his goodness, his glass eye, the weather from all his seasons on the water like a mask. She reached up and touched his coat sleeve. "Are you going to marry me?"

"I'll steer this boat into Two Harbors and marry you this day, if it would please you."

She smiled again, though the truth was she didn't want to marry Odd. She didn't want to have a baby or live in a brick house. She didn't want anything, nothing she'd left behind, nothing out in front. "Don't stop in Two Harbors," she said.

*T*he threat of weather that had hung over the first half of their voyage gave over to an afternoon more akin to an autumn day than a late-November evening. The temperature was near fifty degrees, the clouds had broken, and now a dusk as pale as snow settled in the east. The sky above them trickled into darkness. They sailed on in silence. Odd never more at ease in his life, his girl and his boat and a pocketful of cash money all right there.

They passed Two Harbors and Odd lit the lantern and hung it from the cockpit in lieu of running lights. In the moving shadows of the kerosene light they watched Duluth come closer. Still neither of them spoke. The glow from fifteen miles away became clearer with each passing swell. The light spread for miles to the east, to what he knew to be Wisconsin. He'd never seen so much unnatural light. All it held was promise.

Before long they were passing the east-end mansions, everything coming clear in the night. It was enough even to lift Rebekah from her spot in the cockpit. She stood beside Odd, her hand looped in his arm. The evening hadn't cooled much. It was still almost muggy. It took a half hour to get from the first houses to the harbor entrance. Danny had told him to go until the lake ended. And that was what it did. Marked by the aerial bridge and the breakwater lights, the city to his right unlike anything Odd could have imagined. He throttled down and passed through the canal at a crawl, the swells rising and falling gently, the boat riding them easily.

He followed the harbor east, hugging the shoreline, staying clear of the shipping lane. It was a thin spit of land between the harbor and the lake, lined with houses, a well-lit road running its length. After a half mile they came to the Duluth Boat Club, a Victorian-style building not unlike Grimm's apothecary, with several empty slips and a long dock on the harbor.

He turned the boat wide and sidled into one of the slips, resting against the fenders that hung from the pilings, then killed the engine and rounded the cockpit to tie the boat to the dock. He came back and tied a sternline as well.

"Where are we?" Rebekah said.

"The Duluth Boat Club, near as I can tell."

"What's a boat club?"

Odd crossed his arms and looked up at the building. "I don't rightly know, but it's a place to dock her. It's lit up. I'm hoping they can at least steer me to where I might pull her out of the water for winter."

As Odd spoke a dockhand came from the boat club. He was dressed in a blue blazer and khaki trousers. He wore also a blue cap in the style of a naval officer and black boots.

"Good evening," he said. "Welcome to the Duluth Boat Club. I don't think I've seen you before."

Odd looked at Rebekah, then at the dockhand. "Hello," he said without confidence.

Now the dockhand was standing beside them. "That's a fine boat," he said. "Looks brand new."

"She just spent her first day in the water," Odd said.

"Where'd you all come from?"

"We're up from Gunflint."

"A good day for a cruise," the dockhand said.

"A good day for sure," Odd said.

An uncomfortable silence passed between them. It was Rebekah who spoke next.

"We're on our honeymoon," she said.

"Well! Congratulations. Where are you staying?"

"We haven't made arrangements," Rebekah said. "Could you recommend a nice hotel?"

"Downtown here you've got the Spalding Hotel. It's as fine a hotel as Duluth has. There's a good dining room there called the Palm. It'd be a good place to honeymoon."

"Where is it, exactly?" Rebekah said.

"Corner of Fifth and Superior."

Rebekah turned to Odd. "It sounds like a fine place."

"Sure does."

The dockhand put his hand on his chin and said, "How long will you be in Duluth?"

It was Rebekah who answered. "We're not sure."

The dockhand said, "I only ask because most everyone has their boat out of the water by now. The harbor will probably be frozen before long."

"I reckoned that," Odd said.

"We offer wintering services," the dockhand said. "Get your boat out of the water, store it for the season." He pointed up past the boat club, at a storage yard that Odd had somehow missed since they'd been standing on the dock. Masts reached into the evening, the boats beneath them covered with snug canvas. There were dozens of boats there, sitting for winter.

"That's just what we need," Odd said. He turned to Rebekah. "I'll have her put up for winter, right?" It was a question loaded with significance. More significance than Odd could even imagine, one Rebekah understood with a sense of dread. But there was only one answer. At least for now.

"Of course," she said.

So they went into the boat club and Odd made arrangements to winter his boat. They'd hoist it from the water the next morning and store it in the yard. There were fees for the hoisting, fees for the storing, fees for the tarp, for everything. By the time Odd and Rebekah were standing outside, awaiting a cab to bring them downtown, Odd was forty dollars lighter in the pocket than he'd been on arrival. It irked him for a spell, spending all that money on something he could have handled himself in Gunflint, but as the carriage pulled up, and as he helped Rebekah onto the bench and heard the horse neigh, and as the cabdriver cracked the reins and the carriage started up St. Louis Avenue, heading for the city lights, Rebekah's hand on his, he realized he'd have emptied his pockets entirely if it meant this scene played out forever.

*I*n no time at all the road ended under the bridge, the cab stopped, and the driver climbed down and lit a cigar and told Rebekah and Odd that they had to wait for the gondola to carry them across the canal. Odd looked out the canal, at the lighthouse on the end of the pier. The wind had come around from the north. He felt it on his face, knew winter would trail that breeze.

"It's getting cold," Rebekah said, as though she could read his mind.

"We just beat it," Odd said.

The gondola hung from the truss eighty feet above. By some magic of cables and pulleys that Odd could not decipher in the dark, it would cross the harbor entrance. The cabdriver walked the horse by the reins and set the carriage brake and the gondola started across the water. Rebekah and Odd remained on the plush seat in the back of the carriage, their hands warm in each other's. The surface of the water just beneath them.

When the gondola reached the downtown side of the canal the cabdriver unset the brake and cracked the reins gently and the cab moved toward the hills, toward the city. As they moved into the lights, onto the busy streets, among the ten-story buildings, Rebekah lifted Odd's arm around her and settled into him. He felt hopeful after that. And as they drove up Superior Street, behind the streetcars, under the gas lamps lining the street, all he could see was the beauty of it all.

They'd been twenty minutes in the cab before the driver stopped in front of the Spalding Hotel, seven stories of stone and leaded glass that was all the proof Odd needed of his insecurities. Still, he stepped from the cab, offered his hand to Rebekah, who took it and jumped down, landing beside him.

"Sir," a bellhop said, stepping from beneath an awning, "may I take your bags?"

Odd looked at him, this man dressed like a Mountie, and said, "You bet."

The bellhop retrieved a rolling cart and loaded their belongings. Odd and Rebekah moved cautiously behind him.

Odd heard Rebekah's breath catch as they entered the hotel. The chandeliers hanging high above the lobby cast a refracted light on the Oriental carpets, the long, elegant sofas and beautiful mahogany tables, each with a vase of fresh flowers at its center, the guests lounging on those couches, their muslin dresses and fine English suits lit by the chandeliers above as though made for that express purpose. All of it was gorgeous and elegant in a way that Rebekah couldn't have imagined. If the downtown lights, as they approached them in the cab, had softened her, the loveliness of that hotel lobby melted her.

At the counter a man with a handlebar mustache and slicked-back hair greeted them. He wore a black suit and a black tie and a boutonnière of blood-red roses blossomed from his lapel. "Good evening," he said. "Welcome to the Spalding Hotel. Will you be checking in this evening?"

"We will," Odd said.

Rebekah said, "We're on our honeymoon!" and curled her arm into Odd's.

The man looked from Odd to Rebekah and back again at Odd. "Your honeymoon, yes." He looked again at Rebekah. "Well, congratulations from all of us here at the Spalding." His mustache curled up with his forced smile. "Let me see what rooms we have available." He opened a ledger on his desk and ran his finger up and down a column of numbers. "We have a suite on the seventh floor. How long will you be staying?"

"Can't say," Odd said. "Three or four nights, anyway."

The man behind the desk checked the ledger again and said, "A suite is a must for your honeymoon." Now he raised his hand and snapped his fingers and the bellhop who had unloaded the cab stepped quickly to the desk. "Bring their bags to the Harbor Suite. Draw the curtains and turn down their bed."

The bellhop nodded and was gone with the rolling cart of their luggage.

The man behind the desk pulled his watch from his vest pocket, checked the time, and replaced the watch. "Will you be having a late dinner in the restaurant? Or would you like dinner brought to your suite this evening?"

Again Rebekah and Odd looked at each other. They must have appeared as children, so giddy were they.

Rebekah said, "Bring dinner up. Roast beef and potatoes and something sweet for dessert."

The man behind the desk leaned forward, glanced once in each direction, and whispered, "Would you fancy a bottle of champagne? To celebrate your nuptials?"

Rebekah's eyes spread wide and a broad smile came across her face.

"Very well," the man behind the desk said.

He had Odd sign the registry and snapped his fingers again. Another bellhop stepped to the counter. "Bring Mister and Missus Eide to the Harbor Suite. See that their needs are satisfied." Then to Odd he said, "I hope you enjoy your stay. If there's anything I can do— *anything*—please don't hesitate to ask." He handed the bellhop the key.

*T*he Harbor Suite was perhaps even more elegant than the hotel lobby. There were three rooms and a turreted sitting area overlooking Superior Street and the harbor below. An enormous four-poster bed covered in silk with a dozen pillows at its head filled the sleeping chamber. The bathroom was twenty feet square with a marble-topped table in the middle of it, a crystal vase with a hundred flowers sat atop it. The tub was claw-footed and cast iron and large enough to bathe a bear.

Rebekah moved from room to room with her finger pressed to her lip. She appeared to be levitating. He stood at the window in the turret, watching her, marveling at the contrast between this place and all the other places he'd ever been. He rolled a cigarette and stood there long enough to smoke it while Rebekah inspected every inch of the suite. As he stubbed the cigarette in an ashtray there was a knock at the door.

He crossed the room and opened the door. A waiter in a white coat pulled a linen-covered cart into the room. Two covered plates and a basket of bread sat on the cart. Odd's mouth started watering at the smell of it.

"Would you like me to set this in the sitting room?"

"Sure," Odd said.

"Over here," Rebekah corrected. She was sitting on a sofa with pink paisley pillows on it. "Put it on the table here." She patted the coffee table before her.

The waiter wheeled the cart across the suite and covered the coffee table with another linen. He set the plates of food on the linen, set silverware on either side of the plates, put the bread basket and a ramekin of whipped butter and bowls of salt and pepper on the table. From the second shelf of the cart, covered by the linen, he removed a silver bucket filled with ice and a bottle of champagne. There were two coupes in the bucket as well, and he set one before each plate on the coffee table. He uncorked the champagne and poured each coupe full and said, "Is there anything else I can do for you?"

"No, thank you," Rebekah said.

He bowed and was gone.

When the door closed behind him Rebekah stood up and said, "Look at this!"

"They think we're the king and queen of someplace," Odd said.

"You mean we're not?" Her smile was luminous.

"Let's eat some of that food." Odd sat beside her.

They removed the cloches in unison. On each plate was a slab of roast beef and a crock of au gratin potatoes, a pile of broccoli florets, and a sprig of parsley. Before Odd picked up his knife and fork he lifted his champagne and raised it before him as he'd seen folks in the Traveler's Hotel saloon do. He looked at Rebekah with all the earnestness he could muster and said, "This is it, Rebekah. This is the first night of our happiness. The first of a million." He chinked the rim of his glass against hers and drained it. "Now," he said, "I aim to fill my belly up with this here plate of food."

Rebekah didn't say anything, only sat there beaming, sipping her champagne. Odd cut into the roast beef, sprinkled the forkful of meat with salt and pepper, and started eating.

"We've never had anything like this. Not once," Rebekah said, looking around. "All those nights in your fish house, sitting on fish boxes." She shook her head. "I can't believe it."

Odd said, "I told you so."

Rebekah finished her champagne and poured them each more. Odd quaffed his between a bite of potatoes and meat.

"You're supposed to sip it," Rebekah said.

"These glasses are nothing more than thimbles," Odd said. "I can't help it."

She smiled. She could not stop smiling.

"Ain't you gonna eat?"

"I can't eat right now."

So Odd ate alone, first his plate of food, then half of hers. Rebekah nibbled on a crust of bread, birdlike. They talked and laughed and behaved exactly as if they were on their honeymoon. When they finished the bottle of champagne, Odd fell back on the couch, unbuckled his belt, and let out a deep and satisfied breath.

"I never ate so much food in my life."

Rebekah put her hand on his taut stomach. "If anyone ever deserved a feast, it was you," she said.

"Why'd I deserve a feast?" he said, taking her hand in his.

She spread her free hand before her. "For this. For all of this. For having courage." She took her hand from his and ran it through his messy hair. "How in the world did all this happen?" she said.

Instead of answering he stood up, went into the bathroom, and plugged the drain in the tub. He turned the hot water on and from a bottle on the edge of the tub poured bubbles into the rising water. He went back to Rebekah, took her hand, and led her to the tub. There he left her, walking backward from the room as she undressed slowly, for his benefit, and stepped into the steaming bath.

He returned a couple of minutes later, naked himself, two cigarettes smoking in his mouth, a flask of whiskey and the ice bucket in his hands. There were two crystal glasses beside the bathroom sink, and he filled them with ice from the bucket. He poured the whiskey over the ice and set the glasses on the edge of the tub and took one of the cigarettes from his mouth and handed it to Rebekah.

"I'm about as foul as a man can get, sweetheart."

Rebekah took a long drag from her cigarette and as she exhaled said, "Well, then, I suggest you join me in here."

He had one foot in the tub before she finished talking.

For a long time they sat in the tub without speaking. They finished their cigarettes and Odd drank his whiskey and they rested their heads on the porcelain, the steam from the bath soaking the mirror above the sink. Odd was a kind of happy he'd never been before, loose after the champagne and whiskey, his gal there in the city with him, in the tub, with no more need to speak. He felt the fatigue from the last four days' labor seeping out of his back and shoulders and into the bathwater. He hadn't known, hadn't ever even suspected, that this feeling was in the world to be had.

Rebekah, though, was growing distant. As they sat in the tub she was reminded of the baths she used to take with Thea—*with Odd's mother*—and the weight of those memories, of all their implications, was drowning out the pleasure of being where she was with him. She realized, also, that their lives in Duluth would not be roast beef and honeymoon suites all winter long. Odd was a fisherman, after all, and even if he was flush now, as he claimed to be, he couldn't afford this forever. They'd end up in some tenement with noisy neighbors and the rank smell of sauerkraut in the halls. She remembered that from Chicago even if she remembered nothing else.

And beneath all of these bothers, she felt some strange and distant guilt about Hosea alone in his big shop, moping around the flat plotting his revenge. She didn't know what he was capable of. She didn't want to know.

It was Rebekah who finally spoke. "I suppose he's burned the woods down by now, trying to smoke us out."

Odd cocked his head and looked at her. He thought of saying nothing at all but couldn't help himself. "I guess he ain't found us."

"You know he's been to see Danny. He would have stopped there first."

"And you know Danny would sooner kiss Hosea on the lips than spill."

"I know."

She reached into the bathwater and rubbed Odd's foot, which was resting at her waist. She tried to forsake her doubt. She couldn't. "There's no part of you that sees the folly in all this?"

"Are we going to circle around this for the rest of our lives?" Odd said. "For God's sake, Rebekah, we ain't fifteen-year-old kids."

Rebekah looked at him and the thought of the years that separated them hit her hard. "What are we, then? Tell me, because I can't see. *This* isn't who we are—" she gestured at the lush accommodations, held up one of the crystal low balls "—not by a long shot."

"Of course this isn't who we are," Odd said sharply. "But it's who we deserve to be, for a few days at least. We'll figure the rest out after that." He looked at her softly now, feeling bad for snapping. He saw tears in her eyes. "Listen, Rebekah." He sat up, leaned toward her. He took her head in his hands and kissed her and then put his hands on her shoulders so they were only a few inches from each other. "I told you, I'm going to take care of you now. You and the baby. You don't have to *pay* for nice dresses anymore, for a nice bed to sleep in. I'm going to see to that."

She looked doubtful. Sad. "What if I'm no good with the baby? If I'm only suited to take care of myself?"

"I ain't worried about that."

"*I'm* worried about it, Odd."

She tried to pull away from him but he wouldn't let her. He tried to kiss her again but she turned her head.

"What if the life you describe isn't what I want?" she said, her voice barely above a whisper.

"Is that true?"

"Sometimes. I don't know."

Now he let go of her shoulders. She looked up at him quickly, grabbed hold of his hands. "I'm scared, Odd. I'm scared is all. I don't want you slipping away from me."

"You think I'm going somewhere?" He shook his head, almost laughed. "You think I ain't worried?"

She put her face into his neck and started to cry. "Men don't act like you, Odd Einar Eide."

"The hell they don't." He took her again by the shoulders, made her look at him. "I've been thinking about my mother. About the price she paid for me. Since you gave me those pictures on my birthday I can't stop thinking about her. I owe it to her to take care of our baby, to raise him the way I should have been raised. Never mind what I'm afraid of or how hard it will be or goddamn Grimm."

Now Rebekah softened. She looked down and said, "Your mother and I used to take our baths together. The summer before you were born." When she looked up there were more tears in her eyes. She stood and stepped out of the bath, took a towel from the rack and held it to her chest. "I watched her belly grow with you. I saw you all the time." She removed the towel and put her hands on her own belly. There was nothing there yet. No sign.

Odd stood, too, and stepped from the tub. He stepped to her. "You see? That means you know me all the better." He lifted her chin so they were eye to eye. "You know I'm a good man. And true."

She took a deep breath, turned away from him. She said, "It's not your goodness I'm worried about."

He grabbed her, wrapped her in his arms. They stood like that while she cried, the bathwater dripping from both of them, pooling on the tiled floor. After a while she stopped crying. She took his hands and moved them to her breasts, held them there. His pulse jumped.

She pressed his hands more firmly. Leaned back against him.

"Is this okay? For the baby?" He could feel her own quickening pulse behind her breast.

"I don't know," she said, her voice husky. "But there's nothing in this world that's going to keep me from making love to you on that bed."

XVI.

[March 1896]

*I*t was a morning for slaughter. Thea walked to the edge of the paddock to feed the dog. He did not come off the roof of his kennel for the slop bucket. His muzzle was still pink. The bitch Freya was gone.

She passed through the paddock on her way back to the mess but stopped at the trough. She could not imagine what had happened here. She did not want to. Only knew that the mess of bloodstained snow was in some way related to the awful pain she felt that morning. The memory of Smith lording over her, his brute strength, his rank breath, was with her like her prayers. She had not slept for fear.

Now she fell to her knees and started crying. Between sobs she heard men behind the barn, still twenty-five yards away. Their voices held no alarm. It was as if they were out for their evening smoke. Before she stood again she removed her mittens and plunged her hands in the snow. She left them there until they burned and then left them still another minute. When finally she stood she raised her hands before her. They were roseate and the gentle breeze strapped them like a leather belt. *God forgive me*, she thought. *God protect me.*

Instead of going back to the mess for the rest of her morning chores she walked to the barn. She'd never been inside, but she slid the door open and walked in, the smell of horses and hay thick in the closeness even though the Percherons were already toiling on the ice road. She walked to the opposite end of the barn, following the ray of light shining through the hayloft window behind her. She was surprised at how much colder it was inside the barn than out.

At the other end of the barn she opened the door to a horse hanging from the hayloft pulley, its brown belly split, its guts spilled on the snow. The bull cook stood in a white apron, his cap sprayed with blood, a knife heavy in his hand. Two of the teamsters held either flank of the horse, and the barn boss was reaching for a spade to shovel the guts into a waiting wheelbarrow.

Already in the early morning the snow was dripping from the barn's roof—the *splat, splat, splat* the only sound above the men's heavy breathing. Three wolf carcasses hung by their hind legs from the fence. Thea saw Freya lying under the wolves and for a moment felt a reprieve from the carnage. A second, closer look showed the bitch's throat split from ear to ear. Bloody boot prints trailed all over the enclosure.

"Good Christ, lass, what are ya doin'?" the bull cook asked, stepping toward her, shooing her away with his bloody hand. "This is no sight for a lady. Go on, now."

Thea had already turned. She hurried to the barn door and shut it behind her. She ran through the barn and across the yard to the mess, her hands still stinging.

*A*t her bunk she folded her hands in prayer. Her knees ached against the dirt floor. She opened her Bible. By the light of a flickering candle she read, *Thou shalt not bring the hire of a whore, or the price of a dog, into*

the house of the lord thy God for any vow: for even these are abomination
unto the land thy God. Her fear rose with each word. She closed the
Bible. She hugged it to her breast and closed her eyes.

She could not stop thoughts of Smith. Of his dead tooth, of his
grunting, of the slaver falling from his lips onto her face. *Mercy, mercy,*
mercy, she begged.

Finally she rose and stepped into the kitchen. There were biscuits
to make, and stew to warm, and apples to pare. Perhaps these tasks
would distract her. She donned her apron and smoothed her hair and
lifted the sack of flour from the cupboard beneath the block table. She
cut the bag open and poured flour into the enormous mixing bowl.
She fetched the keg of buttermilk and the salt. Remembering the
stew, she went to the cellar and pulled the vat from its place and lugged
it to the stove and set it to simmer. She fetched a barrel of apples and
put them at her feet. She greased the baking sheets. In this way she
moved forward, her fear and guilt always like a shadow. She could not
raise her eyes because when she did she saw the spot across the room
where Smith had forced her to the table.

*I*t was after lunch when Trond and the bull cook met the constable.
He walked into the mess hall, his hat and gloves already removed, his
wool coat opened, a black belt and holster plain to see. She wondered,
Was judgment so swift? But the men took seats on the other side of the
mess, and except for asking for tea to be served, Trond and the constable and the old bull cook did not mind her at all.

At the midpoint of their meeting the bull cook left, returning minutes later with the barn boss, who was perhaps most aggrieved by the
horse now strung from the pulley behind the barn. His name was

Jacque and he'd come from Quebec. He spoke scant English when he spoke at all.

Jacque was asked: Why was the horse in the paddock at such an odd hour? Why was the horse hobbled? Was it his job to oversee the care and protection of his stable? Oblivious to the insinuation, Jacque answered the questions. He wanted to know himself why the horse was hobbled in the middle of the paddock. Of course it was his job to oversee his stable. Did the constable wish to see his well-kept barn? The horses worked six days each week, they hauled one hundred thousand board feet of white pine down a road of ice every day, and there wasn't a cracked hoof among the dozen of them, not a single harness gall or skin sore to show for their labor.

When the constable pressed him, and when Jacque finally understood the tone of incrimination, he wasted no time indicting the watch salesman Smith, whose own horse was footsore and frostbit and readier for a pistol shot than another step through these woods. Where the hell was Smith? He'd shoot the bastard himself, shoot him right in the knees before finishing him with a bullet in the ear.

The bull cook ushered Jacque from the mess hall. Trond and the constable stood and stretched their backs and poured more hot water into their teacups. They scratched their beards and consulted the list of loggers in camp. The morning passed with a slow parade of men being led into the mess for interrogation. It was a dispirited investigation. The men were simply spent.

After dinner, after the mess hall had emptied, Rolf, the Norwegian, approached the kitchen. He told Thea that the constable and Trond wished to speak with her. He said they would return from their smokes in a moment, and that he would translate for her. He told her not to worry, that they only wanted to know if she'd seen anything suspicious the previous night. He must also have judged some look on her face because he proceeded to elaborate on what had happened: The wolves had come, one of the dogs put down, one of the horses, a crime indeed. They suspected the watch salesman Smith. Thea asked if she could have a moment, she motioned to her room back of the kitchen.

In her hovel she washed her hands and face, brushed her hair, checked her dress in the reflection of the candle sconce. She took her Bible and kissed the cover and opened it to Deuteronomy. That scripture would be her testimony.

These were three beggared men. Each wore a face as drawn and long as the winter had been. Their hands were cracked and folded in front of them. Their lips behind their mustaches and beards were white and bled dry. Rolf's face was mapped with frostbitten scars. The constable licked his pencil tip and turned to Rolf.

"Ask her to tell me her name."

Rolf did, and the constable wrote it down in his notebook.

"Ask her why the Bible."

Rolf turned to Thea, he pointed to the Bible. "He wishes to know why you've brought your Bible."

Thea looked down at the open book. Her pulse was galloping. Trond had withdrawn a pocketknife from his vest and pulled open the blade, the mother-of-pearl handle glinted in the lantern light as he trimmed his fingernails. She whispered to Rolf, "I am a fearful child of the Lord."

Rolf sat back. He looked at her as though he'd never heard a word of Norwegian spoken before. "Says she's feared. Says she's a child."

The constable put the pencil tip to his notebook and began to write but stopped. He lifted his eyes to the ceiling and wrung his hands. He turned to Trond, who was still tending his fingernails. "Christ, Trond, what can this girl tell us? She's a child. She don't know about dead horses nor misdeeds."

Trond turned to Rolf, "Ask the lass if she saw anything suspicious last night."

The constable was already closing his notebook. He'd already put his pencil in his sleeve pocket and was buttoning his vest when Rolf asked Trond's question.

When Thea began to weep the constable stopped readying to leave. He looked at Trond, then Rolf, then Thea in turn. "What's she cryin' for?" he asked.

Thea took the Bible from the tabletop and opened it and found her passage. She handed it to Rolf, who withdrew his glasses from his shirt pocket and held the good book to the lantern light.

He read the verses to himself. When he looked at Thea her face was in her hands.

"What's this nonsense?" the constable asked.

Trond addressed Thea. "What's the meaning of this?" He turned to the Norwegian. "Rolf, ask her what's the meaning of this."

Rolf read the verses again, this time out loud in Norwegian. "If a man find a betrothed damsel in the field, and the man force her, and lie with her: then the man only that lay with her shall die. . . . For he found her in the field, and the betrothed damsel cried, and there was none to save her."

"Good God almighty, let's speak our common language," the constable said.

But Rolf raised a hand as if to ask for silence. He touched Thea's arm and said, "What do you mean to tell us, child?"

Thea looked up at his kind words, at the gentle tenor of his voice. She whispered, "That man. Last night, he came. When the horse was out."

Rolf closed his eyes, then opened them and looked at Trond. He shook his head.

"What is it, old man?"

"If I understand her, we've got a heap of trouble. Sounds like maybe Smith paid her a visit last night."

"What does that mean?" the constable hissed. "Plain English. Tell me in plain English what happened."

Rolf looked disgusted with the constable. He turned again to Thea, who had startled at the constable's sharp words. "Do you mean to say the watch salesman Smith came here last night? When? Why?"

Thea offered the Bible again. She trembled, her fear was stupendous.

"Are you trying to tell me what happened?" He pointed to a word—*skrek*, cried out—and read to her the verse, *"Han traff den trolovede pike ute på marken, hun skrek, men der var ingen til å hjelpe henne."* And the betrothed damsel cried, and there was none to save her. "Do you mean to say that man Smith lay with you?"

Thea put her hands over her face again.

"Child, did that man hurt you?" He took her arm and shook her. "Did Smith hurt you?"

Now she burst into tears and laid her head on the table. Rolf looked up, first at the constable and then at Trond. "We've got ourselves a hell of a mess," he said.

"What's wrong with the girl?" the constable asked. "What kind of a mess?"

"I gather Smith took what weren't his. Her Bible talks about a girl in a field and nobody to help her. I think she's meaning to tell me she were that girl, and Smith laid with her."

The three men sat in dumb silence, each of them looking blankly ahead. Thea sobbed silently, her head still on the table.

It was Trond who spoke first. "What does that have to do with the horse, though? How did the horse get into the paddock?"

They were rhetorical questions. He was thinking out loud. But Rolf misunderstood, and asked Thea if she knew of anything about the horse.

She looked up and said, "I saw a tall man leading a horse last night." She pointed outside. "Before the wolves."

Rolf translated.

"A tall man?" the constable repeated. "Leading a horse, she says?"

"Smith is a damn sight taller than six foot," Trond said.

The constable had taken his notebook back out and was scribbling furiously. "Ask her what time," he said.

Rolf asked her and Thea considered, she told Rolf.

"She says it was late, after ten or eleven. She was done with her chores and readying for bed."

"It makes no sense," Trond said.

"Ask her was it Smith leading the horse."

She couldn't say who it was, she only saw from a distance and through the darkness. She repeated that it was a tall man, that he led the horse by the bridle past the trough, where the horse was left.

There was a moment of confused silence before Rolf said, "He was looking to stir up a commotion. That horse was bait for the wolves."

The constable looked at Trond, "By God, the old man's right. Why else would he do it?"

Trond stood and walked to the door and looked out the window. He'd been in the woods for a long time, he'd solved his share of problems. More than a few of his crewmembers had been sent off the parcel for one misdeed or another, some of those had ended up in the hoosegow. But this was a full-fledged crime if Thea told true. There was a goddamn lawman in his mess hall to attest to it. He had a dead horse butchered; he had a young lady defiled. Things were entirely beyond his experience now. He turned back to the group. "What do we do?"

The constable rose. "I'll bring Jacque and the girl before the magistrate first thing in the morning. They'll give their testimony. We'll put a warrant on the watch salesman Smith. He'll be charged and sought. We'll offer a reward for his capture."

Trond walked back to the table. "If Smith is smart he'll be gone, to Canada or Chicago or goddamn Mexico."

"Then we'll find him in Mexico, Trond."

"What about my horse?"

Rolf said, "Your horse ain't quite as important as it was a few minutes ago, chief." He turned his attention to Thea. "The constable is going to bring you before Curtis Mayfair in the morning. You'll have to travel to town and make a testimony. You can't use your Bible to tell the story. You'll need to tell them what happened in your own words. I'll go with you."

"Tell her to get some rest," the constable said. "Tell her we'll leave with the light."

*T*hey rode the foreman's sleigh up the ice road: Thea, the barn boss, and Rolf on the wooden bench, Trond himself at the reins, one of the Percherons harnessed and stepping lively. The morning was warm even before the light, and the horse proved it with his gait. Before they began the long descent into Gunflint, going over the ice road's last rise, the sun broke over Lake Superior. The trees on either side of the road sagged under the dripping snow and the winter birds were out, their song more evidence of the thaw.

When they were still a mile outside town they passed a farmer mending his fence a stone's throw off the road. A sorry herd of six gaunt Holsteins stood behind him in a small pasture cut from the woods and still pocked with pine stumps. The farmer looked up and waved as if to hurry them along. He had a long beard and hair and like many of the men Thea saw, he bore the scars of frostbite. The farmer took a step toward them and waved his hammer at them and shouted, "Trespassers!" and pounded the packed snow with his sorry boot.

Trond turned to Jacque and Rolf and smiled. "That's Rune Evensen," he said. "Poor fellow's been touched by more than this cold season, I'm afraid."

Thea had been watching the farmer, and when she heard him shout in Norwegian and then Trond announce his name, she turned quickly to look again. Evensen was her uncle's name.

Thea kept watching him as the road curved and began its last plunge into Gunflint. The morning and their errand had been confounding enough without the revelation of a man named Evensen. Now she was as distraught as she'd been during her first hour in this place. Unable to help herself, she turned to Rolf and said, "Sir, I beg your pardon, but did the foreman say that farmer's name was Evensen?"

Rolf only nodded affirmatively.

"Sir, my uncle's name is Evensen."

"Your uncle?" Rolf asked. He was of course not privy to any knowledge of Thea's situation. Nor did he much care. He was sympathetic about what had happened to her, he felt some pride in his role in helping to uncover the extent of the watch salesman's crime, he may have even felt a moment's relief in being spared a day on one end of a double-bitted saw. Even still, he was already dreading the prospect of a day in the magistrate's chambers. He'd spent too much time in courthouses for his liking. "What about your uncle?"

The tone of his voice was stern and suggestive of silence, so Thea said no more, only rode the rest of the way to Gunflint more befuddled than ever.

The constable had left an hour ahead of them, and they met him now outside the livery stable. He looked harried. He carried his saddlebag over his shoulder.

"Mayfair will see us in his chambers straightaway," he told Trond as the two men shook hands. "Stable your horse, then meet us at the courthouse. I'll bring your charge with me."

Trond leaned toward the constable. "Go gently with the lass," he said.

"We've business, Trond."

"She's scared, that's all I mean to say."

The constable looked at her climbing from the sleigh. "It'll be Mayfair's inquest, but I'll vouch for her nerves." He shook hands with Rolf and Jacque and motioned for the group to follow him.

Mayfair's office was on the Lighthouse Road. Though only eight years old, the building was already growing shabby. The dirt road was funneling snowmelt down to the lake, and their boots sucked at the mud with each step.

Mayfair sat behind his desk. He wore a flannel shirt and wool scarf. When he stood to greet them, he had a viola in one hand and a polishing rag in the other. There was a spittoon next to his high-backed chair, and he spit a mouthful of tobacco juice into it. His pants, Thea now saw, had enormous pockets on the knees. The camp clerk in the wanigan had a greater air of respectability than the magistrate did. Except for the dozen calfskin-bound books on the shelf behind him, these chambers looked a lot like the company store.

There were five captain's chairs arranged before his desk, and he motioned for them to sit down. He sat down himself, but not before adding to the spittoon.

The constable spoke first. "Your honor, these are the witnesses in the case of Arrowhead County versus the watch salesman Joshua Smith." He consulted his notebook. "Jacque Chadel, the barn boss up on the Burnt Wood River Camp." He motioned at Jacque, who doffed his cap but said nothing. "This here's Thea Eide. And this here's Rolf Johnson. He'll be helping us translate the girl's testimony." The constable flipped the pages of his notebook as he stepped behind the witnesses.

"Your honor, the night before last one of the horses up on the Burnt Wood River Camp was led into the paddock for no apparent reason. We surmise it was to lure the wolves and cause a commotion. The horse had to be put down yesterday morn. During my investigation, it came to light that Joshua Smith molested the girl here. The suspect fled sometime the night before last.

"Jacque here will testify as to the horse crime. Your honor, Jacque Chadel."

Mayfair had yet to say a word. He looked at Jacque, who looked back. There passed a moment of awkward silence.

"Well, boy?" Mayfair finally asked. "What about this horse?"

"The horse was shot," Jacque said.

The magistrate looked at the constable and shook his head. "You'd think these fellas live in the woods might enjoy a little conversation. Not so." He turned his attention to Jacque. "Would you mind elaborating? I'd like to hear the story of the horse from your perspective."

So Jacque told him in plainspoken English. When he was finished with his one-minute testimony, he concluded with a question: "When will we get another horse? We're going to need us one."

The magistrate was finishing his transcription in a gilt-edged log. When he finished he looked sternly at Jacque. "Do I look like a horse salesman? Did you see a sign above my door that said HORSES FOR SALE?"

Jacque only clenched his jaw.

"Your boss man's in charge of new horses." Again he turned to the constable. "Show this fella the door." To Jacque he said, "I thank you for the fine storytelling." He spit again, then pulled the wad of snoose from his cheek and dumped it into the spittoon.

The constable led Jacque to the door and shook his hand and thanked him properly. He told Jacque that the testimony of the girl might take longer and suggested that Jacque walk up to the Traveler's Hotel and get himself a cup of coffee for the wait. He even offered him a nickel from his own pocket.

When the constable returned, Trond came with him. He wiped his muddy boots vigorously on a rug for such purpose and crossed over to the magistrate's desk. "Curtis," he said, offering his hand.

"Trond. How goes it?"

"Well," he said, looking back at Rolf and Thea, "I can honestly say I've been better. I'm anxious to hear your thoughts on this mess. I saw Jacque on the way in."

"He wants another horse," Mayfair said.

"So do I. But that's a conversation for a different time, with a different man. About this Smith."

"Yes, about this Smith."

The constable repeated for the magistrate the story he'd told earlier that morning, the story of Thea and her strange testimony culled from Deuteronomy. He admitted that they'd not actually heard her say Smith had assaulted her. He concluded by adding, "I trust your interrogation might get it out of her."

Before the magistrate could commence his questioning, Trond quickly added, "She's scared, Curtis, if you'd bear that in mind. And she don't speak our language. But she's a good lass."

Mayfair nodded, then offered his first question. "Did you see the watch salesman Smith on the night before last?"

Rolf translated.

"Yes," she said.

"Where did you see him?"

"In the mess hall."

The magistrate was chronicling her responses in his log. "Why was he in the mess hall?"

At this Thea looked down. "For me. He came for me."

Rolf translated slowly.

Mayfair stopped writing, looked up at her. "What did he do when he got there?"

When Rolf was finished translating Thea put her face in her hands and started to cry.

Mayfair took a deep breath. "My wife and I, we go to church every Sunday." He waited for Rolf to finish translating. "The constable tells me you're an ardent believer yourself. Is that true?"

Thea could not imagine what he meant to ask. "Beg your pardon?" she said.

"Am I wrong that you came to your meeting with the constable here with the good book last night?"

Thea paged through her old testament and offered the judge the same scripture she had offered the constable twelve hours before.

Mayfair listened patiently and when she was finished, he took another deep breath. An uneasy silence came over the room. Finally the magistrate said, "Have you known this girl to be a liar, Trond?"

"I don't know the girl well, but no, I haven't known her to lie. And cookee would have her a saint. She does the work of three."

"Does anyone here object to the statement regarding this girl's integrity?" He went from face to face and watched them shake their heads no.

"Trond, what do you make of Smith's character?"

"I don't have much of an opinion. He's a souse. He was easy pickings at our stud game the other night. He had nice wares in his haversacks. I can't say much beyond that."

"What about you, old man?" the judge asked Rolf. "Do you have any opinion about Smith, accusations notwithstanding?"

"I don't know him from Adam."

Curtis dutifully copied their responses. Now he addressed Thea again. "Is there any reason I should doubt your story?"

Rolf translated. Thea shook her head and looked into her hands on her lap.

Now Mayfair took the viola from the table and held it as though it were a banjo, plucking a few folksy chords. "Good Lord almighty," he said. "That means there's a certified felon running free. I can't see any reason not to put a warrant out on him. I'll offer a reward." Again he sighed. "And I suppose I ought to let them know over at the newspaper. They might want a statement from you, Trond. You mind having lunch in town today?"

*B*y the time they finished lunch at the Traveler's Hotel, the first broadside advertising the reward for Smith's capture hung in the window of the Gunflint *Ax & Beacon*. Trond stood at the window, his hands folded behind his back, bent slightly at the waist, reading the sign aloud:

Attention

Citizens:

THE ARROWHEAD COUNTY CONSTABLE, ALONG WITH

CURTIS MAYFAIR, MAGISTRATE OF GUNFLINT, MINN., OFFER A

$100 REWARD

FOR THE CAPTURE OF THE WATCH SALESMAN

JOSHUA SMITH

for crimes against horses and for assaulting

a young woman at the Burnt Wood River Lumber Camp.

He fled the Burnt Wood River Camp on a one-horse

sleigh in middle-night on March the third.

Convey any information on his whereabouts to

the Gunflint, Minn. Courthouse and the attention

of magistrate Curtis Mayfair.

When he finished reading Trond commented on the swiftness of the court. It was warm enough in the midafternoon sun to remove his coat, which Trond did and then stood with his face raised toward the sun. "Now, if only they'll be as swift replacing the horse." The thaw meant he'd have only another three or four weeks to get the rest of the lumber down from the parcel. Three weeks, most likely. With temperatures like this, the ice road would be gone in three weeks. It would not be enough time to finish the cut.

XVII.

[*November* 1920]

*H*osea trembled as he walked, his heartbeat fluttering, his face cold beneath a sheen of sweat, the swirling lakeside wind rising up to cuff him whenever he turned toward the water. He usually made visits to the fish house an occasion to take his truck out for a drive, but Odd had borrowed the flatbed to haul the boat engine and not yet returned it. So that morning Hosea walked the Lighthouse Road and turned down an alleyway after the outfitters and found Odd's secret path across the isthmus. Hosea had had another bender up at the Shivering Timber the night before, drunk off whiskey he'd supplied, sated by harlots he as much as owned. He knew his appetites were becoming insubordinate, knew he ought to check them but lacked any resolve to do so.

Sundays were Rebekah's day to tend the store. It was open short hours—from ten, when the service was finished at the Lutheran church, until two—and though it was seldom busy, folks did stop in. Hosea used his Sundays to sleep off Saturday nights. He rarely woke before ten or eleven o'clock, when he'd fix a plate of scrambled eggs and buttered toast and drink a pot of coffee.

That morning, though, he woke early and went to the kitchen for a glass of water. He couldn't say why, but as he stood over the sink, his hands trembling, he felt a kind of emptiness in the flat. It seemed colder and darker and in a way hollow on the third floor. He chalked it up at first to the great queasiness rolling around his gut, but as he drank another glass of water, and as the light of dawn began filling the room, he felt the emptiness stronger still. He finished the second glass of water and went to Rebekah's bedroom door and knocked. When she did not answer, he pushed it open a crack. Her bed was empty, the room dark but clearly disheveled. The bureau and armoire were picked through, more than half of her dresses were missing, her jewelry box, her hats and beaver-skin coat. He hurried downstairs, checked the offices on the second floor and the shop on the first, and when he saw no trace of her hurried back upstairs to dress.

When he came out of the woods and into Odd's yard he saw the skiff upturned on the western wall of the fish house, saw a teepee of a dozen or more cedar logs in front of the house, an odd-as-hell way to cure wood, an even odder place to do it, but he thought nothing more of it. His truck was parked at the end of the road. Smoke rose from the chimney.

He knocked on the door and stepped back, his hands joined behind his back to hide their shaking. When no answer came he knocked again and cupped his hands around his eyes and looked through the window beside the door. When after another minute there was still no answer, Hosea turned to face the lake. The sky was low, the wind from the north. The season shifting.

He was about to leave when Daniel Riverfish opened the door.

"Danny?" Hosea said. He leaned forward and peered into the fish house. He squinted, couldn't see much. So he stepped back and cocked his head, looked queerly at Riverfish. "Is Odd here?"

"Nope."

"Where is he?"

"Couldn't say."

Hosea looked over Danny's shoulder again. "His boat's not in there." He turned his head over his shoulder and looked at the cove. "Where's his boat?"

"He launched her this weekend."

"Launched her?"

Danny nodded.

Hosea stood in confused silence for a moment before he said, "Can I come in for a minute, Danny?"

Danny stepped aside and followed Hosea into the fish house, closing the door behind them.

"Can we light a lantern?" Hosea said.

Without a word, Danny went to the bench and put match to mantle and adjusted the kerosene.

Hosea walked slowly around the empty space where the boat had been for the last six months. It still smelled of the homemade varnish, and the fumes were making Hosea's lightheadedness worse.

"You look like hell, Mister Grimm."

Hosea sat on the three-legged stool. He put his elbows on his knees and started wringing his hands. In a raspy voice, he said, "Why would he put his boat in the water now?"

Danny hopped up onto the counter and lit a cigarette.

Hosea looked across the room at him. "What are you doing here, Danny?"

"Odd asked me to watch the place for him."

"Watch the place?"

"While he's gone." Danny would not look away. They stared at each other for a long moment.

Hosea shook his head. "You're a straight-faced son of a gun, Danny."

Danny answered by taking a long drag off his cigarette. He held the smoke deep in his lungs until Hosea began to speak again, then blew it all out in a steady stream.

"I see," Hosea said. He turned his hands palms up. The lie that was his life and that had been lived for so long had come back to get him. The truth was no longer a thing to even imagine.

Hosea stood, looked again at Danny. "Rebekah is gone, too," he said, his voice little more than a whisper now.

Danny didn't respond.

Again Hosea shook his head. He looked around the fish house as though he'd never seen it before. "It's been nearly twenty-five years now that I've taken care of her. I raised Odd. Even you can't deny it. It's because of me he's got this fish house and the farm up on the Burnt Wood." He stood up straight. "He was an orphan. *Orphan*. I gave him a home." He looked again around the fish house. Tears welled in his eyes, a thing he'd not felt since he couldn't remember when. He pressed the heels of his hands into his eyes. "Christ almighty," he whispered. "How did I miss it?" This he asked himself, but the wonder of it turned him to Danny, and he repeated the question. "*How did I miss it?*"

"I don't know what you're talking about, Mister Grimm."

"Did they leave together?"

"All I know is Odd wanted to get his boat in the water. He wanted to put a few miles on the engine. He told me he was going down to Port Arthur. To see about a job for the winter. He asked me to watch the fish house for him. I haven't seen Rebekah for weeks, maybe months, but I watched Odd motor out of the cove alone on his boat just this morning."

Hosea listened intently, but he knew a lie when he heard one and what he'd just heard was a steaming pile of moose guts.

"I guess you and Odd are thick as thieves, aren't you? I could probably get a straighter answer out of a winding river than out of you."

"I thought you knew every damn thing, Mister Grimm."

"Is that what you thought?"

Hosea looked a last time around the fish house and headed for the door. At the threshold he stopped. The consequences of all he'd discovered since he'd woken would take days to parse, but the one thing he knew as he walked out to his truck and started it up was that more than anything else he felt abandoned. However peculiar their coming together had been, however twisted and convoluted, he thought of Rebekah and Odd honestly and lovingly as his children. And now they were gone, without the courtesy of a single word, and he was left to wonder at the world without them. All he saw were the unborn days ahead, their emptiness, and his place among the countless hours. In the instant of that realization, it was as though he aged all the hours yet allotted to him. He put the truck into gear and drove slowly away from the fish house.

*D*espite his sadness and the sting of abandonment, Hosea was geared for deception. Before he was back at the apothecary he had already shaped another ruse: an imaginary sister, deathly ill in Chicago, in need of Rebekah's ministrations. By the time he parked the truck he'd already started believing she existed.

When the first customer came in at ten Hosea was scrubbed and dressed properly and sitting behind his counter, reading a day-old newspaper while his pipe smoldered in an ashtray at his elbow.

Winter arrived with its vengeance and with it Hosea took ill. He spent the week before Christmas nursing himself in his apartment, the apothecary closed for the first time in its twenty-five-year history. When he reopened the day after Christmas, the flood of customers could hardly believe the change in Hosea. He had aged, to be sure, but he also had about him the aspect of a man pulled from the ashes of a great fire. And it was this—ruin more than age—that caused the townsfolk their greatest concern.

XVIII.

[*April* 1896]

*I*n the hills above the waterline the snow in the shadows and meadows'
edges had held deep into the spring. There had been no midwinter
thaw to ease the April snowmelt now, so the Burnt Wood came down
the hills and spilled over its banks and when it reached the lake it
surged against the rollers and boulders as though all the vengeance of
the long winter past had been reincarnated in the river's mad rush.

The jacks had driven the last load of white pine down the ice road
three weeks earlier, and a week after that the camp had been boarded
up. Only the barn boss and bull cook remained, and would until the
fall. They'd tend the horses and repair the buildings and spend as
much time drunk during the warm months as they'd spent sober during the cold.

Thea came down to Gunflint on the back of Trond Erlandson's
wagon with a promise of more work the next fall. Since her day in
Mayfair's chambers, she'd spent much time pondering the nonsensical
life that had been intended for her when she'd left Norway, and when
they arrived in Gunflint having not passed the farm, she was as dis-
appointed as she was perplexed. When Trond Erlandson stopped his
wagon at the livery, and when he pulled Thea's bag from the wagon

bed and offered her his hand for help getting down, her confusion became greater still.

Trond removed his gloves and put them in the back pocket of his dungarees and turned his head to spit a wad of snoose. "Here's where the ride ends, Miss Eide."

She looked at him helplessly. *What do I do now?* she wanted to ask. *Where should I go? Whom can I trust? Where is that man, the watch salesman?*

"Where'll you go?" he asked, as though reading her thoughts. He pulled his pocket watch from his vest and checked the time and replaced the watch. "You've got your earnings. Take a room at the hotel." He pointed up the Lighthouse Road. He looked at her suitcase. He seemed to take stock of his own annoyance. "Maybe Grimm will help. He helped you before."

Now he lifted her bag and carried it the two blocks to Grimm's. When they reached the storefront, he set her suitcase on the stone walkway. "Like I said, you're welcome back upriver come fall. You make a mean biscuit. Keep Grimm apprised, he'll let me know."

Thea looked up at his worn-out face, his complexion scarred by the cold. She smiled helplessly. "Thank you," she said. She reached down and picked up her bag and climbed the staircase to Grimm's porch. She turned once to look at Trond already walking back toward the livery, set her suitcase beside the door to the apothecary, and smoothed her dress.

Hosea's kindness had been her salvation when she arrived in Gunflint, and though she had no right to expect any more of it, she walked into his store. The bell above the door rang. She stood at the threshold, waiting.

There was no one about, so it surprised her when she heard Hosea Grimm's voice from across the room.

"I'll be right with you," he said.

She took a tentative step toward the counter, smoothing her dress again.

"Now," Grimm said, rising from behind the counter, "what can I do for you?" He appeared almost to flinch when he recognized her. It took him a moment to gather his voice. "Miss Eide! I hardly recognized you. How are you?" He looked behind her, as though expecting to see a companion. "Are you alone?"

Grimm walked from behind the counter and stood in front of her. "Now, there's a beggarly dress, Miss Eide." Her dress was indeed filthy and threadbare, its hem undone by the scullery mice in the camp's mess hall. "Of course," he continued. "The camp's shut down for the season. You've nowhere to go."

Thea had yet to say a word.

"You're back where you started. You need a place to lay your head." He put the tip of his index finger to his pursed lips and then raised that same finger to the air. "Excuse me a moment." Now he stepped around her and walked to the base of the staircase. "Rebekah, please come down. Thea Eide is here."

A moment later Rebekah was standing in front of Thea.

"Miss Eide has finished her work up at the Burnt Wood Camp and is looking for a place to stay until she can get her bearings," Hosea said. "What do you think, Rebekah, could we take her in?"

Rebekah tapped her foot as though to a song. She wore quite lovely shoes, Thea noticed: ankle-high brown leather boots with mother-of-pearl buttons. A well-pressed gingham dress with lace cuffs and a matching lace bow in her hair. Thea's own shoes were worn-out brogues. Where Rebekah smelled of lavender, Thea hadn't had a proper bath in eight months and her muskiness was downright rank. But despite Rebekah's pearly skin and the scent of her fine perfume and the lustrous hair braided down her back, she appeared more trapped in her finery than at ease. Thea could not help but feel pity for her. She felt, in fact, that she held some advantage over the druggist's daughter.

"Well?" Hosea persisted, taking Rebekah unkindly by the wrist.

Rebekah shook his hand free. "Of course. We should find a place for her to stay."

*U*p on the third floor of Grimm's apothecary, in the finest quarters Thea had ever seen—the finest by far—Rebekah gathered raiment and hairbrushes and glass bottles of hair oil and bath salts. When all was ready Rebekah led Thea, who had been sitting on the settee with tea, to the bath.

"I thought he'd never shush. He talks just to hear himself. Honestly! Have you ever seen anything like it?" Rebekah was sprinkling the bath salts into the steaming tub. The windows above the tub, looking out over the hills behind their muslin drapes, were clouded with the vapor rising up from the bath. "Be careful of him. Do you understand? Be careful? Especially if he comes around with his camera. He's swine. Sooey, sooey!"

She stopped for a moment and stood before the mirror hanging above the sink, wiping the corners of her mouth with her thin finger. The mirror, too, was beginning to fog. She turned to face Thea. "Well? Get ready for the bath. You must be the dirtiest thing I ever saw. You smell like a horse. Or worse."

Rebekah sat on the edge of the tub. She cupped her chin in her hands and took a deep breath and looked directly at Thea. "You've been through so much. The Evensens and the watch salesman Smith . . ." Her voice trailed off.

At the mention of Smith's name, Thea reddened and turned away. She would have run away were there a place to go.

Rebekah put her fingertips on Thea's shoulder and walked behind her. She began to unbutton Thea's dress. What was left of her dress. When she had it loosened, she slid it over Thea's shoulders and untied her discolored shift and also slid it off her shoulders. For a long moment she let her hands rest on Thea's shoulders. Then she moved around her again and took Thea's hands. "My, what a lovely shape."

Thea reclaimed her hands and crossed her arms at her naked breasts, her chin tucked tightly into her shoulder, her cheeks pink as dawn.

"Why are you blushing? You don't have to be afraid of me."

Thea, her chin still tucked into her shoulder, quickly lowered her stockings and bloomers and stepped into the bath. The water scalded, set her entire body tingling.

Without any preamble, Rebekah removed her own dress and stockings and bloomers and slid into the bath with Thea. If Thea's mother had taught her one thing—beyond piety—it was modesty, and no doubt her expression conveyed this because Rebekah splashed water playfully and said, "Don't be such a grouch, Miss Eide. In Chicago, we girls took our baths together all the time. It's fun! Here—" Rebekah took Thea by the shoulders again and twirled her around so they sat back to belly. Rebekah wet a bath cloth and lathered it with soap and pushed Thea's long braid over her shoulder. She cupped water with her hand and poured it over her back and then began washing Thea with the cloth. "It's a miracle your skin is still so soft, after the winter we had. And you were living up in the woods like a proper creature.

Those lumberjacks must have been quite pleased having you around. I bet they ate you *up!*"

When Thea did not answer, Rebekah continued, "Some of those fellas came into town on Saturday nights. They were all so *strong*. Even in their filthy clothes and with whiskey on their breath, I *loved* it when they came in here." Now she was loosening Thea's braid and cupping more bathwater over her hair. "When Hosea wasn't around I'd flirt with them. Some of them I just wanted to grab hold of."

Rebekah watched as Thea's downy hair spread across her back. She wet Thea's hair, the warm water drawing the stench from those blond tresses the way a cold rain brought out a hound's dank odor. She took the bottle of hair oil and poured a drop in the palm of her hand. "This will get the awful stink from your hair. Honestly, you're as foul as those jacks!"

She hummed as she shampooed Thea's fine hair. "I hope you'll sleep in my bed. With me. Would you do that? We can be sisters. I never had a sister, did you?"

Thea glanced over her shoulder, met Rebekah's eyes, but then looked away. They sat in silence as Rebekah rinsed Thea's hair, as the bathwater cooled and the steam on the mirror above the sink began to run down the glass. "Never mind," Rebekah said. She kissed Thea's shoulder without any warning before rising and stepping from the bath. She crossed the room and turned the doorknob and walked dripping into the next room.

Thea stepped from the tub and wrapped a bath linen around her bosom and stood before the mirror. She saw herself as Joshua Smith must have seen her the night of the wolves, blurred and ghostlike. For a long time she stood at the mirror.

When she finally walked into the next room Rebekah was sitting on the floor, Thea's bag open before her. There were half-a-dozen dresses and skirts from Rebekah's armoire spread across the four-poster bed. They were all pressed and clean and in the height of fashion. Rebekah herself was already dressed.

"Hosea thinks if he keeps me in fine clothes I'll be happy." She paused to consider her wardrobe. "I suppose there are things worse than pretty dresses." Now a complicated smile came across her face. "Pick what you like. Anything. You can have it all if you want." She stood and crossed the room and picked a gingham skirt from the pile. "This would suit you. There are all the undergarments you could ever want in the chest of drawers there." She gestured to the bureau across the room.

Inside the top drawer Thea found a scandalous collection of bloomers and corsets and bodices. Filmy cotton and soft velvet where she was used to coarse wool.

"Hosea says they'll never catch Joshua Smith. Says a man as cunning as that deserves to be free. I guess he would know." Rebekah paused, crossed the room again and stood beside Thea. "I'm sorry. I keep mentioning him." She squeezed Thea's hand and then crossed the room again.

Rebekah lay down on her bed, her arms tucked behind her head, her legs folded up under her skirt, her eyes fixed on the ceiling. "You don't understand a word I'm saying, do you?" The thought had only then occurred to her. She propped herself up on an elbow. "Well, then, I'll have to teach you."

Thea forced a smile, she took a pair of bloomers and a shift from the drawer and went to the bed and dressed in the clothes Rebekah had selected. When she was finished she joined Rebekah on the floor and removed her hairbrush.

"Let me," Rebekah said, patting the floor beside her and taking the hairbrush from Thea's hand.

Thea scooted closer. Before Rebekah began brushing Thea's hair, she found herself talking. "Hosea promised me, when we left Chicago, that I'd never have to be that girl again. Said he'd teach me to read and cook and say the Lord's Prayer. He said I might even find a hardworking husband. A husband! Ha! A fine husband any of these boys'd make.

"I guess I'm not the same girl anymore. He was honest about *something*. I guess that makes him better than Hruby." She leaned over Thea's shoulder and tried to look into her eyes. "That was a man with a mean streak. At least Hosea's not mean." She pulled the brush through Thea's hair. "There's not a true thing about me. Not one." Now she set the brush on her lap. "Guess you don't suffer that, do you?"

Rebekah picked the Bible off the floor and handed it to Thea. "Would you read this to me?"

Thea held it before her as though it were some rare and ancient relic, something not to be dropped or smudged.

"Pick some words. Read it," Rebekah insisted. When Thea sat there still silently, Rebekah opened the Bible, pointed randomly at a passage, and said, "Read."

So, as Rebekah brushed Thea's lovely long hair, Thea read her the eighteenth Psalm. She read haltingly, unsure of the sound of her voice. The fresh smell of her own hair was intoxicating, as was the feel of Rebekah's steady brush strokes. Thea paused midpsalm, she held her place in the Bible with her finger and rearranged herself on the floor.

"Keep reading," Rebekah said. She sounded as though she had just awoken.

Thea opened her Bible again and continued. When she finished, she turned to look at Rebekah. The folds of Rebekah's skirt fanned around her and she was fastening the buttons at the wrists of her blouse. Her eyes were wet.

"Let's be sisters, okay? We'll be sisters forever," Rebekah said.

XIX.

[November 1920]

*F*or all his exhaustion, Odd could not sleep their first night in Duluth. The soft yellow glow from the streetlamps below crept under the curtains, filling the room with a kind of haunted light.

So instead of sleeping he took inventory of the days left behind, of the hours of that night, and of a hereafter that was more than ever hard to see, with only that tawny light filtering up from the street. Already the luxury of that hotel room—the big bed and fine linens, the gourmet dinner, the hot bath—was showing its dim foolishness. He couldn't help thinking, lying there, tired beyond all reason, that it was the season of mending nets, of building new fish boxes, of darning socks and patching his oilskin pants. It was the season for sleeping in past sunup, for long lunch hours at the Traveler's Hotel. It was the season for running traplines with Danny and fishing steelhead on the shore ice. It was not the season for lying hungover in hotel beds fit for governors. He got up and walked to the window and pulled the curtain aside. The street below was empty.

He looked back at Rebekah, sound asleep on the bed. He ought to have felt at ease with her lying there, with the hundred miles between them and the life of lies they'd left behind. The truth, though, was that the distance and finality of their coming here served only to deepen the lies. Up in Gunflint at least part of him was true. His boat and fish house. His knowledge of the land and lake and Burnt Wood River. His feelings for Rebekah. The ghostly presence of his unknown mother.

He paused on this last thought—*his mother*—and went to his duffel bag to retrieve the pictures of her. The picture of them together. He went back to the window and angled the photographs to the light. Was it possible that he had once been that babe? That his mother, with all that love in her aspect, with all that kindness and goodness plain for any fool to see, could be speaking to him in that hour before dawn? Was he capable of listening if she *was* speaking to him? Could he start his life over, down here in the city, with the child curled in Rebekah's belly?

He looked between Rebekah and the pictures of his mother and whispered to himself, "I wonder what she'll look like holding our child." Before he could answer the question he set the photographs back in the duffel bag. He dressed in a hurry and left the suite with his coat in his hand.

*O*vernight the winds had strengthened and now were barreling from the northeast. The lake came up with the wind and as he reached the canal breakwater to await the gondola, the piers were suffering heavy seas. It was snowing, too, and cold now. Odd turned his collar up.

He reached the boat club fifteen minutes later. Dawn was up but the sky with the clouds and snow was hunkered in grayness. In the boatyard he found two men standing under his boat.

"Good morning," Odd said

"How do?" the one in a Duluth Boat Club uniform said. "This your boat?"

"She's mine."

"Fitz told me you'd be stopping by."

Odd nodded, stepped back, and looked at his boat hanging from the davits. She looked a hell of a lot larger out of the water than in it.

It was the other man who spoke next. "Where'd you find her?" His voice was gruff, his eyes the color of the concrete sky.

"Find her?" Odd said. "I built her."

The man bunched his lips up, nodded.

Odd read the man's expression as skeptical, said, "She took her maiden voyage yesterday."

The man nodded again and ducked under the boat so all Odd could see was his feet. He walked around the stern and came back to face Odd. "I've never seen a keel like that."

"I dragged a piece of white pine from the woods, cured it, whittled it down. Now it's backboning my boat."

"You come from where?"

"Gunflint."

"You got lucky with the weather." The man looked up into the snowfall, harder now than even a few minutes before.

"No arguing that."

The man with the eyes settled them on Odd. "How'd she go?"

"I'd take her to war," Odd said.

"I believe it." He stepped forward and offered his hand. "Name's Harald Sargent."

"Odd Eide."

"What kind of name's that?"

The question took Odd aback.

"I mean no offense, I've just never heard of anyone called Odd."

"My mother came from Norway."

"*There's* some folks can build boats," Sargent said.

"I've heard that said." Odd turned now to the man in the boat club uniform. "I need to fetch a couple things before you cover her."

"Give me a half hour to get her on the rack, then you can go aboard."

"All right."

Sargent said, "Come inside, have a cup of coffee with me while you wait."

Again Odd said, "All right."

They walked into a grand dining room. Thirty tables under white tablecloths, fine silverware, and napkins folded to look like swans. Sargent chose a table at random and hung his coat over the back of a chair and removed his hat. He sat down and motioned for Odd to join him. It wasn't more than a minute before a waiter appeared before them.

"Gentlemen," he said.

"I'd take a cup of coffee," Sargent said.

"Two," Odd said.

The waiter nodded and left.

"I'm a boatwright myself," Sargent said. "Sloops and cutters, once in a while a runabout or skiff. Build a lot of boats for members here." He spread his hands before him, suggesting the boat club.

"Is that right?"

"For more than ten years now," Sargent said. He coupled his hands on the table in front of him, leaned in. "I've never seen a boat like that one out there. What's it for?"

"I'm a fisherman," Odd said, the half truth of it caused his stomach to drop.

"A fisherman from Gunflint wintering up in Duluth?"

"My wife and I, we're honeymooning." He felt his voice falter.

"I might have chose Key Largo," Sargent said.

"I never even heard of Key Largo."

"I suppose not."

The waiter brought a tray with two cups of coffee. He set one before each of the men and then set a bowl of sugar cubes and a creamer between them.

Sargent said to Odd, "You want a Danish? Some eggs?"

"I'm fine with the coffee."

Sargent turned to the waiter. "How about a couple of Danishes?"

Again the waiter nodded and left. Sargent doctored his coffee with the cream and sugar. He took a cigarette from his shirt pocket, offered the pack to Odd, who took one. Sargent struck a match on his boot sole and lit his cigarette and offered the match to Odd. They both took long drags and sat back in their chairs.

"Mostly it's yachtsmen and rowers belong to this club. You're paying ten dollars a month for what would cost ten dollars for the whole winter upriver."

Odd looked through the cigarette smoke at Sargent, whose eyes were even more forbidding inside the boat club.

"It was the first place I saw entering the harbor last night."

"I see," Sargent said. He took another long drag from his cigarette. "Where are you and the missus staying?"

"The Spalding Hotel."

"Nice place."

"Awfully so," Odd said.

They sat in silence until the waiter brought the pastries. Sargent took an enormous bite, took a long drink of his steaming coffee.

"What kind of motor's running that boat of yours?"

"A Buda. Company out of Illinois."

"Six-stroke?"

"Four. She don't speed along, but usually the fish are waiting for me in the nets."

Sargent smiled. "Most of the fishermen I know between here and the Soo fish in skiffs. What you got is more like a lobsterman's boat."

Odd took a final drag from the cigarette and stubbed it out. He leaned back in his chair and looked at Sargent. He was feeling defensive, as though Sargent suspected him of something. "I've been a herring choker almost as long as you been building boats. Spent enough time soaking wet to want a little dryness. So I built a bigger boat with a cockpit. Here I am."

Harald Sargent only nodded, took another bite of his Danish.

Now Odd shifted in his seat, leaned forward instead of back. "I'm not sure I understand you, Mister Sargent. I've got the feeling there's something you're wanting to say."

"You should come take a look at my shop."

"I'm not really in the market for a new boat."

Odd felt pierced by the boatwright's gaze, by those eyes as heavy as granite seeing right through him. In a way it was a relief. Sargent stubbed out his own cigarette and finished his Danish. "Son, you're spending money faster than you could throw it into the lake. On a fisherman's wages—if fisherman is what you are—you're going to need a job. I make no judgments. I don't even want to know what you've left behind or where you think you're heading. But if you honestly built that boat, then I'm in some sort of company. I got a crew of seven and I need eight. Even if it's only for a few months, through the winter, I could use the help. I've got two dozen boats to deliver by springtime.

"Now"—he leaned forward again, knocked the tabletop with his big knuckles—"you steal one single screwdriver, one drop of paint thinner, I'll throw you right out the back door." His look softened.

"But if you're ready to live an honest life, making an honest buck, and if you can be up this early every day, then come see me." Sargent reached into his coat and withdrew his wallet and from a pocket in his wallet took a business card. He handed it to Odd. "We're the last stop on the Oneota-Superior line, on the west end, out at the mouth of the St. Louis River."

Odd looked at the business card. He wanted to say thanks. Instead he flicked the card against his finger, said, "The coffee is on me, Mister Sargent."

Harald Sargent stood up. He took his coat from the back of his chair and pulled it on. "Are you familiar with the good book, Mister Eide?"

"We've got believers down the shore."

"Are you one of them?"

"There's plenty I believe in."

"But plenty you don't?"

Odd shrugged.

"Because I've seen that boat of yours, and because I can tell you're a decent fellow, I forgive your mother for not showing you the way of the Lord. But the words of scripture are succor in the worst of times, and I'll leave you with this wisdom from King Solomon." Sargent raised three fingers. *"There be three things which are too wonderful for me, yea"*—now he raised a fourth finger—*"four which I know not: the way of an eagle in the air; the way of a serpent upon a rock; the way of a ship in the midst of the sea; and the way of a man with a maid."* He pulled his fingers into a fist. "You puzzle over that, you think about my offer, and then come see me. I'm there every day but the Sabbath. I thank you for the coffee."

Odd wanted to say something, anything, but Sargent's words and his look steadier than ever made him dumb. Instead of speaking he nodded, knowing certainly, as he watched Sargent walk away, that he would find the shop the next morning.

*O*dd was still sitting there when the boatyard custodian came into the dining room. He told Odd that his boat was on the rack and that he could now retrieve whatever it was he needed. Odd thanked him and laid some coins on the tabletop and followed the custodian out into the boatyard. There was a ladder leaning against his boat and Odd climbed it and went to the thwart before the motor box. He lifted the seat and removed the lid from the false floor inside and from within that secret compartment he removed a small metal box that held within it a roll of cash money and the diamond ring he'd bought off old man Veilleux when his ancient wife had passed in July of that year.

He climbed down off the boat and watched as a crew of three boat-yard custodians covered his boat with a canvas tarp that flapped in the stiff breeze until thirty or more cords of rope held it tight. Then he walked back toward the gondola, where he waited to cross the canal again. By the time he returned to the Spalding Hotel there was two or three inches of snow on the ground and no sign of it lightening.

XX.

[*August* 1896]

*S*he'd begun measuring the passage of time by the movements of the baby in her belly. Each morning she'd wake to the fluttering below her ribs and reach her hand to settle the child, to settle herself. She'd rise and change from her nightdress to housedress and brush her hair and go to the kitchen and in the first light of the day would make breakfast for Hosea and Rebekah. Often as not Hosea was already up, a kettle of coffee warm on the stove and his footfalls soft on the floor below her. Rebekah would only wake with the smell of the bacon and biscuits.

Together they'd take breakfast, Hosea reading the *Ax & Beacon* while Rebekah and Thea sat in silence. After the biscuits and bacon, the canned fruit and coffee, the buttered oatmeal and poached eggs, Hosea would adjourn to the store on the first floor while Rebekah tended to her exhaustive toilet. Thea, meanwhile, would clear the breakfast dishes and wash them in the porcelain sink. After the cleaning, she'd simply retire to the davenport under the bay window and take up her crocheting needles. The morning moved slowly and in those halcyon hours the only thing to distract her from her ease was her lingering fear regarding the whereabouts of Joshua Smith. Of the father of this child.

It had been Rebekah who'd first noticed Thea's rounding belly. One morning in June, after Hosea had gone downstairs to open the apothecary, in the privacy of their shared bedroom, Rebekah rose from the bed while Thea was changing her dress. Rebekah crossed the carpet and put her hand on Thea's belly.

"Look at this," she whispered.

Thea did look down. She'd been missing her monthlies all that spring and so knew what was coming to life inside her. But her knowing was surreal, and it took Rebekah's noticing to bring the dream to life.

Rebekah was wide-eyed. She looked from Thea's belly to her eyes and back again. "It's scandalous," she said, still whispering, a devious grin turning up on her lips.

Thea felt the color rising in her cheeks. She removed Rebekah's hand and quickly dressed.

Rebekah, from the other side of the room, wide-eyed and calculating, said, "Is this from the watch salesman? Is this Joshua Smith's child?"

Thea, with Hosea's help, had been learning English those days, but the bedlam in her mind left her uncomprehending.

"Your child will be a bastard," Rebekah said. "The son or daughter of a fugitive." She was walking toward Thea, who stood before the mirror attempting to gather herself. Rebekah's voice was barely above a whisper now. "What will you do, Thea?"

Thea turned to face Rebekah. She felt her eyes welling. But it was not sadness stirring in her. On the contrary, it was elation, as though her privation this last half year was being rewarded, as though her meager life was now as large as these woods and wide waters.

Now the baby kicked. She set her needlepoint down and rested her hand on the wiggling child. She closed her eyes in a kind of ecstasy and thought only of the feeling coming up into her hands. When the tremors ceased she took her hand from her belly and wiped her eyes and looked out the window onto the harbor and the Lighthouse Road. There was traffic in and outside the marina, like Hammerfest during the fishing season.

While she sat there a thirty-foot boat flying a Canadian ensign entered the safe water. She stood at the window as it motored along the breakwater to the Lighthouse Road. An officer of the North-West Mounted Police stepped ashore and tied the boat fore and aft to the cleats on the road. Two other Mounties stepped from the boat and were greeted by the county constable, whose shabby garb cut a marked contrast to the sharp red coats of the Canadians.

The four of them stood on the Lighthouse Road and lit their pipes and seemed as jolly as they were official, and after several minutes one of the Mounties stepped back aboard the boat and disappeared below-decks. Thea could not say why, but an uneasy feeling had settled on her and to quell it she put both of her hands on her belly. The Mountie emerged again, this time trailing his prisoner. Thea knew who that shackled man was by the gooseflesh on her arms.

*I*t was late in the afternoon when Hosea came. Thea had been feeling qualmish since she'd watched the captive come up the Lighthouse Road earlier that day, and when Hosea stepped into the kitchen and said softly, "Miss Eide, Curtis Mayfair has sent word that the unlikely capture of Joshua Smith has come to pass. The Canadian authorities have brought him here. He wishes to interview Smith before he's extradited to Duluth."

He went to her side and continued, "He'd like to speak with you as

well. He's summoning Selmer Gunnarson to help with the testimony." He paused, looked at her. "Do you understand? You might
have to see Smith."

"I'll go with her," Rebekah said. "I'll help her get herself together."

"I'll go with you as well," Hosea said. "I'll meet you both downstairs in five minutes."

Rebekah took Thea to their bedchambers. She closed the door behind them and held Thea's hands and said, "You understand what's
happening?"

Thea shook her hands free and went to her bed. She lay down on
the bed and curled into a ball, her hands resting on her stomach. And
she might have wept for fear or sadness or loneliness, but the baby
kicked, and whatever else she felt vanished, was replaced with a new
pride and purpose.

"He cannot touch you here. He cannot hurt you again," Rebekah said.

Since the night of the wolves every unexpected shadow had caused
her to flinch, but now she felt ready to face that man.

"Do you understand?" Rebekah repeated.

Thea stood, pressed her eyes, and walked to the door in answer.

*T*he magistrate's chambers had been rearranged since Thea's last
visit. The captain's chairs that had previously sat in a half circle before
his desk now sat behind two tables facing each other. There was a
lamp on each table and on the table opposite Thea there were papers
and a leather valise. She'd been brought into the empty room and told
to wait while Hosea and the constable left through a door behind the
magistrate's desk. The room was hot with the afternoon sun and in the

gingham dress she wore Thea began to perspire. She removed a handkerchief from her sleeve and daubed her forehead. She pulled a chair
from beneath the empty table and sat down.

It must have been a half hour before Curtis Mayfair and Hosea and
the constable returned. Mayfair was dressed now in a linen shirt with
a fine collar and a pair of seersucker trousers, the matching coat of
which hung over the back of his chair. Spectacles sat low on his nose
and magnified the pouches beneath his eyes. He looked spent in every
way, but when he spoke it was with much energy.

"Miss Eide, very good to see you again. Hosea tells me you've been
studying English, is that so?"

Thea looked at Hosea and back at Mayfair and nodded. "Yes,"
she said.

"Selmer Gunnarson is on his way just in case we need help with
your testimony. Do you understand?"

Again Thea nodded. Again she said, "Yes."

The magistrate took a deep breath and shifted in his chair. He removed his pocket watch and checked the time and shook his head. To
Hosea he said, "It's as though the time of day held no consequence to
these people. Old Gunnarson's got so much going on he can't make
his appointments?"

"He'll be here presently, no doubt," Hosea said, and as though his
voice had summoning power, in walked Selmer Gunnarson, flushed
and breathing heavily.

Before he could apologize for being tardy Mayfair said, "Thank
you for joining us, Mister Gunnarson. You remember Thea Eide."

Selmer took a seat beside Thea and said hello.

Mayfair removed his spectacles and set them gently on the blotter
before him. He joined his hands and cocked his head. "Miss Eide, you
testified in March regarding incidents at the Burnt Wood Lumber

Camp involving the watch salesman Joshua Smith." He paused, nodded to Selmer, who quickly translated, speaking softly into Thea's ear.

Judge Mayfair continued, "Mister Smith fled Gunflint for Duluth, where, on March the sixth, he set fire to the Rathbone sisters' lodge rooms. The consequences of that blaze resulted in the Parsons Block burning to the ground." Selmer translated as the judge spoke. "The Meining Hardware Company lost its entire inventory as well as its storefront; Crowley Electric likewise lost everything; the lodge rooms of the Knights of Pythias were destroyed. In all, some forty-five thousand dollars in damages."

The magistrate shook his solemn head. "The watch salesman Joshua Smith managed to flee Duluth for Port Arthur, Ontario, where he took employment in a hotel livery. Ten days ago he was found unlawfully entering a dry goods store. When the authorities searched his boardinghouse room, they found several hundred dollars in currency and several hundred more in stolen goods. It seems Smith is in the habit of taking that which don't belong to him."

Now Mayfair stopped talking to read a document on his desk. Thea, more confused than ever, looked between Selmer and Hosea, neither of whom replied to her questioning look.

Curtis Mayfair set the document back on the blotter. "Miss Eide, Joshua Smith is being extradited. The North-West Mounted Police are in the process of delivering Smith to federal authorities in Duluth, where he'll be tried for arson and grand larceny, among other things. But before they deliver him, they thought enough to stop and collect the hundred-dollar reward we've offered for his capture.

"I figured, as long as we have to pay the reward, we may as well get our money's worth and charge him for his crimes up at the Burnt Wood Camp." He paused a moment to let Selmer catch up, then put his spectacles back on and looked firmly at Thea. "Miss Eide, I hope I can rely on your testimony this afternoon in our case against the watch salesman Joshua Smith."

The magistrate studied Thea for a long moment. When she did not respond—how could she? What was being asked of her?—Mayfair simply turned to the constable, nodded, and sat back in his chair.

Thea kept her eyes on the door as though the building would crumble if the weight of her stare weren't on it. When Joshua Smith came through—his head hanging low, his eyes covered with greasy and unkempt hair, his shoulders slouched, his hands in the pockets of his worn dungarees, his dirty boots unlaced and shuffling across the floor as though weighted with stones—Thea saw a different man than the one who'd violated her. Smith was gaunt and twitchy. The constable pushed him into a chair opposite Thea, where he collapsed with his chin on his chest.

Her impulse was to fly, to raise her shawl like wings and catch a breeze to carry her home. He hadn't even noticed her sitting there. Seemed not even to know where he was.

"Your honor," the constable began, he was standing behind Smith, his big hands on the fugitive's jutting shoulders, "this is our man." He hit Smith on the ear. "Identify yourself, you goddamned vulture."

Smith had looked up with the slap, his sight landing on Thea. Immediately he sat upright, he pushed his hair from his eyes. He looked from Thea to the magistrate and back to Thea. The constable hit him again.

"I said identify yourself."

"I'm Joshua Smith," he stammered.

Mayfair spoke. "Mister Smith, do you know why you're sitting in my chambers?"

"Sir?" Smith said.

"From the look on your face, you've got some idea."

Smith finally turned his attention away from Thea. He looked at Mayfair. "Sir?" he repeated.

"Enough already with the pleasantries. I asked if you know why you're here."

"I reckon it's got something to do with the cook here."

"'The cook here'? Are you crazy, boy? You're in the custody of an international police regiment. You're being extradited. Do you know what that means? You're being taken to Duluth, where you'll stand trial for crimes that are going to land your skinny ass in the penitentiary for twenty years. The 'cook here' is the very least of your problems."

Smith shrank into himself. "Sir, then what am I doing here?"

"That's more like it." Mayfair removed his glasses. "You're here to give an accounting of what happened up on the Burnt Wood last March. You're being charged with despoiling Thea Eide. You're being charged with animal endangerment. Do you catch my drift, Joshua Smith?"

Smith nodded solemnly.

"I'd like you to tell what happened on the night of March the first of this year."

Smith sat up in the chair. He stole another glance at Thea, who hadn't moved since he'd entered the room. She couldn't move. "I can't say I remember much of what happened the night of March the first," Smith said.

Though he'd not intended to sound contrary or at odds with Mayfair, he did. Mayfair seized on him. "Allow me to refresh your memory. You tried to feed one of the horses to the wolves, then you feasted yourself on this helpless young lady. Does that course of events sound familiar?"

Smith ran his hands through his hair. "Sir, there's some truth in that. Some truth, I admit. But that ain't the all of it."

A broad and sarcastic smile came to Mayfair's face. "By golly," he said, "he's a slow learner. Mister Smith, why don't you tell me the all of it, then? Enlighten us."

"May I have a cup of water?" Smith said. "I'm parched something fierce."

"For the love of Christ, get the mutton chop some water." Mayfair threw his hands up, shook his head. While the constable went for a glass of water, Mayfair packed his pipe and lit it. When the constable returned he set the water before Smith, who scooped it up almost as it was set down. He guzzled the water like there was a fire to put out.

The magistrate took a pull on his pipe and through the smoke he squinted and said, "All right now, Smith, let's have your side of the story."

Smith wiped his lips with his sleeve and pulled himself up in his chair. "Well," he began, picking grime from his fingernails, his eyes intent on the task, "you all were here last winter?" He looked up, from the judge's face to Grimm's to Selmer's. When he got to Thea he looked down, then quickly back to the magistrate. "You all felt that cold?"

Mayfair waited silently, still chewing on the pipe stem. The constable went for another glass of water. He returned and set it before Smith and said, "Drink that. If it don't loosen your lips, we'll presume what we've heard to be true. You can add another twenty years to the sentence you'll be getting in Duluth. You'll never see another day of freedom so long as you live."

Smith drank the water.

"Listen to the constable," Mayfair said. "And be aware, my patience is about gone."

"My brother and I, we bought this outfit selling watches and pocket-knives to the lumberjacks. Had a little supply office in Duluth and two horses and two sleighs. He took the Wisconsin and Michigan camps, I took the Minnesota camps. Me and that old mare with the suspect hooves. A goddamn sleigh and a map and that winter enough to freeze a man's reason right out of his head." He paused, ventured a look in the judge's direction. "That's what I mean, you all felt that cold. Colder than this world was ever meant to be." Again he paused, as though the mere remembrance of those nights was enough to freeze him up.

Thea was not listening to Selmer translate Smith's testimony. She understood everything he said through her lessening fear. He was pathetic, and she had the strength of her child swimming in her womb to bolster her. She sat up straighter.

"It's a long way from one of those camps to the next," Smith continued. "A long ways and a lot of dark. I'm just a man from Duluth looking for the next logging camp. Selling watches to men who spend all their time chopping down trees." He shook his head. "You know how far it is from Duluth to Gunflint? You know how much wilderness is between here and there? It's a long way to go just you and a horse. Well, you and a horse and all the sounds in the woods. The shadows. Caribou jumping out of the trailside woods. Ravens everywhere you go, day and night. Enough snow to suffocate you. And the *cold*. Christ almighty." Again he paused. "Why do they need watches? They're crazy about watches. How about a change of drawers? How about new boots? Watches?"

Mayfair interrupted, "With all due respect to your travails, Mister Smith, what bearing does any of this have on your actions?"

"It has everything to do with it. Maybe you sit in your warm office, you light up your pipe without frostbitten hands, you loosen your shirt collar to cool off, maybe you do all that and you forget about what's there—" he pointed out the window, up the hill, at the trees and the wilderness they held—"and what it all means. What it *means.*"

"Mister Smith, I've lived in this town for twenty years. I built the first house, I named the first street. Lectures on how cold the winter is are lost on me. I'll offer you a last chance to make your case." He held his index finger up, wagged it at Smith. "One more chance."

"I had wolves following me day and night. They were after me. Their tracks were on the trail before and behind me. They'd howl. How they'd howl. You put the wolves after the cold, after the wilderness." He shook his head.

"There are wolves in these woods just as there's cold in winter, Smith. It's true."

Joshua Smith risked interrupting Mayfair. "They were taunting me. I needed them to stop. That's why I set the horse in the paddock. To feed them. It was me or the horse."

"Mister Smith, if it's true the wolves were taunting you, then all the hounds of hell must have besieged you in Duluth. Why else burn a city block? I think we've heard enough about the horse. Tell me, what were your intentions when you went to the mess hall?"

"My intentions? I went to the mess hall," Smith said, speaking more softly now, "because the cook's beautiful. There's no great mystery in it. She was kind to me and she's beautiful and I was a man caught in that season. I don't know what I expected. I don't know."

"I'm sure we'd all agree Miss Eide is lovely to look at, Mister Smith, but I'd venture to guess we'd none of us do what you did. The cold and the wolves and the trees don't grant permission of that sort. No one does, nothing does."

"Permission—" Smith began, but Mayfair interrupted.

"Do you know the girl's enceinte?"

"Enceinte?"

"The girl's with child, Joshua Smith. While you're doing your time in a federal penitentiary, she'll be raising your misbegotten child."

Smith's mouth hung open. He leant forward, tried to look at her belly under the table opposite him.

"There are five people in this room with better things to do with their time than listen to your stories about being cold. I'll write a decision to send with the Mounties." Mayfair moved papers around his blotter, took his pen from his shirt pocket, and began to write even as he continued speaking. "This world is dreadful enough. It doesn't need the help of monsters." He paused in his writing, looked squarely at Smith. "Mister Smith, you are a monster. I can only hope the sight of this woman and the child growing in her belly tames some small part of you."

To Thea and Hosea and Selmer, Mayfair said, "You're all free to leave. I'm sorry for the waste of your time." Then to Thea he said, "Miss Eide, my wife and I pray for you. We pray for your unborn child. People are unkind, but if you can rise above the unfortunate nature of the conception of that babe, and if you can love it with a pure heart, with an unsullied conscience, then the stain of its paternity will fade. The good people of Gunflint will rise above their ignorance and make the child one of us. I promise you that."

Selmer finished translating Mayfair's last words and rose. Hosea followed. Then Thea. They stood for just a moment, long enough for Joshua Smith to get a glimpse of Thea's belly, of the swell that sealed the rest of his life with a barred fate. He knew that much. He knew, also, that he was right about the cold and the trees and the wolves.

XXI.

[*December* 1920]

*E*very morning that December Odd woke in the darkness and padded down the hallway of the brownstone they'd rented on East Sixteenth Street. He'd stand over the sink in the bathroom and shave around a lit cigarette dangling from his lips, the wonder of hot running water and the steam it aroused a minor miracle each morning after all those years of hauling buckets of icy water up to the fish house from the lake.

He'd go quietly down the hall from the bathroom to the kitchen and start a pot of water on the stove and while he waited for it to boil he'd patch his lunch together: a cheese sandwich and garlic pickle wrapped in wax paper, a tin of sardines. He'd pack it in his lunch pail and brew the coffee and pour himself a single cup to drink with his oatmeal and pour the rest in his thermos. He did all this in utter silence, mindful of Rebekah still sound asleep. When he finished his breakfast he went back to their bedroom and feathered the hair off Rebekah's forehead and kissed her, hoping the touch of his lips might impart some contentedness. Might sweeten her dreams.

His morning ritual, conducted in that silence and dim light, made each day seem holy. And each day when he stepped from their home he did so feeling devout. Though Harald Sargent had done his share of proselytizing, he'd failed to convert Odd, who had decided early in that season and in the face of Sargent's sermons that he'd take his heaven on earth. And he'd found it in his and Rebekah's domesticity, in their quiet and honest life together. He'd never felt so at peace, not even during his best moments in the skiff.

After he closed the door quietly behind him he'd walk the four downhill blocks to wait for the streetcar on Superior Street. Already in the days before Christmas more than a foot of snow had softened the yards and in those hours before dawn the whiteness cast a ghostly hue on the morning.

When the streetcar arrived—the first of the morning—he'd jump on and drop his token in the fare box and nod hello to the motorman. He'd walk to the smoking compartment on the back of the streetcar and roll a cigarette and while he listened to the plangent clack of the wheels, to the shrieking brakes, he'd watch the snow come up like a wake behind them. Given those early hours he was often the only passenger. But even still—with the sleeping city all around him and Rebekah and the babe in her belly behind him—he felt the world was waiting to happen.

By the time he reached Sixth or Seventh Street the same streetlights that had, for those first few nights in Duluth, shone up into the hotel room at the Spalding Hotel now shone in his eyes, the brooding buildings—rising like a river gorge on either side of the trolley—shadowy behind the light. He might have been in Russia for how foreign it was.

His thoughts inevitably turned to the child, to those days ahead when he'd have a chance to redress his mother's stolen maternity. Whether here or in Gunflint, whether as a boat builder or fisherman or any other thing, Odd would teach the child, would raise him, would love him. This he vowed solemnly each morning on the trolley. He was desperate for the time to come.

As sweet as the promise of those days was, there remained Rebekah's melancholy. There were evenings when, upon Odd's return from his workday, she seemed happy enough. She'd have dinner ready and her hair washed. He might find her sitting on the davenport in the small sitting room, her needlepoint on her lap, ready with a faint smile to meet him. But more often he found her sitting at the kitchen table. Sometimes with a glass of half-drunk whiskey soaking up the amber glow from the electric light. Those nights she was distant and unaffectionate. And Odd did not know what to do.

By the time the streetcar passed the Spalding Hotel and halted at the Union Station stop, he'd exhausted himself with worry and joy. It was at that stop that his morning solitude came to an end, where the stevedores and railway workers and other harbor rats jumped the streetcar and found seats and unfolded their newspapers. In the now crowded trolley he watched the shipyards and loading docks pass. The grandeur of the east end, of the downtown buildings and lights, gave over to the drab harbor on the south side of the tracks and to the shabby houses on the north side of the line.

The terminus of the Oneota-Superior line came at Raleigh and East Seventieth streets. He'd step out the rear door and onto the cobblestones and turn his collar up against the wind off the river. There was a doughnut shop where he paid a nickel for a fritter the size of his hand, and he'd eat that on the way to Sargent's, which was on the water just past the Zenith Furnace Company. He punched in at six o'clock each morning. He was never once late.

Sargent was paying Odd fifteen dollars a week to pinch oakum into the seams of small boats, a job that left an indelible stink and stickiness on his fingers but one he took seriously and performed with a kind of manic attention. Aside from the sealing work Odd also bent boards, did some finishing, and found himself learning things he wished he'd known when he'd built his own boat.

Sargent had customers all across the Great Lakes, with backorders enough to fill a year of work. He could have added another shift, in fact, but preferred to oversee the building of every boat himself. Each morning he met with his crew before manning the storefront chandlery and setting to work on his accounts. Even still, he passed through the workroom every hour, inspecting and praising the work being done.

They gathered around a table in the back of the shop at noon, where Sargent said a blessing before they all ate in silence. Most of the crew at the boatwright's had been eight or ten years in Sargent's employ. They were a hardworking and earnest bunch of men, not given to much conversation. After lunch, however, as they stepped outside for a smoke, Sargent would pass among them, asking after their families in a hushed voice that belied his fierce eyes. But for Odd they were all family men and churchgoers. Between the two subjects and their common vocation they had fodder enough to chat for the length of time it took to smoke their cigarettes.

On Christmas Eve, after a busy week, when half the crew had taken the day off, Sargent found Odd after lunch. Sargent lit his pipe, offered Odd the match.

"How will you and Missus Eide be spending the holiday, Odd?"

Odd, remembering those lonely Christmases at Grimm's, said, "I suppose Rebekah will cook up a feast. After dinner we'll sip some of that apple wine you gave us and sing a few carols. How about yourself?"

Sargent turned his eyes into the light snowfall, a smile came to his face. "Ah! The boys will be on the train this evening. No doubt Mother's got a feast of her own planned." Now he looked at Odd. "Of course we'll go to church. Wake to presents under the tree. Mother still spoils those boys rotten."

"Where are your boys coming from?"

"They're in college down in Minneapolis. Michael's a senior, Jonathon a sophomore."

Odd nodded, took a drag on his cigarette. Sargent looked south, his eyes faraway, as though he might see his boys boarding the train in Minneapolis.

"Sounds like a swell time," Odd said.

"It's my favorite time of the year," Sargent confirmed.

They stood there smoking.

For all the thought Odd had given his own child, he'd not once imagined a Christmas morning with him. Perhaps it was because Christmas had always been the time of year when the pity from the townswomen was most tender and their dotting on their own children made him ache with envy. He felt the same tenderness from Sargent, and, more enchanted with him than ever, Odd said, "I reckon I'll be spoiling my own child this time next year."

Sargent's head swiveled, his smile broadened. "Congratulations, my friend."

"Thank you, Mister Sargent."

"Mother will be so happy to hear your news."

Odd returned Sargent's smile. What he saw in that instant and knew with certainty was that here was an empathetic man, a selfless man. He was, Odd realized, a man to model his life after.

"Are you nervous, son?"

"I think Rebekah's a bit nervous, but I'm pleased as punch."

"Well, what better gift could she give you?"

"I know it."

Sargent emptied his pipe bowl and looked again into the falling snow. He took a deep breath, put his hand on Odd's shoulder. "Not that you asked, but let me give you a piece of advice, Odd. Someday your child will be full of wants. What they'll want more than anything, whether they know it or not, is for you to cherish them." He squeezed Odd's shoulder now. "I doubt you'll have much trouble with that." He took his hand from Odd's shoulder, reached into his coat pocket, and removed a gift wrapped in Christmas paper. "This is from Mother and me. For you. And Rebekah. And your child now, I suppose. Merry Christmas, Odd."

Odd held the gift. "Thank you. Thanks for everything." He paused, looked between the gift in his hand and Harald Sargent.

"What is it?" Sargent said.

"I've been wondering, why were you at the boat club that first morning? I can't quite parse it out."

"Well, I've much business at the boat club."

"At six o'clock in the morning? On a Sunday?"

"You ask as though you're suspicious of me."

"I ain't suspicious, just curious."

Sargent smiled. "The truth is, I was there to offer you this job. The boatyard custodian is a neighbor of mine. We met in the alleyway on Saturday night, putting the trash out. He told me about your boat, said I ought to see it. So I came to see it, and here we are."

"Why'd he say that?"

"You're not aware of what you've accomplished, are you? You don't see the beauty in that vessel you built."

"I see a cockpit. A little more room for fish boxes. A heavier keel in big water."

"A heavier keel. Precisely."

"You're speaking in riddles, Mister Sargent."

"There's no riddle at all, Odd. You built something worth seeing.

I thought I'd take a look. The rest of it, the fact that we've become friends, that you've ended up here—" he knocked on the wooden wall of his shop—"that's just the Lord working in strange ways."

"Strange ways indeed," Odd said.

"I'm just glad it worked out, son. Now, in honor of the birth of our Lord Jesus Christ, take the rest of the day off. I'm closing the shop early today." Sargent took a step toward the shop door but stopped. He turned back to Odd. "And tell Rebekah I send my congratulations, will you?"

"I will. Thanks."

*W*hat Odd found when he returned to their brownstone could have felled him. There was Rebekah, sitting on the davenport stringing popcorn, a short and misshapen Christmas tree standing in the window. He stood in the doorway, smiling, dumb, holding the packages he'd stopped to buy on the way home like some kind of working-class Saint Nick.

After a moment Rebekah stood and crossed the small apartment. "Hello. You're home early."

"Sargent closed shop for Christmas. What's this?" Odd said, nodding his head at the Christmas tree.

"Mister Johnson walked down to the lot with me and carried it home. He helped me set it up. I bought the bulbs at the hardware store on the corner. Isn't it nice?"

Odd stepped in, closed the door behind him. He kicked off his boots and walked across the parlor. He put the packages under the tree and turned and crossed the apartment again. He took Rebekah in his arms and held her for a long time.

When finally he let her go he said, "It's perfect. And what's that smell?" He turned his nose to the small kitchen on the other side of the flat.

Rebekah grabbed his arm and pulled him toward the tree. "That's a surprise. Here—" she forced him to sit on the davenport—"help me with these popcorn strings."

Odd picked up a threaded needle and started stringing the popcorn. He'd never had the sensation of being awake in a dream but he did now. He said as much.

Rebekah sighed and said, "I've been difficult."

"Well, now."

"One minute I'm happy, the next I'm—" She turned away, her eyes widened and then closed. She shook her head and looked back at Odd. "I'm terrified of the baby. Even more terrified that this is no life I want, much as I *do* want you. I feel like a different person every day of the week." She stopped talking as suddenly as she'd started, picked the strand of popcorn back up and began stringing it with a new kind of haste.

Odd did not know what to say, or at least had no words to say what he wanted.

More calmly, Rebekah continued, "It's Christmas. I at least wanted to make a nice go of it. I thought a tree would make me happy."

"Has it made you happy?"

"Let's finish with the popcorn."

So they finished their strings and hung them and stood in the end of the daylight looking at the scrawny tree. Odd was thinking it the most wonderful tree, greater than any of the two-hundred-foot white pines left in the forest. But he didn't say anything, only stood there on tenterhooks, hoping Rebekah saw what he did.

"It needs candles," she said, her voice suggesting nothing.

"It looks awfully good to me."

She squeezed his hand.

"It's early for dinner, but if you're hungry, it's ready."

"The smell," Odd said.

Now a very pleased look came over Rebekah's face. She almost blushed.

"Rabbit stew!"

*T*he kitchen table was so small the rims of their bowls touched. The table and two chairs, a davenport, a Murphy bed and armoire in the bedroom, these were the only furnishings in the apartment.

Their bowls were steaming. Parsnips and potatoes, mushrooms, onions and garlic, tender chunks of rabbit, barley malt, all of it held together with buttery roux. It was their secret, this feast, harkening back to their first time up at Rune Evensen's farm.

As they sat there under the cheap chandelier, he thought her face was as changeable and temperamental as a stormy sky lowering over Lake Superior. And as distant. So except to thank her for the stew, Odd had not uttered a word since they'd sat down. He reckoned even the possibility of her contentment was better than the moods likely possessing her. She stirred her bowl of stew absently, once or twice dipping a crust of bread into it and raising the bread to her lips before setting it back on the edge of the bowl uneaten.

When Odd finished the first bowl Rebekah rose automatically and fetched the Dutch oven from the stovetop. She ladled him another helping. She also topped off his mug of apple wine.

"It's delicious, Rebekah. A real treat." He said this without lifting his head to look at her.

"Have more."

He finished the second bowl and wiped it out with a piece of bread and ate the bread. He sat back with his apple wine and looked at her.

"Want your presents?" he said. "I know it ain't Christmas morning yet, but I doubt Saint Nick will mind."

He got up and stood before her, his hand outstretched as though he were asking her for a waltz. They walked to the davenport this way. Outside, the snow had started again. It was almost dark so he turned on the electric lamp. Odd took the gifts from under the tree. He put them next to her on the davenport and sat before her on the floor.

"I didn't get you anything," she said.

"As if I could want more."

She reached down and ran her hand through his hair.

"Go on, now. Open 'em up."

She took the smallest gift from the top of the stack and opened it. She smiled when she saw the chocolates and set them aside directly.

Next she opened a hatbox and pulled a cloche with pink ribbon from the tissue. She put it immediately onto her head, cocked it just so, and looked down at Odd flirtatiously.

"Looks real nice, Rebekah."

"It's very smart," she said.

"There's a whole department store full of them just down the road. Got about every color in the rainbow."

She removed the hat, held it before her, inspecting the soft felt and silk ribbon.

Odd sat up, took the hat from her, and put it on her head again. "There's one more. Go on."

She took the big box on her lap. "I feel bad I didn't get you anything."

"I told you I got all I want. Now, open that last one."

She tore the big box open and pulled a dress from the tissue. It fell before her, catching the lamplight. "Oh, my!" she said. She dropped to her knees and wrapped her arms around him. "It's *so* pretty!" She stood up as quickly as she'd knelt and held the dress before her again.

"Go put it on," Odd said.

Her face was bright as she hurried to their bedroom.

Odd climbed up onto the davenport, took a cigarette from his shirt pocket and lit it, and laid his head back while he smoked. *God almighty,* he thought, *let her be happy tonight.* He closed his eyes tight and pinched the bridge of his nose. After a couple of minutes he shouted, "You come on out here when you get that dress on, let me see how it looks."

A moment later she reappeared wearing the dress. "Let's see." He took her hands as he stood, shifted her to the left and to the right, looking her up and down. "I ain't *never* seen something so pretty before. My goodness." He reached behind him, took the cloche up, and put it on her head. "There now," he said. "My goodness," he repeated.

She seemed suddenly bashful, running her hands along the beaded chiffon, adjusting the shoulder straps and the hat, her eyes cast down, standing there in her bare feet.

"You like it?"

"A whole bunch," she said, smoothing the belly of the dress.

"It's the right size?"

She took a deep breath, stepped back. There were tears in her eyes.

"Hey, now. What are you crying for?"

She sat down, felt the dress tighten around her waist. "You're such a sweet boy."

He sat down beside her. "I got to tell you, Rebekah, you're getting harder and harder to understand. One minute you're calling me baby, the next you're calling me a boy. You're cooking up our rabbit stew, then you're sitting here crying. Do you not like the dress?"

She took another deep breath. "It won't be a month and the dress will be too small."

"Well, let's get a different size," he said, oblivious.

"It's the right size, Odd. It'll be too small because of the baby."

"That's a good reason to outgrow a dress." But he knew she was lost for the night. This was how it went: Once she settled on the pregnancy—on her fear of it, on how it would change her—she drifted off into a world of sad thoughts where he wasn't welcome. "That Glass Block store is full of a hundred dresses. We'll go find some good ones."

The apologetic smile she gave him was sincere but unmistakable. He had to look away.

Odd sat there for a long time, staring at his hands folded on his lap, thinking it was easier to read the lake than this woman. For the first time since they'd been in Duluth he felt angry with her. His reason and sympathies were being devoured by her moodiness. For all the thought he'd given it—and he was thinking of it again now—he didn't see how being here, with him, with all that was in store for them, could be worse than being in Gunflint. He got up. He wanted a drink, started for the kitchen and his stash, but stopped at the sound of her voice.

"I love you," she said. "I've loved you every way a girl can love a boy. Every way a woman can love a man."

He didn't stop walking but went into the bedroom instead of the kitchen. He took the lockbox from the bottom drawer of the armoire and the key from his pocket and unlocked the box. He moved the wads of cash aside and took the small velvet bag in his hand. He put the money back in the box and stowed it again.

He returned to the parlor. Rebekah hadn't moved. She sat on the davenport with her feet up beneath her, the cloche still on her head.

Odd knelt, took from the velvet bag the diamond ring he'd bought from the widower Veilleux, and held it before him. "I want you to marry me," he said, his voice cracking as though he were twelve years old. "I want you to be my wife and be happy with me. We can be happy."

"No," she said, as though he had proposed three hours ago and she'd had all that time to consider.

He didn't move.

She stood up, took the hat from her head, and dropped it to the floor. She reached behind her and unbuttoned the dress and let it fall and pool around her ankles. She reached behind her back and unlaced her corset, she slid her hands beneath the waist of her panties and slid her panties from her hips. They too fell in the mess of clothes on the floor.

"No," she said again. "I don't want to get married. I can't be happy and you can't be happy with me."

Odd was stunned, both by her nakedness and what she was saying.

She lay back on the davenport. "Stand up," she said. "Put that ring away."

As though Odd were hypnotized, he did as she said.

"Now, come here," she said.

When Odd stepped to her, she reached up and unbuttoned his trousers. She tugged them down and lay back again on the davenport.

"Come to me," she said.

She left him alone in the parlor when they were finished.

He lay there for a long time before he thought to get up and pour himself that drink he'd first craved an hour earlier. On the way back to the sitting room he stopped and found a new pack of cigarettes in his coat pocket. He also found Sargent's gift. He took both to the window and lit a cigarette and took a sip of his whiskey. He looked at the package. He looked at Rebekah's dress and hat and undergarments still piled on the floor.

He felt aged, like ten years had passed since he'd got home from work, like in all that time the world had changed without his knowing. He drank and smoked and looked out on the Christmas Eve. There was the snow.

He looked over his shoulder, thought of her sleeping—*how could she sleep?*—back on their bed.

Almost as though he were surprised, he felt Sargent's gift in his hand. And because he could think of nothing else to do, he tore off the paper. It was a Bible. There was a note, too, written in Sargent's impeccable script: TURN TO LUKE. BLESS YOU. H. SARGENT

Odd opened the book and scanned the names—he might have been reading roll for the old men in Gunflint: Joshua, Samuel, Isaiah, Jeremiah, Daniel, Hosea—until he found Luke and turned to the corresponding page. At first he was put off by the high style of the King James version. It reminded him of those Greek poets he'd been made to read in school what seemed like a hundred years ago. But as he settled into it he found himself in a kind of communion with the gospel.

And so he read the story of the life of Christ. He read for hours, until the first light of Christmas morning was showing on the edge of the dark sky. When finally he put the book down and laid his head back, he realized that his own sorrow and suffering were nothing next to the world's. If Rebekah would renounce him, if she would renounce her child, he would be father enough when the time came to raise his baby.

He set the Bible on the floor, stood up and gathered Rebekah's new dress and undergarments from the floor, folded them neatly, and put everything in the department-store box.

XXII.

[*October* 1895]

*I*n an examination room on Ellis Island, an immigration official asked Thea her final destination.

"Gunflint, Minnesota," she said.

The Norwegian-speaking immigration officer checked one of a dozen ledgers on his desk. "Gunflint, you say?" He checked another of the ledgers. "There doesn't seem to be a place with that name."

Thea was of course confused. She told him her aunt and uncle lived there. She gave him their names as though that might prove its place on a map, its place in a ledger.

"How will you be getting from here to there?" he said.

She told him she would be taking a train from Hoboken to Chicago. From Chicago she'd take a steamer to Duluth. From Duluth another steamer up Lake Superior to Gunflint. She told him her uncle raised cattle.

The immigration officer consulted an atlas of Midwestern states. He summoned another official and, after a brief consultation, they settled on Duluth, Minnesota, for Thea's final official destination.

Five hours later she was on a barge bound for Hoboken. She would not remember these days, or would remember them only as a blur, as though she had passed through the train station in Hoboken in a dream. The locomotive was another dream, and the two days it spent on its way to Chicago were still other dreamlike days.

In Chicago, at Union Station, she stepped from the train into the strangest world yet, a building so grand and in such contrast to anything she had ever imagined that it frightened her. All that noise and motion and clamor like a taut string about to snap.

And outside Union Station was another kind of tension, another kind of dream. The buildings above her were shrouded in fog, a kind of rain fell and drenched the penny map she held before her. On Michigan Avenue she walked north to the river and found the docks of the Chicago, Soo & Duluth Line. In the ticket office she bought a third-class berth on the *Sault* for seven dollars. She had only four hours to wait for her three-day cruise to Duluth.

*T*he *Sault* passed through the locks onto Lake Superior in the middle of the night. It rode out of Whitefish Bay, the moon on the horizon its lodestar. It was cold and even as the boat sailed ahead, a breeze came up the stern, hitting Thea's face and bringing tears to her eyes. The *Sault* docked in Marquette at midday. For half an hour stevedores unloaded and loaded cargo, a dozen passengers debarked, another dozen boarded. In the dark of night they docked again, this time in Ashland. The same exchange of passengers and goods. Another half hour spent in harbor.

The following morning Thea stood on the stern deck again. Again she watched the sunrise behind them. Still the stiff breeze trailing. It was fully day when the *Sault* landed at the Chicago, Soo & Duluth Line docks in Duluth harbor. She thought the fledgling city rising before the tall hills looked something like Tromsø. Even the air had an arctic quality, chill and damp.

The offices of the North Shore Ferry Service were located right on the harbor, behind the livery and the enormous Board of Trade building. Thea entered and waited while a man behind a barred window sold billets to two families in line ahead of her. When finally it was her turn, she approached the window. She had clutched in her hands the phrasebook she'd been given for just such purposes.

In a halting whisper she said, "Gunflint, Minnesota. Please."

"Speak up," the man said.

Thea collected herself and repeated her request.

"*Opportunity* sails tomorrow at seven A.M. Passage is two dollars twenty cents." He spoke in a loud voice, avoiding her pleading eyes. "Will you take a ticket? There are others awaiting my services here." He gestured to the queue behind her.

Thea reached for her purse, pulled some crumpled dollar bills from it, and put them on the tray under the bars. The ticket vendor looked at her finally, exhausted. He took a deep breath.

He shifted his visor and said, "Do you understand the boat leaves tomorrow?"

She answered with an unconvincing nod.

He took another deep breath and shifted his visor still again. "Wait a moment." He stepped into an office behind him and returned in a moment with his own phrasebook. He made his best effort to put the same question to her in Norwegian.

In English she said, "Yes. Tomorrow."

He nodded and set about preparing her boarding card. He made change for her payment.

Thea, emboldened by the exchange, added, "I am new in America."

Without looking up the ticket vendor said, "I'd never have guessed."

*S*he walked up Lake Street past Superior Street, dodging the mule-drawn streetcars, slipping on the rain-slicked cobbles. Farther up the hill, on the corner of Lake and First, she paid a quarter for a room in a boardinghouse, another dime for a hot bath. It was her first proper bath since leaving Hammerfest and as she soaked in the tub she was overcome with fatigue. So rather than going out for a hot meal, she finished her bath and dressed in her freshest clothes and, by the light of a window, read her Bible. She read it with a fervency she'd not felt in ages. Starting with First Corinthians. She read for a long time. Even as her eyes felt heavy and the softness of her rented bed called, she read.

When finally the evening fell and the light from the window waned, she laid herself down and slept, the good book clenched to her heart, for more than twelve hours. When she woke before dawn she felt a moment of panic before she realized where she was. She quickly gathered her belongings, washed her face, pulled her hair back, and donned her bonnet. By six A.M. she was back on Lake Avenue, headed for the docks.

The *Opportunity* was a two-masted schooner and her crew was drunk and quarrelsome even as the passengers boarded. The rigging and masts were plagued by a colony of gulls and the singing of the lines in the wind was a song that brought Thea back to the harbor in Hammerfest. It reminded her of why she was making this journey. She stood on deck, her bags between her feet, as the *Opportunity* was tugged through the canal and out onto the lake. The sails were raised and they filled and she felt the old pull of a boat borne by the wind.

The boat moved into a quartering breeze, its progress slow, the roll of the water sharp. The spray rose above the decking, met her waiting face. Four hours later the crew was already lowering the sails. The weather the wind had brought in turned cold and foggy, the conditions worsening the crew's already sour mood. They weighed anchor and dropped a tender and announced Two Harbors. For an hour she stood on deck and watched as the tender made trips in and out of the fogged harbor. Ten travelers debarked, none boarded.

The rest of the day was slow moving. At sunset they anchored outside Otter Bay. All afternoon Thea had had the strange sensation of going back in time. Whether it was the way the boat moved under sail, the sharpness of the cold wind, or the prehistoric wilderness they were traveling past she could not have said.

At midnight they stood at anchor outside the settlement at Misquah. The boat's captain told Thea and the three remaining passengers that they would have to wait until morning to sail to Gunflint, so Thea went belowdecks and found a bench to rest on, using her carpetbag as a pillow.

The ship heaved all night, even as the wind died and the rain began. Sleep was impossible, and not only because of the ship's rolling. She felt, after this long month of travel and tribulation, the relief of being so near her destination. She felt the excitement that should have been accompanying her all along.

In the morning they woke to more heavy fog. The lake was now coming in slow undulations. The lines rang up on the masts, the gulls swarmed in the brume, and the crew was hungover and at odds over whether to weigh anchor or wait for the sun, which showed promise in the east, to come burn off the fog.

They waited for two hours, the fog more blown away than burned, and raised sails under a southwesterly breeze that brought as much warmth as it did smooth sailing. They traveled the last thirty miles of shoreline in little more than three hours. As they turned toward shore outside Gunflint Thea saw the town spread sparsely along the harbor:

the fish houses, the hotel and apothecary, the church steeple up the hill. From the quarter mile offshore, with the exception of the trees, it looked just like Hammerfest, and as her heart raced it also sank. The boats rowing out to meet them looked exactly like her papa's fishing skiff, the water was as hard and as cold as the North Sea. The wind, even as it brought a warmer day, had every quality of bitterness that the air back home had. Had she really traveled so far to end up where she'd started?

Rather than dropping anchor again, the crew reefed the sails and turned for harbor. It seemed a difficult maneuver, as the ship was large and the harbor entry narrow, but the crew was practiced and sidled her right alongside the Lighthouse Road. Two of the deckhands jumped ashore with lines and tied her off on the cleats.

On the Lighthouse Road several townsfolk had gathered. Thea, standing behind the mizzen shroud, her heart aflutter, looked from face to face for the welcoming smiles of her aunt and uncle. She panned the crowd twice, each time coming away empty. She sat on a crate on deck, disbelieving.

"Last stop," one of the crew said. "Gunflint, Minnesota."

Thea looked at him. He had a wind-worn face, his hair was a tousled mess, his coat was open and sagging on his large shoulders.

"Miss," he said, as he stepped nearer, "all passengers must get off the boat now."

Thea understood enough to grab her bags and land. As she rose, clutching her handbag and shouldering her carpetbag, she noticed the man with the camera box standing below her. He had the lens pointed at her and snapped a shot. It was Hosea Grimm, his Kodak at the ready as it was every time a boat landed in Gunflint.

Thea moved to the plank that had been laid down as a gangway. She crossed onto the Lighthouse Road and stood with the *Opportu-*

nity in the background. Hosea Grimm took another picture, then flashed her a puckish smile.

*I*t was not long after the crowd had dispersed, after the crew of the *Opportunity* had unloaded their cargo, after Hosea had collapsed his tripod and boxed his camera and arranged delivery of a pallet of dry goods for his apothecary, after the sun had come out full and all the morning's mizzle had been burned away, it was not long after this that Thea sat on a bench on the Lighthouse Road with her bonnet crumpled in her fists. Her sobs were there for all the world to see and hear. Hosea approached her with his hat in his hands. He had been watching her from the corner of his eye as the crowd scattered, watching as the expression on her face shifted from expectant to nervous to despairing.

He knew all at once that he must help her. Simply help her. So he stood silently before her a long time, his feet surely in view of her downcast eyes. When finally she looked up, Hosea said, "Hello, miss. I trust, based on this attitude of despair, that your landing has not met your expectations."

She looked back at her bonnet in reply.

"My name's Grimm. I'm a merchant in town. I'd help. However I might."

Now Thea met his eyes—an act that spoke as much to her situation as her tears, for she'd long been taught to avoid the gaze of men—and in a tremulous voice said all at once what a horror her journey had been. She talked a full minute before Hosea interrupted her.

"Beg your pardon, miss, but you're speaking a language I don't understand. Do you not speak English?"

She returned her blank stare to her bonnet.

"You've come from far away, I'd bet. From Norway, I presume. Judging by that gibberish you speak. Or Denmark. Or Sweden." He was speaking as much to himself as to her, and he kept his chin in his hand as he studied the masts of the schooner tied to the Lighthouse Road. "Probably Norway if you're staking a claim here." Now he knelt before her, played his hat brim through his own hands. "Norge?" he said.

Thea looked up. She wiped her eyes dry with the backs of her hands, cleared her throat, and said, "I am new to America."

Grimm smiled. "Welcome," he said. Without asking for permission he lifted her carpetbag and said, "Come along with me." With his spare hand he lifted his tripod and camera box and started up the Lighthouse Road. Thea followed because she knew no other option.

Outside the offices of the Gunflint *Ax & Beacon* Hosea stopped, set down all that he carried, and opened the door, holding it for Thea. There were four men sitting at desks, one of them was Selmer Gunnarson, who did the typesetting. He'd been in Gunflint for eight years, before there was a Lighthouse Road or brick building. He'd emigrated from Bergen eight years before that.

"Selmer," Hosea said, "I need to borrow your old tongue, friend. This here young lady landed at noon, she speaks hardly a word of English."

Selmer rose from his desk, wiped his huge hands on the apron he wore, and came to stand before Thea. He removed his spectacles and addressed her in Norwegian: "Hosea tells me you've just landed. Who were you expecting to meet?"

Feeling a surge of relief, Thea spoke rapidly, "I've come from Hammerfest, my uncle is Rune Evensen, I've come to help on his farm." She paused, withdrew a letter from her purse addressed to Mrs. Rune Evensen She offered it as some kind of proof. "My auntie was to meet me." She paused for a moment, then asked the question she now feared the answer to. "Why wasn't Auntie here to meet me?"

Selmer looked at Hosea, who stood with his hat in his hands. "The lass is here for Rune Evensen. She's his niece. She's come an awfully long way."

Thea looked from Hosea to Selmer and back again. To Selmer she said, "Is Auntie okay?"

Looking at Thea, Selmer addressed Hosea again. "What should I tell her?"

Hosea stood with his finger tapping his pursed lips for a long moment, then said, "Tell the lass the truth. Tell her how her aunt hanged herself from the barn trusses. How old Rune has lost his mind. Tell her she can stay with me until we figure out what to do." He paused. "Tell her about Rebekah, that she'll have a friend."

She spent two days and nights boarding at Grimm's. At the end of her second day he put her on the back of a wagon bound for the lumber camp on the Burnt Wood River.

The previous morning Hosea had asked her if she could cook. He did this with the typesetter translating again. When Thea said yes, of course she could cook, he told her that Trond Erlandson needed help at the camp. He told her that for around a dollar and a half a week she could winter upriver. She could take stock in the spring, after her season in the woods, and decide on her future then. All of this, he said, was provided she did not wish to return to Norway presently.

Thea sat there dumb, trying to see herself in the woods. And because she could not return home, and because it was harder to fathom an alternative than the prospect before her, she agreed to go.

XXIII.

[*January* 1921]

*T*he weeks after Christmas were drudgery for Odd. The days came and went with little more than the small changes in Rebekah's temper to mark them. It was a temper as bleak as the cast-iron sky.

In the middle of January Rebekah's belly and breasts started to round. She was tired all the time and fell into a pattern of sleeping during the day and staying awake through the night. During those nights, alone in the world but for Odd's snoring in the next room, she felt herself coming apart. As she paced the small apartment it began to seem she was chasing herself, that she had literally become two people: the one pacing—worried and weak and vacant—and the one she used to be, a shadow, trying to keep up. She knew she had to close the distance between herself and the shadow. How to do that, though, was entirely beyond her power of imagination.

Finally she went searching for an abortionist. When she found him in a rank office above a harborside warehouse, her misgivings met the squalor of his surgery and she knew enough to leave. But now she carried a new and cumbersome shame around during her insomniac nights. She'd seen plenty of the women in Gunflint lose their minds.

She knew what it looked like. It looked like her. But she had enough wits remaining to want to fend it off.

So she did the unthinkable: She wrote Hosea. In all her life she'd never had reason to write a letter, though she had spent many of her days slotting mail into the townsfolks' boxes behind the apothecary counter. She could see Hosea, standing there in his starched apron, the hat he'd worn every day for twenty-odd years. Was he getting along? Did he think of her? If he did, was it with fondness or that meanness she alone in Gunflint knew?

In the middle of the night she found one of the pencils Odd carried behind his ear. On the back of a brown paper sack, without salutation or date, in her childlike scrawl, Rebekah wrote: *I was never who you said I was. But this is not me neither. I am having a baby. A baby. What has happened . . .*

She folded the paper sack and hid it beneath the davenport cushion and continued her restless pacing.

The next morning, hours after Odd left for work, she went to the mercantile on Superior Street and bought envelopes, stationery, and half-a-dozen two-cent stamps. It was the first time she'd left the brownstone in days, and the cold came biting like a small dog on the way back up the hill.

In their apartment she hurried to the davenport, took the folded sack out, and placed it in the envelope. She addressed it the only way she knew how:

Mister Hosea Grimm

Gunflint, Minnesota

and placed the postage in the corner and put the envelope back under the davenport cushion. She hid the stationery and envelopes in one of her hatboxes and went to bed to try for sleep. When it did not come she dressed again and went back to the mercantile to drop the letter for delivery.

Each of the next five nights she wrote another letter to Hosea. They got longer as her confidence grew but never asked for or told much.

If she thought writing the letters would slow her unraveling, or appease her guilt for leaving Hosea, if she thought it would help her understand the bitter feelings she had for the unborn child, she was mistaken. Instead of finding solace she found further proof that there was no reckoning with this life of hers. The sleepless nights grew longer and longer, spilling into the mornings, when her guilt was worst. Until those mornings she had been able to separate the causes of that guilt—leaving Hosea, betraying Odd, abhorring the child— but now it became the only state of mind she possessed. Her guilt ravaged her, and she gave up any resistance.

*M*eanwhile Odd did his best. He still tried to woo her, brought her things to satisfy the cravings she announced randomly, still spoke to her gently and imploringly. But there was no hope in his plea. He knew better. When he took Rebekah to the Lyceum hoping the troupe might succeed where he failed, and when she became sick from the cloud of smoke in the theater, he decided his only hope was that the child—when he was finally born—would compel her to happiness.

So he got up each morning and took the trolley across town and found his relief in the long, philosophical days at Sargent's. At night, after he and Rebekah shared their silent suppers, she would retire to her needlepoint and he to the Bible Sargent had given him at Christmas. He read every night, not because he was becoming a believer but because any story was better than the one he was living.

It was around Saint Valentine's Day that Odd came home with a dinner invitation from Sargent. Rebekah was sleeping on the davenport, her needlepoint fallen at her feet. He watched her for some time, remembering how he used to revel in her childlike ability to sleep at a moment's notice, how he'd once loved watching the sleep come over her. What he saw now could hardly have been the same woman. She kept him awake at night, her pacing like she was some kind of caged animal.

She woke with a start to see him there, his hand on his chin.

"Odd," she said. She sat up as though she'd been dreaming of fire.

"Hey, Rebekah. Didn't mean to wake you. How you feeling?"

She rubbed her eyes, looked out the window. "You're home early."

"Harald gave me the afternoon off. He's invited us to Sunday dinner. I told him we'd be there."

"I can't go to dinner—"

"Nonsense," Odd interrupted. "You can and you will and we're not going to hem and haw about it. This Sunday. You'll behave yourself, too. These are good, upstanding folks. Put on a smile."

"I don't have anything to wear," she protested.

"We'll head downtown this afternoon and fix that. Now, go and get yourself together." He looked at her fiercely. "Now, Rebekah. Up. Let's go."

Rebekah rose slowly, paused in front of Odd, and went to their bedroom. She came back out ten minutes later. Odd had not moved.

*S*unday they had dinner at Harald Sargent's home. Rebekah wore her new dress, sitting at Sargent's bountiful table. Harald wore a heavy woolen suit and necktie, his wife, Rose, an equally heavy woolen dress.

Sargent, his eyes clenched shut, his hands clasped together, intoned the blessing. "Dear God, my savior and my light, with all my love I give thanks to thee. For the bounteous fare set upon this table, for the warmth of this home, for the love of my wife and sons, I give thanks to thee. For my wayward guests, may you show them the way to your heart, may you deliver their unborn child into a world of goodness and show him the way to your love and forgiveness. Yea! May you show us all your love and forgiveness. Amen." Sargent opened his eyes and smiled at his table, his eyes serene where they'd always appeared set in stone before.

"Amen," Rose said.

Odd and Rebekah both smiled demurely, seemed almost to blush in unison. "Smells good," Odd said.

"Thank you, Odd. Help yourself," Rose said. She handed him a plate of pork cutlets. "Harald insists on pork and gravy for Sunday dinner. I could make it in my sleep after all these years." She turned to Rebekah, smiled. "A good Sunday dinner is about all it takes to please a man, that's my free advice to you, young lady." Here was a woman so cheerful and good-natured that Rebekah indeed felt like a young lady.

"Odd could eat bread and butter for Sunday dinner and not care a whit," Rebekah said.

The mere sound of her voice buoyed Odd. He took her hand on the table and smiled.

Rose leaned toward Rebekah and said, "He leads you to believe that because he wishes to make your life easy." She winked. "Don't believe him, make him meat and gravy."

"Bread and butter's fine, but this here's a right feast," Odd said. "I thank you kindly, Missus Sargent."

"Harald, pass Odd the creamed corn and hominy bread. Here's a young man who knows how to please his hostess."

After the pleasantries at the start of the meal the table settled into a formal silence interrupted only by polite requests for second helpings. By the time they finished with supper, dusk had settled with still more snow. Harald requested coffee to go with the pudding, and Rebekah joined Rose in the kitchen to help prepare it.

In the dining room Sargent took out his pipe and packed it. He poured each of them another glass of apple wine. Odd could see the bare branches of the apple trees through the dinning room windows.

"Rebekah was to see Doctor Crumb?"

"She was."

"He's the finest physician in all of Duluth. Educated at the University of Chicago."

"Seemed a fine fellow."

"He was a help?"

"Rebekah's right private about that business."

Sargent nodded. "Do you mind if I ask you a question, Odd?"

"Shoot."

"How old are you?"

Odd had to think about it. "Guess I'm twenty-four years old."

"I had you pegged for older than that." He paused. "Mind if I ask how old Rebekah is?"

Odd smirked. "Old enough to know better than to get stuck with me."

Sargent smiled. "I apologize if I seem impertinent. I was just curious."

"I can't even begin to imagine what impertinent means, but your curiosity is no harm to me."

Sargent took a deep breath. They each took a drink from their wineglass. "You've been studying the Bible?"

"I've read some."

"Is it helping you toward peace?"

Odd stared long on the empty apple-tree branches.

"Thoughtful," Sargent said.

"There's plenty of good stories in that book. But I find my peace on the boatwright floor. Out on the lake hauling nets." Odd turned back to the window. "In the expectation of my child."

"Then your heart is full of love. If it is full of love, it is full of peace."

"All I'm full of right now is apple wine and pork chops. That's enough for me."

Sargent let a knowing smile play across his face.

Rose served the coffee and pudding and when dessert was finished they adjourned to the sitting room. Odd could tell from the bleary sheen of her eyes that Rebekah was tipsy. She'd had two full glasses of apple wine. Once that look would have set his heart to thumping, but now it filled him with dread. She'd behaved so far, but he knew how careless she'd become lately, knew she felt there was nothing left to lose. He knew also that there was nothing she loathed so much as pious folks.

"I hope that meal pleased you, Rebekah," Rose said.

"You are a wonderful cook. A wonderful hostess."

Sargent said, "Mother takes it to heart if her dinner guests don't leave with a bellyache."

Rose put her hand on Sargent's arm. "Rebekah's belly is home to a child of God, there's no ache in the world capable of upsetting her."

Rebekah flashed a false smile. "No ache in the world," she sang.

"Rebekah," Odd said.

Rebekah turned to Sargent's wife. "My belly aches all the time. I feel awful."

Odd leaned forward.

Rebekah continued, "My back aches. I can't sleep. I—"

"You bear those things so your child needn't," Rose interrupted. "Put those cares from your mind."

"Put them from my mind," Rebekah repeated. She sat back in the overstuffed chair, wrapped her hands around her abdomen.

"Besides the love of God, the love of a child is life's greatest reward, Rebekah," Sargent said.

Odd buried his face in his hands.

Rebekah looked up at Sargent. "There's no reward in this life," she said. She turned slowly to Rose. "I ought to envy you. I know that. But it's pity I feel."

"Rebekah!" Odd shot from his seat on the davenport. "Enough!" He turned to Sargent, turned just as quickly to Rose. "I beg your pardon. I don't know what's come over her."

Rebekah stood unsteadily. "You're lucky. . . ."

"Rebekah!" Odd repeated. He took her forcefully by the arm. "Don't say another word."

He walked her to the front door and took her coat from the rack. He put it over her shoulders and opened the door and pushed her outside. When he turned around Harald and his wife stood in the foyer, their faces full of sympathy.

Odd looked at the floor. "I wish there was something I could say."

"Nonsense," Rose said. "When a woman is with child she says things she doesn't mean. It can be a very difficult time."

"Odd," Sargent said. He moved toward him, put his hands up, and shrugged. "Mother's right. Rebekah is alone in a strange place. She must be anxious about the child. Go home with her. Read the Bible with her. Stand by her without malice or fear of your own. That is your duty now."

Odd pulled his coat over his shoulders. "Thank you, Mister Sargent. I will take care of her." To Sargent's wife he said, "Missus Sargent, I apologize for Rebekah's foolishness. Don't matter how out of sorts she is, she oughtn't behave that way. It's me she pities, not you. I know that. Me and her own self. I'd explain if I could, but I can't. Not even one of them Bible writers could explain it."

Odd walked out with his head slung low. When he got to the end of the Sargents' walkway he turned to look back at their home. From the warm light of the foyer he saw both of them silhouetted in the window, and he knew that no such scene would ever play in his life.

*T*he wait for the trolley on a Sunday evening was intolerable. Odd and Rebekah stood under a grocer's awning on Superior Street in an awful silence. Odd's anger had given way to resignation while Rebekah's sharpness turned dull. He could no more look in her direction than find words to express his sadness. By the time the streetcar emerged Rebekah was nearly sleeping on her feet. Odd took her by the arm and led her onboard.

They still hadn't spoken as they entered their brownstone half an hour later. Odd would normally have taken her coat off, hung it up, and asked her if she'd like a drink or for him to draw her a bath. Instead he kicked his boots into the small foyer closet and walked to the sitting room window. He heard Rebekah remove her own boots and walk slowly to the davenport. Odd kept his back to her, kept his eyes fixed on the darkness.

"All those prayers and talk of the Bible," she said. It was as though she expected Odd's complicity, as though she hadn't embarrassed him.

"I guess their decency undid you," Odd said.

"Decency? Ha!"

"Because they believe in something bigger than themselves you write them off? I suppose all the lies you've lived, all the shit you ate, that's better?"

"Don't forget, darling, you're right here with me, living the biggest lie of them all."

He thought to say, *But I want to change. I see our chance.* Instead he only set his jaw.

Some time passed before Rebekah said, "I can't understand how it's come to this. For all my life I can't."

Odd said nothing. Since Christmas he'd said all there was to say. He'd said it all twice.

Some more time passed before she continued, "I thought of getting an abortion. I went all the way to his office before I lost my nerve. Now it's too late."

An automobile rounded the corner outside, its headlamps sweeping past their window, filling the room for a moment before leaving it in darkness again. He heard a match strike the box and Rebekah light a cigarette. He heard her exhale.

"I wrote letters to Hosea."

"The hell you say?" Odd said, spinning around.

"I told him about us. About being pregnant."

"Goddamnit, Rebekah."

She took a long drag from her cigarette. "I asked him if I could ever come back."

He turned his good eye toward her, flashed a gaze so fierce it made her shudder.

"Don't look at me like that," she said.

Now he spoke with his teeth clenched, "Does he know where we are?"

"No."

"When did you last write him?"

"A month ago. Maybe."

He ran his hands through his hair. He felt dizzy with rage. He looked at her without blinking until she stood and started for the bedroom. He spoke to her back: "I forbid you to ever write him again. This is our new life here. Do you understand? This is our life and it has nothing to do with what we left behind."

She stopped and turned and looked at him, thought to say more, but turned again without saying a word.

XXIV.

[*April* 1907]

*T*here were secrets cankering at Grimm's.

One of Hosea's strictest rules was that no one—not Odd, not Rebekah, not any visitor—enter his offices on the second floor of the
apothecary without his accompanying them. He kept the doors locked
and carried the keys on a chain that hung from his belt loop. As a
young boy Odd had been given the strap for merely testing the glass
doorknob. He'd never been much curious about what was in those
rooms, but something had gotten hold of him that spring. So Odd
played sleuth.

Late one Saturday night, after he figured Hosea had left for the
Shivering Timber, Odd crept out of his bedroom and went down to
the second floor. He felt pure of heart but still his pulse quickened. At
the bottom of the staircase he paused, tried to stay his quivering sight,
and realized that one of the office doors was open. A swath of bright
light fell on the hallway floor. Odd could hear voices.

He sat on the bottom step and looked again down the hallway. On
his hands and knees he crawled halfway to the light.

"Good, now," he heard Hosea say. "Yes. Very good."

"As if there's a good or a bad," Rebekah said.

A flash of light came from the doorway, followed by the chemical smell of magnesium and potassium chlorate.

"Why are you such a contrary girl?" Hosea said.

"Why, indeed."

They were silent for a moment. Odd pushed himself against the wall, the light from the open door not ten feet down the hallway.

"Will you remind me to order more castor oil tomorrow? The Johnsons have near run us dry of it," Hosea said.

"Of course."

"Pull the peignoir off your shoulder. There, good."

"The Johnson kids have been near to death all winter long. Are they going to be all right?"

"The Missus Johnson prefers quackery to doctoring. I've given up on her."

There was another pause in their conversation. More flashing came through the doorway. Odd inched closer to the light on the floor.

"If you're going to keep me awake all night, you might consider uncorking a bottle of champagne. Anything to hurry this along."

"You're difficult enough sober. Inebriated you'd be impossible."

"Nonsense. If you gave me something bubbly to drink you might actually get a smile out of me."

There was another flash, then the sound of a match being lit, then a moment later Odd could smell Hosea's pipe smoke.

Now Odd was only an arm's length from the doorway. He felt unnaturally calm given the intrigue, but still he was not quite ready to show his face. He knew instinctively that the goings-on in that bright room were none of his business.

"Odd sure is turning wise, isn't he?" This was Rebekah speaking, and whatever edge had gotten hold of her voice was gone when she spoke of Odd.

"He's a fine boy."

"Do you want me to take this off?"

"Yes, take it off. And put the boa around your neck. Straddle the arm of the divan."

Now there was more quiet, only the faint sound of Rebekah moving around the room. Odd slid so that his left shoulder was only a few inches from the doorjamb. If he'd extended his leg, his foot would have rested on the edge of the light on the floor.

Two or three full minutes passed without a word from either of them. All of the powers of his imagination failed Odd now. He'd never heard the word *peignoir* nor *boa*. He could not dream up what was happening in all that flashing light. He had always supposed that Hosea's medical equipment was stored in the rooms along this hallway, knew that one of the rooms two doors down was his surgery, the room in which Odd himself had been born. But even to his ten-year-old mind there was no logic that might explain a medical procedure of any sort that needed be conducted now, some hours after midnight.

"That'll get a rise from the perverts," Hosea said. He clucked his tongue, then added, "Hold your bubs. Push them together."

"Are we almost finished?"

"We'll be finished when I say so."

"Just hurry."

All Odd heard for the next five minutes was the click and snap of Hosea's camera and flash. When Hosea said, "That's enough for now," Odd jumped to his stockinged feet. He ran to the dark end of the hallway and crept quietly back upstairs. He slid into his bed, the flashing lights from Hosea's office stayed with him until he closed his eyes and fell asleep.

*H*osea was stirring the hash when Odd came down for breakfast the next morning.

"It's Sunday, right?" Odd said.

Hosea startled at the sound of Odd's voice, turned from the stovetop to see the lad. "There's tea in the kettle, boy-o. Grab a cup. Eggs and hash in a jiffy."

"Why are you awake? Why are you making breakfast?"

"There was business to attend to last night. I missed my frolic. Here I am full of vigor. We'll be off to church after breakfast."

"I don't want to go to church."

"Why not?"

"Why would I?"

Hosea poured the bowl of whisked eggs into the hash. He sprinkled salt and pepper over it and turned to face Odd. "Why would you, huh? That's what you want to know, is it, boy-o?" He turned back to the hash, stirred it for a few minutes, then took the skillet off the stovetop and brought it to the table, where he set it on a trivet. He spooned a plateful for Odd, then a plateful for himself, then sat down across the table from Odd. "You might want the Lord on your side, son."

Odd said nothing, only stared back at him.

"For the fight."

"What fight?" Odd said.

Hosea blew on his plate of steaming hash. He forked it around his plate. "'What fight'? Good Christ, what's wrong with you this morning?"

Odd picked up his own fork and held it before him. "I'm tired out. Couldn't sleep last night."

Hosea's eyes shot up and into Odd, who didn't flinch. Hosea stared at the boy for a long minute. He smirked. "The fight, boy-o, is this life of ours. I don't know if you're equipped to tussle with the big boys, that's why I say you should have the Lord on your side."

"I'm ready to fight," Odd said.

"I'm only speaking as an impartial observer, Odd, but you don't inspire confidence."

"I can fight!"

Hosea shook his head. "Eat your breakfast. Then we'll go to church. And let's refrain from these boasts, this backtalk. Your virtue is in your tractability. Let's be a good boy." He flashed Odd a condescending smile, took a large bite of his hash, then a big swill of his hot tea.

*O*dd did not go to church. After he finished his hash, Hosea told Odd to make a plate for Rebekah, told him to put it on the stove and to get his church clothes on. Hosea then went to ready himself. When he returned fifteen minutes later, Odd still sat at the table, his legs crossed, a week-old newspaper spread before him as though he were actually vested in the happenings of this town. Hosea said nothing, only walked down the staircase. Odd heard the bell chime and the front door slam shut. He pushed himself back from the table and walked to the sitting room window. He watched as Hosea marched up Wisconsin Street. He watched until he turned north, toward the hillside church, and disappeared.

Odd stepped to Rebekah's bedroom door then. He put his ear to it to hear if she was awake. After a minute, content that she was still sleeping, he went down to the second floor. All of the excitement of the night before was gone. His heart beat slowly and his sight was steady and clear.

He walked down the hallway and stood before the locked door that had emitted Hosea's and Rebekah's voices the night before. He tried to shoulder it open, then took a few steps back and glowered at the door.

It was only a minute before Rebekah came downstairs. He turned to watch her walking toward him. She looked sleepy, still wore her nightdress.

"What are you doing down here, Odd?" she said. Her voice was soft, gentle. It always was with him.

All the balky instincts that had arisen with Hosea that morning were gone now. He felt boyish again. Shy. He looked down at her feet. "What's a bub?" he said.

Rebekah's eyes widened and she couldn't help but laugh. "*What?*"

"A bub. What's a bub?"

"Where did you learn that word?"

He turned away. Looked back at the door. "How 'bout a pervert? What's that?"

"Oh, my," she whispered.

"How come you and Hosea were up in the middle of the night?"

Rebekah sat down. She sat down right on the floor and crossed her legs. She took Odd's hand and pulled him down, so they were each sitting cross-legged, their knees touching. She looked right at him with her sleepy eyes.

"I couldn't sleep last night, so I went exploring. I heard you two down here."

"Did you see anything? Did you look into this room?" Rebekah nodded at the door without taking her eyes from Odd.

"Last time I tried to get in there Hosea caught me. He gave me the strap."

"Did you look into this room last night?" she repeated.

"No. I did not. I only saw the lights flashing and heard you talking." He looked away. "Will you tell me what a bub is?"

"Oh, dear," she said. She bit her lower lip and took a deep breath. "Let's see. Do you and Danny ever talk about girls?"

Odd looked back at her. "What do you mean?"

She took his hands, held them over the tangle of their feet. "You know, are there girls in school that you talk about? Pretty girls?"

"Danny says Sarah Veilleux's pretty."

"Do you think Sarah Veilleux's pretty?"

"I don't know. She's not as pretty as you."

Rebekah blushed.

"Danny says you're pretty, too. Everyone thinks you're pretty."

At this the blush washed from her cheeks. "Yes. Well." She paused, bit her lip again. "People don't know much."

"What do you mean?"

"You're only ten years old," she said.

Odd knew she was just thinking out loud, something she did all the time.

"Ten years old, raised by a misfit and me." She put her hand on his chin and raised his face. "You hardly have a chance, do you?" She shook her head.

"Why do you and Hosea keep saying things like that?"

"You're a very fine young man. And so sweet. Maybe too sweet, I think that's what I mean."

"You still haven't said what's a bub."

"You'll learn about bubs soon enough."

"What's in there?" Odd said. Again he pointed at the door. "Why ain't I allowed to see it? How come you can go in there?"

Rebekah stood up, she offered Odd her hands and pulled him to his feet also. "For once I agree with Hosea. You don't need to see the grown-up things in these rooms. Not now. Not yet."

"That's stupid," he said. He was angry and confused and tired of all the roundabout talking.

"Trust me, sweetheart. It's not dumb."

"Quit acting like I'm stupid and a kid."

He turned to stomp off but Rebekah caught his arm. "You are a kid, Odd. That's not a bad thing. It's a *good* thing. I never got to be a kid." This last she said in that way of thinking out loud again. She let go of his arm and he went away as quickly as he had the night before.

*I*t was three days later that he broke into the room. A Wednesday, in the evening. The days were just beginning to seem like summer. Odd had rejected Hosea's invitation to dinner with Rebekah and him at the Traveler's Hotel with a snide and impetuous "I'd rather eat alone." Hosea hadn't even tried to persuade him.

Odd, as he had the Sunday morning before, stood at the window looking down onto Wisconsin Street. He watched as Hosea and Rebekah turned onto the Lighthouse Road, watched as they stopped outside the hotel to talk with Curtis Mayfair and his wife, the rose-colored sunset from above the hilltop faintly lighting their faces. When they walked into the hotel Odd ran downstairs. He fished the filched skeleton key from the pocket of his dungarees. The key fit easily into the keyhole.

He stood on the threshold. It was a windowless room. Dim. Even if it was oddly arranged, if all the furniture was pushed to one side of the room, nothing seemed overly queer. There was a davenport along the back wall, a floor lamp with a lacy shade, a rug on the floor, the divan Odd had heard mentioned the other night. He stood there for a moment, looking around in disappointment. But as the light from the hallway gathered, as Odd's eyes adjusted to the dimness, he stepped into the room and began to see the curiosities. He lit the sconce on the wall and shut the door behind him.

Along the wall to his right were dozens of wigs, a birdcage filled with faux flowers, a rocking horse built for an adult, a rack of silky undergarments and another of strange costumes. A coat stand draped with furs. There was a chest full of lifelike animals. When he looked closer, Odd saw they were indeed real animals. Dead and stuffed and piled in the chest. A fox, an otter, a beaver with his tail stiff behind him. He walked over to the wigs and inspected one of them. He set it back on the shelf and looked across the room.

Hosea's photographic equipment was stored along the opposite wall. There were shelves with cameras and jugs of who knew what. Next to the shelves was a closet door. Odd crossed the room and opened the door. The closet was lined with shelves and the shelves were lined with boxes. Each box was the same size. Each had a type-written label taped to the front of it. Odd took a box labeled BEAVER/ DECEMBER 1905 from the shelf and walked back into the room. He stood under the light of the sconce.

Until that moment he'd only been confused. Such an odd assortment of bric-a-brac Odd had never seen, but taken together it seemed merely peculiar. Another of Hosea's strange hobbies. It wasn't until he opened the box that everything came together.

It was full of postcards. Odd took one from the box and looked at it for a long time. There was Rebekah. She lay on the divan, wearing one of the wigs that he quickly identified on the shelf across the room. She was naked, her breasts full and lying across her chest. One hand was behind her head, the other held the stuffed beaver on her leg. A

caption stamped in gold lettering under the photograph read, THE
BEAVER TRAPPER.

Even as he tried, he could not take his eyes from the postcard. He
looked at the faraway cast of her eyes, the lilt of her chin. He couldn't
say she appeared sad, though there was an undeniable quality to her
expression. Or at least a quality to the look in her eyes. Like she could
see from where she lay the full bright moon.

He switched his stare to her breasts and it was then he felt his pulse
quickening. Just like that. From a glance. And once his pulse started
strumming, his vision went blinky and he had to sit down, which he did
in the light from the sconce. His guts stirred and he closed his eyes,
rested his head against the wall. Why the beaver? Why was she lying that
way at all? Why was there a picture of it? And, most confusing of all, why
did he have this feeling? He put the picture back in the box and sat there
for some time. By some simple instinct he knew that what he'd seen was
beyond his capacity to understand, so rather than trying to make sense of
it, he pondered the simpler question of how he could keep it a secret.

And so it happened that Odd—only ten years old—passed from
childhood. During the following days, he no longer wanted to spend
the rainy days sitting on the davenport reading storybooks with Rebekah. He no longer thought it a lark to help Rebekah mix a batch of
cookie dough and while away an afternoon eating the cookies as fast
as they came out of the oven. He no longer challenged Hosea to chess
matches after supper. And he was no longer willing to abide by the
rules of the house. His chores went unfinished. He did not eat what
didn't taste good. He no longer trusted the felicity of his young years,
no longer trusted much of anything.

In the years to come he would sneak into the closet whenever the
chance arose. He went despite his shame. The way a beaten dog will
still take scraps from the flogger's hand.

XXV.

[*November* 1896]

*T*hose first days and nights of their life together it was hard to tell who was newborn. Odd would nuzzle and fuss and by purest instinct stretch for Thea's breast, where he would give suck until he was exhausted. Then he'd fall into a fitful and unsated sleep because Thea's milk had not come in yet. She would hold him on her belly, swaddled in a blanket, a knit cap on his small and misshapen head, until he'd writhe again, still hungry or hungry again, and she'd put him back to her breast. And despite the new winter seeping through the windows, despite the frost left on the panes each dawn, the child was like a hot stone in her lap. When she was alone, or when Rebekah was there, asleep on the other side of the room, Thea would remove her nightdress and rest her babe's soft face on the sweat-damp flesh in the crook of her neck.

For four dreamlike days and sleepless nights this continued, the child never really at rest, until the fifth day, when she felt first a tingling and then a weightlessness in her breasts and the nursings that had once lasted an hour lasted fifteen minutes, after which Odd fell into an engorged sleep. Her happiness in those hours, with the contented boy in her arms, was her new religion, their communion her new salvation.

Sitting in her bed under the window, looking out over the isthmus that separated the harbor below her and the cove to the north, looking out over the great lake and her shimmering waters, she thought often of who she used to be. It seemed, in those sleep-deprived daydreams, with her boy on her lap, that the travails of the last year were trifles beside her feelings for Odd. He was her reward for the loneliness she'd endured. This thought filled her with peace. She saw the distance between Hammerfest and Gunflint as the way to this peace and so her regrets and misgivings dissolved in the warmth between them.

Though the look back was clear, the one ahead was dark as the devil's lair, and thoughts of the easiness of her love inevitably gave way to worries about what would come in that darkness. She had every cent she'd made at the Burnt Wood Camp saved in her purse. Seventy-five dollars in all, though what it amounted to she had no idea. She'd been told that returning to the camp on the Burnt Wood was not possible. She would have known it without having been told. She knew finding a husband would be nearly impossible now, too. She knew, finally, that she could no sooner return to Hammerfest than resurrect her childhood. It was as though the way back had been swallowed by the wakes of the boats that had brought her.

Hosea's generosity had saved her more than once, but she knew she could not live with him forever. She would not ask for so much. She'd shift her view from the water to the buildings on the Lighthouse Road. Perhaps she could become a shop girl. Or a cook at the Traveler's Hotel. Perhaps she could even work for Hosea, alongside Rebekah. But where would she live? And how could she take care of her boy while she did any of these things? This last was the question furthest from an answer, the one that cast the darkest pall on her days ahead. It was also the question on which she inevitably turned her thoughts.

She wrote letters to her mother and father, not from a sense of duty but because it spared her any reckoning with the future. Instead of giving them to Hosea to post she folded them and stacked them on the bedside table. She read her Bible without deliberation. She tried to sleep but couldn't. Her days and nights bleeding into each other, her mind wrestling itself, her only clear thoughts arriving when she studied her boy.

His eyes were not often open, but when she caught their glint she marveled at their blueness. In the daylight they were almost transparent, the color of cold, cold snow. At night, with only the bedside lamp glowing, his eyes looked fathomless and dark. She always wished to see them, so she'd feather his full hair back from his forehead. When he did not stir, she'd bend her lips to his face and kiss each of his sleeping eyes. She'd feel her own eyes glossing over with the tears that came at will and without her even knowing.

When his eyes opened he'd search for her and look intently at her as she'd say, "*You're my beautiful boy.*" Her voice would send him back into his blessed sleep. What had he seen, looking up at her? And why could she not stop weeping, with all her joy?

Hosea had begun to wonder the same thing. He'd cosseted her from the hour of Odd's birth, stopping in her bedroom every morning before he went down to the shop and again each evening before dinner. He'd check her abdomen and feel her forehead and then switch his attention to the babe.

"How's the wee lad this morning?" Hosea might say, not expecting an answer.

Thea would not even look up.

"Dear me," Hosea would say, checking the boy's forehead. "I'm worried about you, Thea."

Down in the shop, during the late-morning lulls, he was consulting Burton's *Anatomy of Melancholy* and Charles Daniel Fox's *Psycho-*

pathology of Hysteria. He'd made a preliminary diagnosis of postpartum melancholia but knew such a diagnosis wasn't complete. There was no question she cried often, almost incessantly. She talked to herself, he knew from passing her room, and she seemed to have no eagerness to rejoin him and Rebekah at table or in ordinary conversation. She was overly protective of the boy, seemed paranoid, was even twitchy at times. Yet despite these symptoms, he was mystified by what he could only think of as an aura. Though she'd always seemed, in some way or another, angelic, in those first days after Odd was born she literally had a sheen about her, a radiance that as much as lightened the air around her.

When two weeks passed with no change in her aspect—two weeks he'd spent immersed in his books, mulling options for her cure—he decided something had to be done. Before he went downstairs to open the shop he stopped in to Thea's room.

"Good morning, Thea."

She adjusted Odd's cap.

Hosea thumbed the wee boy's little toes, spoke his baby gibberish, then stood up and looked down at Thea. In his clumsy Norwegian he said, "Has two weeks of rest given you your strength back?"

Thea did not answer.

He continued in Norwegian, "You've hardly spoken at all since the child was born. Are you feeling well? Are you happy?"

She turned her attention back to the child, touched his face gently, then looked back at Hosea. "Very happy," she said.

Hosea stepped forward and knelt at her bedside. He put his hand on her arm. "Join Rebekah and me at supper tonight."

Thea nodded, smiled.

"Very good!" Hosea said in English now. "Rebekah will prepare a feast."

And she did, fish soup and buttermilk biscuits, apple strudel for dessert. Thea came to the table for supper with Odd in her arms. She appeared sleep-starved and nervous, and when Rebekah asked—as she'd been instructed to—if she could hold the boy, Thea shook her head and held him closer.

"Now, Thea, you can't hold him forever," Hosea said in Norwegian, his voice jolly, his line rehearsed. "Rebekah wants a turn with the little one."

"Sleepy," Thea said in English. "Odd. Sleepy."

"Okay, child," Hosea said, his tone full of sympathy.

By the time Rebekah served the strudel, the boy was indeed asleep. Thea held him close while she nibbled on the baked apples, tending constantly to the blanket wrapped around him, to the knit hat he wore on his head.

"I've got something for Odd," Hosea said, setting his empty coffee cup on the saucer. He stood and wiped his mouth with the napkin off his lap. He went into his bedroom and returned a moment later lugging a birch-wood bassinet. He set it down next to Thea. "A place for the boy to sleep," he said, rearranging the muslin canopy. There was a scalloped skirt hanging under the ticking.

Thea leaned forward, looked into the bassinet, at the plush bedding. She looked doubtful, seemed to be holding the boy closer.

Hosea did not hold much hope she would put the child to bed properly. "You must get some rest. Your humors are not well." And with those words Hosea left Thea and the boy at the table, carried the bassinet across the flat.

*R*ebekah stayed up late that night. She trimmed the apothecary with holly and mistletoe, with candles in all the windows and a ten-foot spruce covered in tinsel and strung cranberries. When she came up-stairs after midnight Thea was changing Odd's diaper. He was fussing, sending up his little howls, punching the air with his balled fists. After Thea finished wrapping his bottom and straightening his layette she lifted him and started to sing.

Her voice was lilting and faint and it put the boy at ease. She went to the rocking chair next to the window and lifted her nightdress. Her full breast shone in the winter moonlight. Odd as much as lunged for it, and in an instant Rebekah could hear him suckling.

Thea began another song, her voice even fainter from across the room.

"What does it mean?" Rebekah asked, her voice upsetting the deep silence enough that Odd pulled off Thea's breast.

Thea guided his head back to his feast. "A bear sleeping," she said softly.

"It sounds pretty. You sing nice." Rebekah could see Thea's smile in the moonlight, could see her glassy eyes. "It's a lullaby. A song you sing your baby. It's called a lullaby."

"Lullaby," Thea repeated.

"You're making me sleepy."

Again Thea smiled.

Then there was only the sound of Odd suckling, of Odd catching his breath when he was finished. Thea put him over her shoulder and stood and walked around the room as she patted his back. She stopped at the window and stood there with her son, the moon gone higher but still shining through the glass.

Rebekah watched them for what might have been an hour. Long enough that the moon no longer gave them light. When Thea finally returned to her bed with the sleeping boy, she did so still whispering the lullabies. She fluffed her pillows and lay down. She pulled the bedding up over her legs and sang to him more.

And Rebekah might have fallen asleep listening to Thea sing but she was intent on enforcing Hosea's will. So she struggled to stay awake. When no sound had come from the other bed for some minutes, Rebekah slid from her bedcovers, crossed the room, and stood above Thea and her son. It was the first time she'd seen Thea sleep since the child had been born. Odd lay in her limp arms, wrapped in his blanket, the cap falling off his head, his hair winging out after his bath earlier that night.

Neither Odd nor Thea woke when Rebekah picked up the boy. She held him as she'd seen Thea, setting him in the crook of her arm, holding his head with her free hand. His lips puckered and he reached for his face with his bunched hands and she was sure he'd wake bawling but he only settled deeper into her arms. The floor creaked as she stepped off the carpet, into the whispered light from the window.

Thea slept soundly, her head fallen on her shoulder, her breathing slow and tremulous. There were no dreams there. And there were none in the boy, either. She could see that. All of that sleep absent of dreams saddened Rebekah deeply. She laid the boy in the bassinet and tiptoed to bed, thought she might conjure dreams for all of them. Lord knows she had them.

*R*ebekah woke to Thea's screams and the light of morning. Her eyes flashed open and the first thing she saw was Thea thrashing in her bed, kicking and tearing at the bed linens. "Odd! Odd! Odd!" she said, her voice shrill and piercing.

Rebekah threw her covers back and jumped from bed, not remembering her antics in the middle of the night before. They reached the bassinet at the same moment and looked together into its emptiness.

Thea hollered as she ran from room to room in the flat, her panic rising alongside her shouting, Rebekah trailing the desperate mother.

By the time Thea reached the second floor her shouting had given over to sobs. She went down the hallway from door to door, stepping into each room to check for the boy. It was in the fourth room, in the surgery, that she found him, lying on the table, Hosea standing above him with a pair of eight-inch nickel-plated shears in his hand. On a tray next to the boy lay a pile of bloodstained gauze and a long needle and syringe. The boy was naked and wailing.

Rebekah managed to get her arms around Thea before she reached the table. Before she reached her boy. Thea's cries mixed with Odd's and Rebekah hugged her tight.

Hosea spoke. "Dear child, there's nothing amiss." He set the shears on the table, turned and reached out for Thea, took her hands in his, and tried to pull her to him.

"My boy!" Thea shrieked, fighting to free herself from both Rebekah and Hosea. They held her tight. Her crying had sapped her breath and she went limp in their arms and could only muster a whisper as she said, *"Good Lord, my boy."*

Hosea ushered her to a chair and urged her to sit. To Rebekah he said, "Apply an ample dose of Vaseline to the boy's prepuce and wrap him up." Turning to Thea he said, "Miss Eide, listen to me."

Thea seemed to have no breath left in her.

"Miss Eide!" Hosea shook her by the shoulders. "Miss Eide, listen to me. Odd is fine. I gave him an examination this morning, I circumcised him. There's nothing wrong with the boy that a little nap won't cure. You've nothing to worry about. These are things the child must have done. Do you understand me?"

Of course she did not.

On the table on the other side of the room Rebekah had wrapped the boy's bottom, had dressed him in his layette and his knit hat. In her clumsy way she picked him up and carried him to Thea, who pushed Hosea out of the way and stood and took her boy in one motion. Odd stopped wailing as soon as he was in his mother's arms. Thea hurried from the surgery, ran up to her bedroom, and closed the door behind her.

Hosea and Rebekah stood in the surgery, looking at each other, shocked though they ought not to have been.

After a moment Hosea said, "There's no use denying it any longer. She's suffering badly. Postpartum melancholia. Worse than I've ever seen it." He looked at Rebekah and said softly, "Will you check on Thea?"

*H*osea read deep into the night, consulting his old medical journals and further chapters in Fox's *Psychopathology of Hysteria*. Around midnight he'd decided there was but a single course of action: He must remove her ovaries to quell the madness. It was a decision that greatly eased his concern, and after he reread Battey's "Oophorectomy: A Case Study" in the *British Medical Journal* he made notes in his surgeon's journal. Before he retired for the night, he wrote a long explanation in Norwegian and practiced it twice.

Early the next morning, after only two hours' sleep, as soon as he heard stirrings in Thea's bedroom, he knocked quietly on the door.

He knocked, put his ear to the door, and listened to her feet hurrying softly across the floor. "Miss Eide?" he said quietly. He knocked again when she did not answer. "Miss Eide, I must speak with you. May I come in?"

When she failed to answer again he pressed the door open. She sat on the bed, Odd clutched in her arms. She had the look of a cornered animal.

"Thea, dear, what do you think I've done? Do you not understand that I took Odd yesterday only to perform perfunctory and essential examinations? That if I'd failed to perform those examinations I would have been in breach of the code of ethics by which my profession is governed?"

He'd intended to spare her his lecture on professional ethics, to cut right to the matter at hand, but he couldn't help himself.

She only looked at him fearfully.

He proceeded in Norwegian, reading from the notes he'd prepared late the night before, notes he hoped would convey not only his sense of urgency but his profound affection for her and her boy. "Miss Eide, I am your friend. I have tried to help you. And your boy." He paused, judged the look on her face, and took a step closer.

"Thea, I was helping your boy yesterday." He paused again, looked at his prepared remarks, looked at Thea, still clutching Odd on the bed, her eyes swollen with tears and lack of sleep, and thought he loved them both. He wished he could tell her, wished he could convey the honesty of his feelings. Instead he returned to his remarks.

"Thea, you are sick. Postpartum melancholia. You must get well. If you don't, you will be unable to care for the boy."

This last made her clutch Odd tighter still.

"I would like to perform a surgery called Battey's Operation to re-move from your body what's causing your morbid condition. I will remove your ovaries. It will cure you. Do you understand what I'm proposing?"

She only looked more frightened.

"Miss Eide, without this surgery, you will go insane." This last he said in English as he shook his solemn head.

*A*nd so two days later Hosea Grimm held a sponge to Thea Eide's nose. She breathed in the chloroform and went into a catatonic sleep and he, with his sure hands, removed his scalpel from a bath of carbolic solution, took measure of her *linea alba*, and made a small incision from which he removed the first of her ovaries. He stanched the flow of blood and stitched the incision. He gave her another dose of chloroform and made a matching incision on the other side of her abdomen and repeated the procedure within and without. An hour later, after Thea woke vomiting and feverish, he injected a dose of morphine into her thigh and set a cold compress on her forehead.

He stood back, wiped the sweat from his brow with the sleeve of his shirt, and believed honestly that his methods were sound and that Thea Eide, asleep again on the table, awaited a kinder fate thanks to his steady surgical hand.

*I*f Thea had spent her life in prayer and devotion in hope of finding God's grace, and if God's grace meant everlasting life in heaven's gentle glow, then what she found in her fever dreams those ten days after her surgery were her hopes dashed. Whatever bacillus took root in her womb was swift and voracious. A riotous fever set in, and in her delirium there were no trumpets, no bronze altars, no jasper and carnelian, no unapproachable light. There was only the Cimmerian wilderness of her fever and Odd's howling. She wanted to reach for him, wanted to take away his sorrow, but she was too weak to say so, much less do it.

Odd's care had fallen to Rebekah. And Eleanor Riverfish, who became Odd's amah, and who visited five times a day to nurse the boy. It was in this way that Odd Einar Eide and Daniel Joseph Riverfish became brothers, and it was in Eleanor's arms that he forgot the warmth of his mother's lap and the soothing sound of her singing voice.

The only song that remained was the dirge of her final hours. She sang in time to her slowing heart her last true words: *My boy, my boy, my love.* Odd would never hear those words, though one day he'd learn them in his own way.

Finally her fever boiled and her brain burst and she left him. She left all the world. And wherever else her sorrow scattered in the hereafter it went first to Odd's infant heart and found shelter there.

XXVI.

[*June* 1921]

*T*he first time Odd saw Rebekah with the child, he read the end of their story in the look on her face. Her gaze rested on the boy with the same vacant ambivalence she used to train on butchered capons before roasting them. The child lay in her arms, stunned, staring through the slits of his own eyes upon a mother he would never know.

Odd had been at work, finished with lunch and back at the steam box bending planks for the lapstrake hull he was working on. During his time at the boatwright his responsibilities had grown, and now, seven months later, he was as close to a foreman as the shop had.

Sargent was in the chandlery office when the call came. Odd could see him talking into the telephone mouthpiece, could see him turn quickly and motion with his elbow. Odd pulled one of his mates to the steam box and hurried to the chandlery office as Sargent put the telephone earpiece back on the hook.

"Grab your lunch pail, Mister Eide. Your wife is in labor."

Odd stood there dumb.

"Hurry, now. I'll drive you." Then Sargent put his head into the workshop, "Willy! Get over here, man the chandlery while I bring Odd to the hospital." He turned back to Odd, put his hands on his shoulders, and said, "The Lord has blessed you this day." There appeared almost to be tears in his eyes. "Now, let's go. You'll want to be near your wife."

They climbed into Sargent's flatbed—the same truck Hosea owned—and started up Raleigh.

Sargent said, "Would you like to pray?"

"You pray for me," Odd said. "Pray for Rebekah and the child, too."

So they drove in silence across town.

Sargent parked the Ford on the street in front of the hospital. Together they hurried up to the third floor, where Doctor Crumb's office and Odd's fate awaited. Sargent sat in the reception room while a nurse led Odd into the surgery. It was there he found Rebekah and the child, there he saw the look on her face.

It was Doctor Crumb who spoke first. "Mister Eide, meet your son."

Odd stood where he was, looking now on the child. "My son," he said or thought, he didn't know which.

"He's big as a bear, Mister Eide. I've never seen one bigger."

Odd took a pair of unsteady steps toward the surgery table, toward Rebekah and the big boy. *A boy.*

"He's well?" Odd finally managed.

"I'm surprised the lad didn't come out with teeth. Or hair on his chest. He's nine even pounds according to my scale. And he's fine, way ahead in the race and only just in it."

Odd walked to Rebekah. "And you?" he asked, knowing with unwelcome certainty the answer to his question.

Rebekah, confirming all, said nothing, only lifted the baby to Odd's hands.

He'd never held a child before, never suspected that something that had weighed so heavily in his mind could be so light in his hands. But as he looked down on the boy, on his puckered lips and pale skin, Odd felt a preternatural strength rising in him. He felt as though someone could have handed him a bowl with all the water of Lake Superior in it and he would still have been able to bear it.

"I've a few details to attend to," Doctor Crumb said. "If you've a name for this one, the time to tell me is now."

Odd kept his eyes on the boy, said to Rebekah, "Any ideas?"

"He's your son. You name him."

Her words felt like a punch, but he'd been sure of the boy's name for months. "We'll call him Harald Einar Eide."

Doctor Crumb said, "He'll live up to his stature with a name like that."

"I hope so," Odd said.

Odd walked the boy to the window. It was late afternoon and the summer sky was squally. Odd knew surely there was a thunderstorm up there, might have been able to say the exact hour at which it would begin to rain. He whispered to the boy, "Look up there, son. You see? That's a thunderhead. Means rain."

Together they stood at the window looking at the weather. Odd pictured his own mother, recalling that photograph on the windowsill in the brownstone. The picture of him in his mother's arms. He saw that beatific look in her eyes and knew the same look came now from him. From his good and his bad eye both. After a few minutes Odd returned to Rebekah's bedside and looked down on her with all the courage he had to spare.

*F*ive days later Rebekah and little Harald came home from the hospital. It was a hot and low-down day, the first heavy weather of summer. The humidity stuck for a week, and whether it was because of the atmosphere or Rebekah's disposition, the first few days of having the baby home were some of the unhappiest of Odd's life. The only sounds that made their way around the flat were the hungry yowls of the boy and Rebekah's sullen sighs. She seemed to have a complaint for every-thing. Her sincerest and most regular grievance came whenever it was time for the boy to eat. Her breasts were sore and engorged, her nipples cracked, and Harry, unnaturally big as he was, demanded regular suck.

The looks she cast on that boy. His hunger, his fear and vulnerabil-ity, all of it like a badge he wore. And still she looked at him as though he were a cancer. He'd spit her nipple, grab at her breast, wail. And Rebekah with that poisonous and unforgiving stare would scold him. Odd wanted to help, would have done anything, but was always in the way, making Rebekah more agitated.

On the occasions Rebekah could slake the boy's hunger, he'd fall into a heavy infant slumber. Rebekah would call Odd, hand Harry to him, and lie down on the davenport, shielding her eyes from every-thing with her arm.

"My breasts feel like they're going to catch right on fire," she said one June evening after Harry had eaten and was sleeping in his papa's arms.

"I sure am sorry, Rebekah."

She looked up at him from under her arm. "What are you sorry for?"

"Sorry you're not feeling well. Sorry you're so tired. All that stuff."

"All that stuff . . ."

Odd had walked Harry to the window. Together they stood look-ing at the Norway pines on the side of the house.

"It was so easy for your mother. When you were a baby. To feed you. You latched right on and ate like there was no tomorrow." She might have groaned, Odd couldn't tell. "I can't stop thinking what a twisted-up thing this is."

"Haven't we about covered that?" Odd asked from the window, not even turning to look at her.

"Oh, sure, we've covered it. Or you have. Mister Everything Will Be All Right. Mister We Don't Need No One. You've covered it, all right."

"What the hell do you want me to say, Rebekah? What in fuck's name is going to get the sulk out of you?"

She didn't say anything, only lay there on the davenport with her arm over her eyes. Odd and Harry still stood at the window, Odd whispering to Harry an account of a gray squirrel husking a pinecone on the bough of a tree.

"That first day her milk came in, and you ate and then filled your diaper and slept for six straight hours, she held you the whole time. She always held you. Sang those fool songs." Her words trailed off. Odd turned to look at her.

"I want to understand, Rebekah. I do. But I don't see your unhap- piness. It doesn't make sense."

She looked at him for a long time. Eyes as vacant as two stones. She might have been dead for all the life in her.

Odd kept at it. "He's a hundred percent perfect, this one. Sure, he's hard to get fed. I know that. And I know it's you suffering his temper tantrums when he's at the teat. But he's brand-new to this business. Might you give him an inch of rope?"

If it was possible, the look on her face went even more expression- less. Still she would not look away from him.

"Some things just aren't meant to be understood," she said. "Some things are just invisible and out of reach."

Odd crossed the room, offered her Harry. "He ain't out of reach. He's right goddamn here. Take him."

She put her arm back over her eyes. "Your mother," Rebekah began before Odd could say more, "she was real sad after you were born. Melancholy's what Hosea called it. Said she had the sadness disease.

But still she wouldn't set you down. She wouldn't stop ogling you. She was more in love with you than she could even imagine."

Odd had cradled Harry back in his arm. Now he sat on the end of the davenport.

Rebekah tucked her feet up beneath her to make room for him. "Hosea had a way to get the sadness out of her," she continued. "Cut it right out of her, that's how he described it." She shook her head under her arm.

"What are you talking about, cut it right out of her?"

"He did an operation. An ovariotomy, he called it. He cut the sadness out of her."

"Maybe there's a way to cut the sadness out of you." He couldn't help feeling hopeful, still clung to some thought they could all three of them be a happy family.

She looked at him under her arm. "Sadness has no hold on me, Odd. It's something else. Besides, when Hosea got the sadness out of her, he got everything else, too. The whole life of her."

Odd sat up. "What do you mean the whole life of her? What are you talking about?"

"After the operation. She got sick."

"You always told me it was a fever she died of."

"She did. A fever he conjured up, I suppose."

Now Odd stood. "What's that mean?"

"Your mother didn't have any sadness in her, Odd. That's what I was telling you. She was the happiest person I ever saw in those days after you were born. She needed that operation like the lake needs more water."

Odd stood there trembling. He'd always been led to believe that his mother had died naturally. A simple fever that had got the best of her. "Are you telling me she got the fever because of Hosea?"

"I don't know why she got the fever, but it came a day after the surgery."

"He *killed* her?" he whispered. "Is that what you're saying?"

"How could I know?"

Odd looked down at Harry. For a long time he just looked at the boy sleeping in his arm. "How come you never told me before? Why didn't anyone do anything?"

"He was trying to help her."

"He's got every living soul hoodwinked."

"What difference does it make? The how or the why? You're an orphan either way. Nothing was going to change that. Not then, not now."

Odd walked back to the window. The squirrel was still on the bough.

"I believe he thought he was doing the right thing. For what it's worth, I believe that," she said.

"What is that? You and this notion Hosea needs defending? He's lousy. Any way you slice it, he's lousy. And you talking for the hundredth time like he was some upstanding man."

"Where would you be without him?"

Odd spun around. "We're gonna cover that territory again, too? Hell, no." He shook his head slowly. "Hell, no, we ain't. *Hosea our savior.* You must be out of your mind, Rebekah."

"I guess I am," she said. "I guess I am."

*A*nd maybe she was. How else to account for her?

Sargent had given Odd two weeks off, and when Odd returned to the boatwright's on a Monday morning it was with grave misgivings.

The week passed and his misgivings grew, and on Friday evening, after work, after Odd had made supper and given Harry his bath, after Rebekah had fed the boy and put him to sleep in his basinet, she asked Odd to sit down. So he did.

She had that look on her face like the night of his birthday, in his fish house. Like she was about to tell him the end times were nigh. "I'm sorry what I told you about your mother," she said. "I'm trying to—" Her voice emptied out, got lost in one of her sighs.

Most of these conversations during the last week, Odd had just quit. Walked into the bedroom or right out the door. But this night was different. He didn't know why.

Rebekah began again. "I told you about your mother because thinking of her is the only way any of this makes sense to me. The way she felt, that's how I'm supposed to feel. I'm supposed to be as happy as she was. I couldn't get to happiness on a train. Maybe Hosea could make me happy."

"Sure, give him a chance to kill you, too."

She looked up at him. "You could never understand. Not about me, or your mother."

"I *don't* understand, you're right. Not what you're saying. Not how you're acting. And sure as shit not how Hosea could make you happy. Hosea goddamn killed her. He killed her and then tried to be my old man. I hope he's hung himself up by the neck." There was no rancor in his voice. No exasperation. Not even any curiosity. He was taking his own account was all.

"If you really understand about my mother," Odd continued, "then you'd see what you're doing to Harry. He might as well be an orphan. Half an orphan, leastways. How much you hate him."

"I don't hate Harry, Odd." She shook her head, as though he were the biggest fool. "You and me. Harry next. We're all orphans."

Odd stood there in disbelief, mustering the right words to end this season's long conversation once and for all. He simply could not bear it any longer. He smiled at her. Shook his head. Said, "Rebekah, darlin', I love you. I don't care how we got here or what kind of right or wrong it is, but Harry is our boy. That's all there is now. That's all there'll ever be. I know you're mixed up. But here's something you need to hear from me." He paused again, looking down at Rebekah, who was look-ing back up at him with tears in her eyes. "If you abandon our boy once, you abandon him forever. If you walk away, our boy will never know you. Much as it would kill me, I'll see to it. So help me God."

*S*trange that he should find himself standing outside Gloria Dei Lu-theran Church on Sunday morning. Harry was sleeping in his buggy, the canopy pulled up to block the hot sun. Odd himself was shielding his eyes with his cap, looking up at Sargent's church. From inside he could hear the organ piping in harmony with the singing congregation.

He stood there until the doors swung open twenty minutes later and the worshippers came out in their summer dresses and seersucker suits. Sargent appeared midflock, his wife on his arm. They paused on the top step, looked up at the glorious day.

It was Rose who saw Odd and Harry. She raised her hand to greet them, tugged on Sargent's coat sleeve, pointed at Odd. They made their way through the departing throng and joined Odd on the sidewalk.

"Mister Eide, to what do we owe the pleasure?"

"Mornin', Harald. Missus Sargent."

"This must be little Harald," Rose said, peeking under the buggy's canopy.

"That's Harry. Sleeping his fool head off."

Sargent lit a cigarette. "Rebekah's catching up on her own sleep, I gather?"

"I couldn't rightly tell you what Rebekah's doing."

Sargent arched his eyebrows. "Mother, see if you can talk to Pastor Guenther about the bake sale next week, would you?"

She turned a sympathetic eye to Odd. "Mister Eide, it was very nice to see you. And this lovely little boy. What an angel!"

"He is that," Odd said. "He's that if he's nothing else."

The two men watched Rose head back up the church steps. Watched as she took the pastor's arm and headed inside the church again.

Sargent offered Odd a cigarette, which he took and lit and pulled the smoke in. As he exhaled he said, "Rebekah's gone, Harald. Just up and left."

"What are you saying? Where did she go?"

"I have my suspicions about where she went off to, but I couldn't say for sure. Harry here woke up howling this morning and his mama was gone. That's about it."

"She didn't say where she was going?"

Odd looked at him as though to suggest the question was ridiculous.

"What about the boy?"

"The boy's the problem. Or a big part of the problem." Odd tried to gather himself, tried to understand why he was there with Sargent. "It's a complicated business, Harald. It's a sight more than complicated, to tell the truth. Rebekah, she was never keen about having the baby. She was scared and confused. Didn't think she'd know what to do once he came." He paused, took a drag on his smoke.

Sargent had those eyes set on Odd. Didn't even blink as he blew his own smoke out his nose. "Go on, son."

"I guess she was right. See, she was an orphan. We're both orphans, if you want the truth. I suppose she never saw a child being cared for. Never saw how a mother's supposed to act. Anyway."

"Do you mean to suggest that she's gone for good? That she doesn't want to have anything to do with the boy?"

Odd nodded his head.

"That's impossible. A mother can't abandon her child that way."

"Rebekah always had a mind of her own. But I've got a mind of my own, too. I got imagination enough to take care of the boy. Why, hell, just this morning I mashed up some blueberries to feed him. Ate 'em up like that milk from the bub was a long-forgotten thing." Odd tried to smile as though his cleverness was enough. It wasn't. He felt tears welling.

"Son, you can't feed a baby that age blueberries. He needs his mother's milk. Some milk, leastways."

"He ain't never supping at that teat again."

Sargent looked up at the stained-glass window of the church for a long while. Long enough he finished his smoke. He dropped it and rubbed it out with the sole of his shoe, then said, "Are you sure you're not the cause of her leaving, Odd?"

"What do you mean?"

"Did you ever raise your hand against her?"

"Hell, no."

"Did you ever berate her? Demean her?"

"I was never anything but kind and true, Harald. I love her better than anything."

"But she'll come back, son. She can't really leave the boy. Can't leave a man good as you."

"She can and she did, and she ain't coming back. I don't know much, but I know this."

Sargent brought his hands together and hung his head. "Dear Lord, forgive that woman. Forgive her and find peace for her. And for this child, Lord, hold him in your hands. Show him the way." He lifted his face to the sunlight for a moment, then looked again at Odd. "Son, you know you've got a place with me as long as you need. Mother, she can watch the boy until you find other arrangements. I'll call Doctor Crumb. We'll find the boy a wet nurse. Everything will be all right."

"You're right, boss. Everything will be all right. But part of why I'm here is to say good-bye."

"Good-bye?"

Now Odd turned his face up to the sun. "You've been the closest thing to a father I ever had. It ain't even a year I've known you and I'd lay across the tracks for you. But I was always just visiting. I didn't know that until this morning. I'm a Gunflinter, I guess." He lowered his face and took the last draw on his cigarette. "I'm gonna get my boat out of dry dock tomorrow. I'm gonna take this boy home. I'm gonna teach him how to cast a net and build a boat." Now Odd smiled. "I'll build him a skiff so he can run about."

And Sargent couldn't help smile himself. "It'll be a fine boat."

"A damn fine boat."

*T*he next day Odd and Harald motored home. Roundabout Otter Bay, Odd opened the locker in the cockpit and withdrew the box that held the bell. He locked the wheel and checked on Harry and then, nimble as a cat, Odd fixed the bell to the header in the cockpit.

The rest of the way home he talked to Harry. He told him about the lake, the rivers and streams. He told him about the kinds of fish in the lake and the kinds of men in the world. He told him what kind of man he would be. Motoring past the settlement at Misquah, he told him about the boat. Said, "I built this boat for all the wrong reasons, Harry. It's easy to do things for the wrong reasons. My problem? I never know what the wrong reasons are until it's too late. Same goes for your mother, rest her soul." He looked down at the boy in the crook of his arm. The sun on his pale skin. "See, I built it so I could run more whiskey. Catch more fish. Get more. But now I got all I want." He rubbed Harry's cheek with the back of his thumb, a gesture that would become his regular show of affection. "How could I have known when I dragged that tree out of the woods, when I carved this keel, when I bent the first board, that I'd be cruising with you? I couldn't, you see? But now I know what I never could have: that of all the reasons to have a boat, none is as important as using it to carry your son home. To carry you home, Harry."

Before they reached Gunflint Harry started fussing. The roll and pitch of the water and Odd's voice had left the boy sleeping for the better part of six hours but he woke just east of Misquah. So Odd fixed him a bottle. He had fifty dollars' worth of Dextri-maltose prescribed by Doctor Crumb. He mixed it up and offered Harry the rubber nipple.

When Harry had guzzled it all, Odd laid a blanket across the motor box and changed the boy's diaper. "That's my little fella," Odd said, picking him up and resting him on his shoulder. He burped him and then held him in the crook of his arm.

When they came up on Gunflint it was still light. The sun rested on the hilltop. A breeze had been stiffening for the last hour, and as they rounded the breakwater and headed across the harbor, the roll of the boat on the swells set the bell tolling. It was the song of their coming home, and Odd hoped everyone heard it.

XXVII.

[*February* 1937]

*T*he shingle above the chandlery door read, EIDE'S BOATBUILDING & SUPPLIES. Every time Odd walked under it, he thought of Sargent and Hosea, the two men he had had to learn from. Both men had hung such shingles over their doors: Hosea at the apothecary, Harald at the boatwright.

That morning he and Harry walked in together an hour before sunrise, a strange, cold wind blowing away a fog bank outside. They went to their desks and poured coffee from matching thermoses and spent fifteen minutes cracking their knuckles and sharpening their tools before either of them spoke.

Odd said, "We've got a letter here. A query about building a canoe."

"I'm not building a canoe," Harry said.

Odd smiled. "I guess you think they wouldn't pay for a canoe?"

Harry took his adze to the skiff he was building. He put his hands on the gunwale the way Odd always did, walked around the boat twice before he set to shaving a bit off the transom.

Odd still sat at his desk, sipping his coffee, watching Harry. He wondered how the boy would be different if he'd been given his mother.

"You'll be done with that in a week," Odd said.

"Less than that."

"Then you can get to work on the canoe."

"All right," Harry said.

Odd watched him for another spell. Long enough that the boy had set down the adze and was stroking the transom with his sanding block. "I don't see why we wouldn't go out and catch some of those morning trout, do you?" Odd said.

Harry gave up that big, boyish smile. He didn't say anything, just smacked the sawdust from his trousers and went to the door to fetch his coat and mitts. He stepped outside, crossed the yard to the fish house, and pulled the toboggan loaded with their ice-fishing supplies from the barn door.

"Let's walk around the point today. Get some of that sunrise on our ugly mugs," Odd said.

"Let's go, Pops."

*H*ow many times had Rebekah stood at the window as she did that day, her forehead and fingertips resting on the glass? She was watching them walk into the rising wind, out from the point, a sled trailing the boy. They'd been at it often enough since the ice had come to stay in January, and she always watched them go. On some days she stood at the window the whole while they were gone. Others she went to her needlepoint and tried to put them out of her mind.

That morning she would lose hours to the sadness left in their wake. Though she literally could no longer cry, she felt the phantom welling in her eyes. She wondered, *Has the boy ever known? Does Odd ever think of me now?*

Out on the ice Harry said, "You don't feel it?"

"I don't," Odd said. "You sure it ain't the breeze is all?"

"The breeze coming up through my feet? I don't think so."

"Your tongue ain't getting any duller, is it?" Odd asked. He put his hand on the boy's shoulder and smiled to himself. The smile lasted only a moment.

These mornings ice fishing? The summer mornings when they were at their nets before dawn, the only herring chokers still making a go of it out of Gunflint? Or, back across the isthmus, those mornings in their workshop, building boats side by side? Thousands of mornings if you added them up, all begun with the memory of her looming above him.

If Harry knew of the grief that attended his papa, if he saw it in Odd's bowed head, he at least had the wisdom to witness it in silence instead of badgering his father about it. Odd took pride in his son's stoic silence. The whole world, it seemed to Odd, was garrulous. But not Harry.

Out past the breakwater Odd said, "That *is* a strange wind."

"And cold."

"Did you ever know a February wind to be otherwise?"

"I'm just saying."

"I know it."

They walked another fifty rods before they stopped. Odd turned to the shore to take measure of where they were. He turned to the lake to do the same. "What do you think?" he asked Harry.

The boy answered by lifting the auger from the sled. He set the blade on the ice and started to drill. He was a long-armed, well-built kid and it wasn't ten minutes before the auger broke through to water. It came splashing up through the hole.

Odd and Harry looked at each other. "Maybe we should go a little closer to shore," Harry said.

Odd inspected the horizon over the lake, the sky above them. He pulled the sleeve of his coat up, took off his mitten, and knelt. He stuck his hand into the hole in the ice to measure its thickness. He stood up. "I think we're all right."

Harry started another hole ten paces from the first. He'd inherited his father's habits of calm and diligence, and he went about the work of making a fishing hole with an old man's patience. When the second hole was augered he brought his papa's stool to it. He brought the small ice-fishing rod and the box of jigs.

"You rig it," Odd said.

"I know."

Odd's hands were worthless in winter. He could hardly tie his boots anymore, let alone jigs onto fishline. So Harry baited his papa's line and handed him the rod. He tied a jig to his own line and in no time at all they were both fishing for steelheads. They'd eaten nothing but trout dinners for two weeks, and still they had a freezer full of fish. Times were better on the ice than in the open water, something Odd brought up every day.

"You give any thought to Veilleux's offer?" Odd asked over his shoulder.

"I give it some thought, sure."

Already Odd had a strike and he set the hook and started reeling. He loosened his drag and then, as though nothing were happening, he said, "It'd be a good move. He's a good man with a good business. His family has been here from day one."

Harry was peering into his own hole on the ice, more intent on hooking a fish than on his papa's pitch. Even still he responded, "You know how much I like fishing and boatbuilding."

"And I can't say I blame you, Harry. But there ain't much of a living to be made any longer. Neither enterprise pays for itself nowadays.

Not small operations like ours. You apprentice with Veilleux and you can make money all year long. You could still fish some. Obviously we'd keep filling boat orders. Canoe orders. You'd just have another wagon to hitch your load to."

Odd pulled the fish from the hole, unhooked it, and threw it on the ice a few feet away. He took his knife from this belt and knelt before the fish, thumping it on the head with the hilt before he sliced the guts from it. He threw the offal as far as he could, with the wind. He did this in twenty seconds and in twenty seconds more had his jig back in the water. A colony of gulls descended from the clearing sky and went to work on the fish guts.

"Besides," Odd continued, "you keep telling me how you want to build something out at Evensen's farm."

"I could build it without apprenticing. I ain't talking about a castle."

Odd looked up into the sky, took a gulp of the cold wind, noted the snow squall on the eastern horizon. "You're sure and steady with a hammer and nails, there's no denying that. But there's more to building a house than a hammer and nails. And it ain't like building a skiff. Trust me on this one, buddy."

Harry felt a hit on his line but he failed to set the hook. "Shit," he said.

"I don't know how many times I got to tell you don't horse it."

"I know."

"You know."

They sat for a spell jigging in silence. Finally Odd said, "I'm telling you it's a good move."

"I'll go see Veilleux this afternoon. See what he has to say."

Odd said, "You got some saying to do yourself, don't forget that. Sure, he knows you and he's the one offering, but you stand to gain here. Don't go over there acting like you deserve it."

"I wouldn't."

As he spoke Harry hooked a fish. A big one. The short rod arced.

"See? You listen to your old man and good things happen."

Harry was too pleased to say anything back.

But it was moments like this when Odd saw most clearly what his hardheartedness all those years ago had wrought, when their joviality felt most suspect. *Good Christ*, Odd thought. *What have I taken from this boy?*

*J*ust as Odd had foreseen, Rebekah had left Duluth back in the summer of '21. On a Sunday morning after she'd fed the four-week-old Harry, while Odd still slept on the Murphy bed, she went. Odd woke hours later to the boy's hungry lamentation—it couldn't have been called a cry—and knew as soon as he stepped out of bed that Harry was his alone.

When the questions started three or four years later, when Harry wondered about his mother, Odd told him what he'd told the towns-folk the autumn they'd returned, that he'd met a sweet gal up in Port Arthur, Ontario, married her, then lost her nine months later when she'd given birth to Harry. That lie and the others it spawned came easily to Odd and he realized that his deceit was different from Hosea's only by degree. He was not proud of this, but neither did he ever tell the truth. Not to his son. And not to anyone else.

If the townsfolk had ever wondered about Harry, if they tried to make sense of the rift between Odd and the Grimms, they did so in the privacy of their own homes. Hardly a suspicious glance had ever come Odd's way along the Lighthouse Road. He'd never heard so much as a snigger.

Maybe this was because of the visit he'd paid Rebekah and Hosea the day he'd returned to Gunflint with Harry. Odd had come down from Duluth, turned into the harbor with his boat bell tolling, tied up on the Lighthouse Road, and marched up to Grimm's. He found them sitting at the kitchen table—the same kitchen table where he'd taken almost all his childhood meals—and held the boy before them.

"Look at you two," Odd said, feeling as sad as he did angry. "Couple of quacks." He shook his head fiercely. "I want you to take a gander at my boy here." When neither of them looked up, Odd said, "All right. You mind your own business. That's good. We'll all mind our own business. From this day forward, don't utter his name. Don't even look at him. If you pass us on the Lighthouse Road, walk on by. If anyone asks about him, about me and Rebekah, you shrug your shoulders and don't know a damn thing. Understand? You never breathe a word about this."

He'd not waited for them to respond, those loonies sitting there holding hands above the linen tablecloth, only cradled the boy and turned and went about his life. And so Harry became, like his father a quarter century before him, Gunflint's motherless son, the heir of their blind-eyed sympathy.

Odd looked over at him and wondered again what his hardheartedness had done to the boy.

"Hey, bud," Odd said. "Hell of a morning for catching fish, ain't it?"

"It's unnatural, the way they're biting."

She was fifty-seven years old as she stood at the window. Except for that year in Duluth with Odd she'd spent almost forty-four of those years living here, the last ten of them alone. The apothecary had devolved first into a general mercantile, then a clothier, and finally a haberdashery before it became nothing more than a madwoman's madhouse. That was what people thought, anyway. What the high school–aged kids said as they roamed the Lighthouse Road on Friday nights. Sometimes they threw rocks through the big front window, once they painted a large owl on the clapboard siding. She thought nothing of their mischief, was only relieved to know that Harry was not among the vandals.

She looked up and down the shore at the snow in the pines. Some of the trees had grown in the years she'd been there, others had been felled, but the shape of the wilderness had stayed the same. The shape of the lake, too. She took comfort in this, felt some affinity with the years.

But it was a comfort short in lasting. As soon as she settled her gaze back on the ice fishermen, the vagaries of time that a moment ago had provided solace were now as cruel as the wind.

Out on the lake the ice fishermen were hauling them in, one after another, even as the fissures spread like veins through the ice, even as the wind stiffened from the northeast.

Odd said, "That wind is coming around now, ain't it?"

"Maybe we should call it a day."

"Look at that pile of fish. We've never had a day like this."

"Still. The wind."

"We'll be all right."

And because Harry believed every word his papa ever said, he dropped his line into the lake again.

ACKNOWLEDGMENTS

To Gillian van Leuven, Laura Jean Baker, Thomas Maltman, Emily St. John Mandel, and Kevin McColley, my gratitude. Thanks and admiration to Greg Michalson. To Caitlin Hamilton Summie, Rich Rennicks, Rachel Kinbar Grace, Steven Wallace, and all the other fine folks at Unbridled, much appreciation for all your hard work and commitment. Matt and Jenae Batt, I owe you. To Laura Langlie, a bouquet of flowers. Pops, I have another question for you. . . .

Finn, Mac, and Liese, you're my inspiration.

And to Dana, what thanks could ever be enough?